and a Half
Just Won't Do

Ninety-Nine and a Half Just Won't Do

Kimberly T. Matthews

URBAN BOOKS

http://www.urbanbooks.net

This is a work of fiction. Any references or similarities to actual events, real people, living or dead, or to real locales are intended to give the novel a sense of reality. Any similarity in other names, characters, places, and incidents is entirely coincidental.

URBAN SOUL is published by

Urban Books
10 Brennan Place
Deer Park, NY 11729

ISBN-13: 978-1-59983-022-3
ISBN-10: 1-59983-022-1

First Printing: November 2007

10 9 8 7 6 5 4 3 2 1

Printed in the United States of America

Prologue

The Him Book

Genesis Taylor dug a black-velvet-covered journal from the bottom of the chest at the foot of her bed. The unique book, made purposefully for keeping track of men and the memorable things about them, had caught Genesis's eye two years before as she browsed the journal section of the bookstore for a new home for her thoughts. Each page of the journal was set up to represent a different man, but with nearly 250 pages, there was no way Genesis planned on filling the book up in that manner. Instead, she dedicated several pages to a single man, adding photos and meticulously documenting her thoughts regarding him, his behaviors and actions toward her, and most importantly, his point value.

Along the bottom of each page a one-to-ten rating scale was printed, but Genesis found that a ten-point scale just didn't cut it for her. She needed something bigger, broader, and more detailed. She developed her own hundred-point scale. That gave her plenty of room to track each man's performance when he gained points by taking her to dinner or massaging her back, lost them by showing up late for dates, cheating, and the like, and sometimes redeemed them again.

Before making a new entry, she flipped through the pages, revisiting both in her mind and on paper notes she'd taken on men she'd dated in the past. Most guys never made it past the fifty-point mark, and those who did only made it because Genesis was temporarily mesmerized by some trivial quality that she thought he possessed. Like Jose Rodriguez. The Latino brother was so fine that Genesis awarded him thirty points straight out of the gates. He'd earned minor points here and there until a few weeks later when they'd made love, for which he earned an additional forty points, making her feel things she had only read about in Zane's novels. Some days later when she had to be treated for gonorrhea, his point value dropped from eighty-two to a final score of negative one hundred, which was printed in bold red letters at the bottom of his final page of documentation. It was a difficult lesson, but Genesis found out that fine in looks certainly didn't mean fine in health, and she learned to be far more careful with whom and how she shared her body.

She looked several pages forward to Chauncey Gardner's page. He'd started off pretty well, although he earned very little points for looks. It wasn't that he wasn't attractive, but after getting a shot in the behind, cute simply didn't count for anything. Well, maybe something, but definitely not thirty points. She'd dated Chauncey for seven months, which seemed like heaven at the time. He had swooned her with romantic dinners, weekend getaways, and small gifts, all which had been recorded with positive point values, scribbled down the sides of his pages. He had actually made it up to seventy-nine points, with only a few minor deductions, before Genesis found out that he had a wife. A wife he was separated from. They were in the middle of a divorce that had been delayed by two years, but in the meantime they lived under the same roof. *Blah blah blah*, Genesis had scribbled as a final entry note, then ended his score with a flat zero.

Turning a few more pages, she ran into Payton Turner's entry. Payton was all the things Genesis thought she wanted and needed in a man—professional, smart, funny, well dressed—and almost instantly she fell head over heels in love with him. Her love was unreturned, however, as Payton couldn't have shown her that he wasn't interested in her any more if he'd have hauled off and slapped her in the face. They'd dated (or so she thought) for about a year before she finally got the message that his interests were not in her. In that twelve-month span of time, Payton was often late for dates, sometimes "forgot" his money to pay for meals, neglected to get her anything for her birthday or Valentine's Day, and had even borrowed her car a few times and forgot to come pick her up from work. Genesis still sometimes scratched her head trying to figure out what it was that she was thinking at the time. Glancing over his point history, she saw that he swayed between five and thirty points, but never more than that.

It was actually that relationship that made Genesis evaluate herself in an attempt to realize what it was she was truly after. Sex? Money? Love? Companionship? Trips around the world maybe?

Unfortunately "The One" had yet to make his appearance. Well, this time points wouldn't come easy. The man she would crown as The One would have to have a full one hundred points. "And ninety-nine and a half just won't do," Genesis said aloud to herself as she turned to the next blank page and began a new entry.

Chapter 1

A roach scurried across the bathroom countertop as soon as Genesis flicked the light on. She picked up her latest issue of *Essence* magazine and smacked at it wildly as it attempted escape. Successful after three tries, she tore off the back cover and discarded it along with the remnants of the roach in a small wastebasket beside the toilet. *Things have got to get better*, she told herself while she pulled a bottle of disinfectant from the cabinet beneath the sink and cleaned the counter. *What do roaches want in the bathroom anyway? There's no food in here.*

She placed a shower cap over her hair, which was still in rollers, then started the low-pressured trickle of water for her shower while she brushed her teeth. Peeking across the hall into her bedroom at the digital clock on her nightstand, she realized she had less than thirty minutes to pull herself together. Her car was acting up again, and this would be her third week of having to wake up extra early to catch the bus. The Omni Hotel was only a twenty-minute drive by car, but the traveling time more than quadrupled with public transportation. Hopefully the neighborhood mechanic would complete the repairs soon. It seemed that the more money she handed him, the more things he found wrong. Nonetheless, Genesis trusted him; he'd been working on cars ever since he'd selected vocational electives back in high school ten years before.

The water cooled sooner than Genesis would have liked, but it really didn't matter; she was in a rush. She quickly slid into her uniform pants and smock, brushed her formed curls into a smooth elongated mushroom, and jammed her stockinged feet into a pair of worn tennis shoes before grabbing her purse and keys and heading out the door to the bus stop.

The scenery outside was typical for a weekday morning. Young uniformed children with book bags strapped to their backs trudged down the sidewalk in small troops headed for Achievable Dream Academy. Older kids clustered on one corner waiting for the school bus, while teenaged boys with their pants too low and teenaged girls with their skirts too high grouped on the opposite corner conversing, joking, and boxing waiting to be transported to another part of the city. Unemployed brothers loitered alongside a convenience store, puffing on cigarettes and getting a jump start on wasting the day. Police cars cruised by every few minutes, driven by officers ready to investigate any suspicious activity. A few disheveled and possibly homeless citizens wandered aimlessly, toting plastic bags from the local grocery store filled with clothing, canned food, and other personal items. Genesis spoke or waved to familiar faces while she waited five minutes for her bus to arrive.

"Hey, Coco-brown." Alton Marshall welcomed her onto the route five bus, waited for her to slide her fare into the collection box, then pulled away from the curb once she took her usual seat just across from him.

"Good morning," she sang. She liked that he called her Coco-brown, attributed to her rich smooth skin tone, so she'd never shared with him her real name. "How's it going today?" She'd learned in the past few weeks that Alton started his route at four in the morning. By the time he picked her up, he'd been driving in a loop for three hours.

"You know, same sites, different day. Your car still acting up, huh?"

"Yeah." Genesis shook her head while her lips twisted to one side. "One of these days, I'm just going to buy me a new one."

"Don't do that, Coco-brown," he teased. "If you do, I won't have anything to look forward to on my route." He glanced over his shoulder at her, then quickly cut his eyes back to the road. She giggled as she looked at his shiny black hair, which lay neatly against his scalp. "Unless you give me your number." His skin was a caramel complexion, darkened on his jaw and around his lips from the continuous growth and cutting of facial hair. His lips poked forward just a little as if he were always ready to blow a speck of dirt out of someone's eye. For a split second, Genesis wondered what they would feel like against her neck. Her eyes traveled to his broad shoulders, muscular arms, and large hands that effortlessly wheeled the bus around the corner before it slowed for a stop. He pulled the bus over to let on more passengers, taking the opportunity to look her in the eye. The quick rise of his eyebrows begged a response from her. She couldn't deny the attraction she had to Alton, but she wasn't quite ready to reveal it.

"We'll see. I don't want Mrs. Marshall knocking down my door." Genesis smiled slyly as she squeezed a dollop of scented lotion from a small bottle into her palm.

"Mrs. Marshall? Pfff!" he blew out, wrinkling his forehead. "There's no such thing. My mama ain't even a Mrs." He gave a half smile, revealing a small segment of straight white teeth. "I'm tryna make you Mrs. Marshall." This brought a burst of laughter from Genesis as she rolled her eyes upward. "Oh, that's funny, huh?"

"I'm not laughing at you, Alton. I'm just blushing, that's all," she said, pushing a headband back over her hair.

"You're cute when you blush, and you know what else—" Before he could finish, Genesis held up a finger, cutting him off to answer her cell phone.

"Hello?" an automated voice response unit replied, dampening Genesis's mood.

"This is a friendly reminder that your cellular phone account is now past due. To make a payment now over the phone, please press the star key. If you have already made a payment, please disregard this message." She held the phone for a few moments longer than the recorded message, commenting every few seconds to give the impression that she was having a conversation.

"Okay . . . yeah, that's fine. Mm-hmm. Bye," she pretended before hanging up. She then made a call to her bank's automated teller hoping to find a few extra dollars. After pressing a sequence of numbers, her balance of $27.42 was called out to her. Though grateful that her account wasn't overdrawn, she sighed at the fact that there never seemed to be enough money to do all that she needed done.

"That was your man?" he quizzed.

"Something like that." She dropped the phone back inside her purse and stared out of the window. She and Alton made small talk between her thoughts of tallying up her next two paychecks and making mental notes of her current and upcoming financial obligations. One thing she was more than happy about was she had learned to live debt-free. Other than general living expenses, her money was her own, but even so, things were tight. She was certain that she'd make it through; she'd always had.

"All right Coco-brown," Alton said, pulling over to her stop. "I'll see you tomorrow."

Genesis gave a slight wave, trading the air-conditioned bus for thick summer heat. As she trotted down the tree-lined street that led to the hotel, she could feel droplets of sweat forming on her back. Digging in her purse past the banana and granola bar that would serve as lunch, she sighed in relief when she saw her emergency deodorant. It was one thing to work alone and not be completely fresh, but today she would be partnered with a few others, and body odor of any kind was simply unacceptable.

Four new girls would be starting today; she was scheduled to work with two of them, which had its pros and cons. While she was always glad to have an extra set of hands working with her, and in this case two extra sets, training two girls at once would surely slow her day, not to mention she would have to split any tips, which were already few and far between.

She walked into the employee break room, placed her banana and granola bar in the refrigerator, then checked the internal job posting board—something that she did every day. A position for a housekeeping manager had gone up two days before, and would stay up for another three days. The thought of applying had been rolling around in Genesis's head, but she was undecided about even going through the process, knowing that she didn't meet the qualification of having managerial experience and/or at least two years of college.

Going to school had always been just a fantasy for Genesis; paying for college just seemed impossible at the time. Raised below the poverty line solely by her grandmother, Anna Marie Taylor, Genesis had no rich parents who had been saving for her college education since the day she was born; her mother had been living from pillar to post strung out on drugs, while, other than his name, she had never known her father. Because she was just an average student, she hadn't been awarded with full-ride scholarships like some of her high school classmates, and never even thought seriously about college until the spring of her senior year. Without the guidance of a caring counselor to help her uncover grant and other scholarship opportunities, the feasibility of taking on the price of books and tuition on her own was beyond unrealistic.

There was nothing that Anna Marie would have liked to give Genesis more than a college education, but the reality of scraping over pennies for decent meals and clothing brought tears to Anna Marie's eyes whenever Genesis would mention school. After a while, Genesis stopped bringing it up, which brought both relief and pain to Anna Marie's heart. She was proud to see her granddaughter graduate from high school, but felt in many ways she'd failed her by not helping her to carve a clear path to a more successful future. The one thing she was able to do was leave Genesis with a roof over her head. While the small three-bedroom, one-bath home wasn't much and hadn't been paid off when Anna Marie passed, it had been willed to Genesis at age eighteen, only two months after she'd finished high school. Right away, Genesis secured a full-time job to make sure she didn't lose her grandmother's legacy. The mortgage was fairly low, and with some frugal budgeting and shopping constraints, Genesis kept her head above water. It didn't matter to her that the house sat just across from Ridley Circle, a public housing complex overrun with low-income families consisting mostly of kids and mothers; Genesis was grateful for a place where she could find safety, refuge, and comfort. In her grief and sudden transition into adult responsibility, the pursuit of college almost immediately dropped from her priority list.

Now, looking at the posting for a job she knew she was more than qualified for in terms of experience, she wished that she'd at the very least gone to a community college and taken a couple of classes that she could try to dress up.

Her eyes roamed over the posting a few seconds longer, until Maureen Singleton entered the room, trailed by four new employees. Maureen had recently turned in her resignation as she was expecting a baby, getting married, and moving to Arizona, which was the reason for the open manager position.

"And this is the break room," she said, lifting her arms as if she was showcasing a grand prize. "The time clock is in here. We don't use an actual clock, but you will log in to the computer there." Waddling on her heels, she walked over to the computer station right where Genesis stood. "Good morning, Genesis," she greeted. "This is Dee-Dee, Simone, Julie, and Amber. They are just starting today, so I am going to team a couple of them up with you."

"No problem," Genesis said, nodding at the four young ladies.

"Have you seen Taunya this morning?" Maureen glanced down at her watch and frowned. Just then, Taunya came bustling in the door on her cell phone.

"I tell you what . . . that mess better be cleaned up by the time I get off work or I'ma beat somebody's ass!" She snapped the phone closed while she switched her way to the refrigerator and deposited a foil-covered plate enclosed in a plastic grocery bag. "Good morning," she said to the group, barely looking over her shoulder. "I'm sorry, them kids of mine getting on my nerves first thing in the damn morning. How y'all doing?" With a mouth as big and loud as Adele Givens's, Taunya could easily have filled in for a speaking part if the actress/comedienne ever took ill.

"Hey, Taunya," Genesis said back, while the others gave a slight wave or mumbled good morning. Although she was not a large woman, her uniform pants fit purposely tight across her behind, and she always made sure to leave a little eye candy out in her bosom area, claiming that doing so netted her more tips from overnight male guests, even the ones with wives. "What's good for lunch today?"

"I cooked some Salisbury steak with onions and gravy last night, and had some leftover macaroni and cheese from Sunday. You still on your breakfast bar diet?" she teased, gathering her long hair up into a ponytail and securing it with a rubber band.

"You know me, I try to eat light."

"Yeah, until you see what's on my plate," Taunya scoffed. "I think you just don't like to cook, girl, but you know I brought a little extra just for you." She turned to Maureen and the group of ladies. "This y'all's first day?" She did a quick once-over of each woman as she walked toward them to clock in. The ladies nodded.

"Actually, they were just getting ready to clock in," Maureen answered. "Do you mind showing them how to do it since you're here?"

"Not at all." Taunya clocked herself in, then guided the group of ladies through the process before turning back to Maureen. "Who going with me? Don't be tryna hold me up in here all day, Miss Maureen. You know I likes to get my stuff done early. I need to be home by the time *Oprah* come on."

"Why don't I send Dee-Dee and Amber with you? And, Genesis, you take Julie and Simone," Maureen stated, scribbling on a notepad she held in her hand. "Then tomorrow you all can switch." She looked at the new girls and continued. "You ladies are in good hands with Genesis and Taunya. I'll be doing a walk-through around midday to see how things are working out for you, but in the meantime I need to have a seat," she huffed, holding on to her belly as she walked toward the door.

"Yeah, you look like you 'bout ready to drop that load," Taunya remarked. "Gone and sit down 'fore somebody have to roll you outta here."

"I'll be in my office working on payroll if you guys need me."

Genesis retrieved her supply cart from the closet and tried to imagine what Maureen did all day. Inter-

view and hire new staff members, produce a weekly
schedule, handle payroll, order supplies, and make
sure everybody else was doing his or her job. *I could do
that*, Genesis thought, making a decision to apply for
Maureen's position.

Chapter 2

Alton looked at his reflection through the driver's-door window for a final self-approval of his appearance. A loose-fitting black knit shirt hung from his shoulders, the top button gapped open, exposing the crew neck of a white T-shirt beneath. His tan cargo-styled khakis were freshly pressed and creased down to the hemline where they fell on a pair of black bowling-shoe-styled loafers. He ran a hand over his waves, then chuckling to himself, twisted the diamond stud in his left ear for good luck; it was a ritual that had yet to fail him. It was their third date, so things could stand to move forward a little, he reasoned. After popping an Altoid in his mouth, he strolled casually to the door of 1615 Ivy Avenue and tapped lightly.

Genesis had been standing on the other side watching his approach up the walkway through her peephole, but counted to ten, tugging at her blouse, before opening the door, not wanting to seem too anxious. She met Alton with a dazzling but shy smile while his eyes absorbed her five-eight, size 6 frame, casually dressed in a pair of white slacks paired with a turquoise blouse with white beading around the neck-line, and white sandals. She'd pinned her hair up into a loose roll, allowing tendrils to cascade down both sides of her face. She felt that just a little eyeliner and lip-gloss was sufficient for makeup; she didn't have much else anyway.

"You look great," he said, having never seen her in anything but her work uniform. The other times that they'd been out had been simple morning coffee dates, when he had personally given her a ride to work on his day off.

"Thanks, come on in. I'll be just a minute." Alton watched the swing of her hips as she sauntered down the short hallway into what he assumed was either the bedroom or bathroom. While out of her sight, he reached down and gave his manhood a reassuring squeeze and twisted his earring once more. He reminded himself that he had at least four condoms in his wallet, but it was his goal to go home with none.

To keep himself occupied, he began giving himself an uninvited tour of the small space she called home. Four steps took him from the living room into a small, outdated but clean kitchen, modestly decorated in a sunflower motif. A small dish on the countertop filled with a potpourri mixture gave off a fragrant cinnamon aroma. Behind the dish were a set of candles of varied sizes, their wicks untouched by a flame. Kitty-cornered beneath the cabinets sat a large portable stereo. A set of wineglasses were neatly arranged along a shelf above her double sink, flanked by an older model electric stove. A Crock-Pot and toaster accompanied the stove as alternate cooking appliances. Alton took note of the half loaf of bread that sat atop the refrigerator, along with a box of cheese crackers and a bag of potato chips. Simply out of curiosity he peeked into the fridge. Two rows of eggs and a package of bacon signified that she cooked breakfast, and a half-empty bottle of white zinfandel suggested that perhaps she was into pampering herself. *Maybe we can finish that wine off tonight,* he thought before easing the door closed. *Then she can cook me a little breakfast in the morning.*

Once back in the living room, he peeked through the miniblinds at his vehicle, for no reason in particular. "Coco, you need some help back there?" He thought for a second of tiptoeing to her bedroom to make a quick assessment, and maybe even skip dinner altogether, but then concluded that patience would be the better card to play.

Genesis tapped down the hallway, presenting herself a second time, this time with her hair cascading around her shoulders. "I decided to let my hair out for a change. It's always up or pushed back at work."

"Good choice," Alton commented, giving a nod of approval. "So, what do you have a taste for?"

She shrugged. "I don't know. I'm not picky."

"Well, what do you like? Seafood, steak, Chinese, sushi? How about Indian?"

"Indian? I've never had Indian food before. Is that like goats and stuff?" Genesis crinkled her nose.

"If that's what you want, I'm sure they can fry you something up." Alton placed his hand on the small of her back, escorting her out the front door and to his car. "I wouldn't recommend it, though, if you've not had it before. They do serve chicken, beef, and meats that you are probably more accustomed to. And it's pretty good eating . . . so what do you say?" He flashed a sexy smile that made Genesis weak in the knees. *Sexy smile, two points,* she noted mentally.

"I'll try anything once." She blushed as he opened the passenger's door, made sure that she was seated, then walked around to his side of the car and got in.

During the twenty-five-minute drive, Alton silently planned his after-dinner strategy. He'd take her back to her place, offer her a minipedicure and foot massage, and work his way up her long legs from there. No woman had ever been able to resist him lapping at her feet. He had read in a massage manual that there was a connection to every part of the body located on the sole of a person's foot; he definitely knew how to work the part that would bring him the most benefit and return on his investment. He had learned that just the right touch in the right place would make a woman's panties nearly dissolve into thin air. He glanced over at Genesis, who sat with one leg crossed over the other, looking as chaste and as pure as she possibly could. She couldn't have looked more like a prude if she dressed like a nun. *I'ma tag that tonight, though,* he thought, folding his bottom lip into his mouth.

They arrived at Nawab's, a restaurant specializing in Indian cuisine. Genesis was immediately intrigued by both the ambiance created by varied lighting arrangements, rich colors, and artwork, and the tantalizing aroma of blended spices, roasted meats, and freshly baked breads.

Like a gentleman, Alton pulled Genesis's chair out and made sure she was comfortably seated before seating himself. They both perused the menu, reading the vivid descriptions of the entrée selections.

"They don't, like, cook dogs here, do they?" Genesis asked with an apprehensive expression.

"I don't know, but we can ask the girl when she comes to take our order," he teased. "But look, how is eating a dog different from eating a cow, a chicken, or a pig? It's still an animal you're stuffing in your mouth." He chuckled at the expression of disdain on Genesis's face. "I mean really, how is taking a bite out of Flossie or Homer any better than sinking your teeth into Toto?"

"Because they aren't house pets," she argued.

"No, *you* just aren't used to them as house pets. I bet if you go to Brazil or somewhere, they got plenty of chickens strutting around the house and in the front yard as pets and dinner! If you were raised in the Philippines, you wouldn't think twice about eating a dog. As a matter of fact, let me tell you what they do to stray dogs. See, first they catch him and start fattening him up by feeding him—"

Genesis held up her hand and cut him off before he could go into any more detail. "Hold on, I don't want to hear anything about anybody eating a dog before I order this stuff I can hardly pronounce. How do you know anyway?"

"I used to be in the army. I've been there and seen it with my own eyes. You wouldn't believe the stuff they eat over there."

"Alton, do you want me to enjoy my meal or not?" She swatted at him with her menu, impressed that he'd had the disciplined background of a soldier. He probably still had some benefits if he was discharged honorably; she awarded him a few more points.

"You're right, I'm sorry. I don't want to spoil your appetite." *And spoil my nightcap.*

Genesis decided on chicken tikka masala, an entrée of boneless roasted chicken served in a mild curry sauce. Alton ordered saag lamb, which was lamb cooked with spinach. They both decided on a side dish of stir-fried rice mixed with vegetables, nuts, and raisins.

"So you decided to post for that job, huh?" Genesis had shared with him during one of their morning conversations that she was looking to move up at the hotel.

"Yeah, I put my application in. The way I see it, the worst thing they could tell me is no, and that's not something I've not heard before." She sipped from her glass of iced tea. "I think I have a pretty good shot at it. I've been at the hotel for, like, eight years now."

"So you're pretty much a professional at what you do, then," he suggested.

"I ought to be, but I don't know if that is saying very much, a professional bed maker? That doesn't sound like something to brag about."

"Your change is gonna come, Coco-brown. Don't even worry about it." Although he had since learned her name, he hadn't discarded his pet name for her.

Steam rose from their platters as they were set on the table before them, and they both dug in.

"Mmm . . ." Genesis murmured. "This rice is really good."

"I told you they had good food here." Alton forked a cube of lamb into his mouth and between bites fed Genesis encouraging lines about her career goal aspirations. Making her feel good about herself now would make him feel good later.

* * *

"You mind if I come in for a little while?" he asked, pulling up in front of her house after their meal. "I won't stay long. I'd just like to end this date on a special note."

"What kind of special note?" Genesis quizzed, giving him a suspicious eye.

"Nothing you have to take your pants off for," he said in a tone that suggested he was slightly insulted that she could even think that of him. "What kind of man do you think I am?" Alton chuckled, trying to keep the mood light.

"I'm just checking in case you had some bright ideas." She dug through her purse for her house keys. "I guess it won't hurt for you to come in for a few."

"You won't be disappointed," he promised, hopping out of the car and then jetting to her side to let her out. "I'm going to need to get a couple of things out of my trunk."

Once inside, Alton set up his workstation in the living room, which consisted of a basin of warm sudsy water, an exfoliating foot scrub, some peppermint oil, and a bottle of lotion. Genesis giggled as he set up, looking forward to the pampering session, then scooted to her room to change into a pair of shorts and a T-shirt, not wanting to roll up the legs of her pants. While she changed, she suddenly heard the mellow voice of Maxwell crooning through her speakers. She couldn't determine if that was a good or bad thing, but once she dipped her feet into their prepared bath, it was all good.

Inside of four minutes, her eyes were closed and she was mesmerized by the soothing touch of Alton's hands on her feet. When the water began to cool, he had another basin of heated water waiting and made a quick transfer. After thirty minutes of his underwater massage technique, he lifted and dried each foot, then continued the massage first with warmed lotion, then with his lips, tongue, and teeth, licking and nibbling on her toes and ankles. Just as he anticipated, before a full hour had passed, he was right where he'd planned to be, on top of her naked body with her legs up and pinned under the weight of his chest.

It was well after midnight when he pulled away, one condom shy of his goal, and packed his paraphernalia. "I'll see you in the morning," he whispered, leaning in to kiss her at the door. He glanced down at his watch and calculated the few hours he had left to sleep before he would have to be at work.

Genesis pulled her fleece robe around her tightly as she smiled, partially from embarrassment that she'd let herself go, and partially from pure satisfaction. "Okay. Drive safe."

Shutting the door behind him, she trekked to her room, pulled out her Him Book, and documented the evening, counting a total of twenty earned points between the dinner, the foot massage, and that little thing he did with his tongue.

Chapter 3

The bus ride to work had only been a little uncomfortable as Genesis and Alton caught eyes. He greeted her like he always did, but a hint of lust mixed with secrecy flickered in his eyes. Genesis grinned sheepishly, took her seat, and made small talk as normal. When Alton pulled over at her stop, she watched as his eyes traveled up and down her body, lingering on the parts that were more rounded.

"You have a good day," he said with a split-second rise of his brow. He licked his lips seductively and pulled away.

"That's a mighty big grin you're wearing on your face today." Taunya started, taking note of Genesis's glowing countenance. "You musta let that man get a prize from the cubbyhole last night."

"Actually, I was the one who got the prize. This man gave me a full foot massage after he washed my feet." Not exactly wanting to share the full details of her evening, Genesis avoided the sex part of her recap.

"What?" Taunya exclaimed, chuckling. "Girl, you had him working on them dogs?"

"I thought for a minute that I was in church, 'cause I looked at my hands and they looked new and I looked at my feet and they did too!" Both women burst into laughter. *And goodness knows that man had me speaking in an unknown tongue,* she kept to herself.

"So, how'd your interview go?"

"I haven't had it yet. I just now changed clothes. It's in fifteen minutes. But what are you doing on this floor?" Genesis asked in surprise as Taunya normally worked on the first few floors of the building.

"I thought you were down in your interview so I came up here to make sure these lazy heifers was up here working." She cut her eyes down the hall at two young ladies who were supposed to be inside a room. One was leaning against the wall snacking on a small package of peanuts. "You got time to lean you got time to clean!" Taunya yelled down the hall. The girl rolled her eyes, stuffed the peanuts in her pocket, and picked up a spray bottle and rag. "I'm tryna make sure you don't stay in here all night. And look at you looking all cute in your interview clothes."

"Do I look okay?" Genesis asked.

"Yeah, you look fine." Taunya smoothed a stray hair down at the nape of Genesis's neck. "You ready?"

"As ready as I'm going to be. I am a little nervous, though."

"Well, good luck, not that you need it. I'm sure you'll do just fine. You should have let me touch up this kitchen back here, though." Taunya pinched at a few tightly curled tufts of hair just above Genesis's collar.

"I tried to gel it down but—"

"You know good and well gel don't work on naps."
Taunya waved, cutting Genesis off midsentence. "Go
'head 'fore you be late."

They split to go their separate ways; Genesis headed
for the Human Resources office, while Taunya walked
toward the stairwell.

"I'll call you when I'm done and let you know how
it went," Genesis said.

Deidra Cox pushed back a headful of blond curls as
she glanced over Genesis's employee file in preparation for the interview she'd scheduled with her for that
afternoon. Her eight-year work history was impecca-
ble: very few absences or late arrivals and performance
reviews reflecting that she exceeded job expectations
consistently, receiving a raise of twenty-five cents per
hour every six months. Now at $8.50 an hour, Genesis
was one of the hotel's highest paid housekeepers. She
then printed off a sheet of prepared interview questions, attached them to a clipboard, and walked out of
her office to greet Genesis, who'd been waiting in the
HR lobby for fifteen minutes.

"Genesis?" she greeted with a corporate smile
pasted on her face.

Genesis tugged at her Wal-Mart knee-length skirt
and cropped ruched blouse as she nervously stood,
then met Deidra's extended hand with her own for a
firm shake. "Good afternoon, Ms. Cox."

"Call me Deidra," she replied, waving a dismissive
hand, trying to ease Genesis's apparent anxiety. In
two seconds, she took in Genesis's neat and clean but
unpolished appearance—a pair of black rubber-soled
flats atop flesh-toned panty hose, basic black skirt,

white blouse, small hoop earrings, and her hair done in way that made each pinned-up section look like a thick silky rope. "How are you doing today?" she asked, leading her back into her office and directing her to a chair positioned opposite of her own.

"Fine, thank you," Genesis answered confidently as she sat.

"So . . . you are interested in the housekeeping manager role." Deidra paused as she glanced over her application again, as if she had not already reviewed it.

"That's right. I really would like to consider the upward mobility opportunities that the company has to offer here, since I've been an employee for several years now."

"Yes, I saw that. Your work history is quite impressive." Deidra pretended to scrawl a few notes down on a sheet of paper positioned just beneath Genesis's completed paperwork. "Well, I just have a few questions for you to help me better understand your experiences here." A pleasant but not so natural smile spread across Deidra's face as she began asking the prepared questions, then jotting down Genesis's responses. She was actually surprised at the answers Genesis gave, backed by solid examples of her leadership abilities. Nonetheless, Deidra's mind floated away from the interview process to her plans for the evening.

It had been a while since she and her fiancé had been out, and his commitment to do dinner and a play that evening had been something Deidra had looked forward to all week. While she nodded in acknowledgment to what Genesis was saying, she was virtually roaming through her closet looking for her black strapless minidress. He loved her in that dress and couldn't seem to keep his hands off her whenever she wore it. She crossed her legs under her desk, as a direct reaction to the pulsing she felt beneath her panties in anticipation of lying beneath her man. Getting more turned on as the seconds passed, Deidra made plans to have a little phone sex right after this interview. The private bathroom that she shared with the training manager next door often became a midday place of escape for her, where she could spread her legs for a few minutes, and while her baby chanted in her ear through her cell phone, her fingers would do some talking of their own.

A smile from Genesis cued Deidra back into the present, so she cleared her throat and jotted down a few words that she thought she'd heard Genesis say.

"Well, that pretty much wraps it up for me. Did you have any questions?"

"Yes, how soon are you looking to make a hiring decision?"

"It could be in as early as three days, or it may take up to two weeks. I do have some other candidates that I'll be interviewing today, and from there, I'll be making second interview selections. I'll try not to keep you in suspense too long." She winked and smiled coyly before rising to escort Genesis to the door.

After Genesis thanked her for her time, Deidra closed the door, then looked down at the poor notes she'd taken. *It really doesn't matter*, she thought, frowning as she examined the backside of the internal application; her lack of formal education was the one barrier that Genesis had yet to overcome. As much as Deidra could have given Genesis a shot at a managerial role, she wasn't willing to. She was still up to her neck in student loan debt with several years of monthly payments to go. It wasn't fair to give someone else the same opportunity that she had to pay thousands of dollars for.

Deidra jotted a few thoughts on a sticky note, documenting experience as a plus but education as a minus. She stuck the note onto Genesis's application, added it to the pile of candidate applications that would receive decline letters, then rushed to the bathroom with her cell phone. She quickly pushed the digits of her fiancé's number, then waited for his answer.

"Hello," he said, his voice heavy with sleep.

"Hey, baby. I missed you so much last night."

"I know, but I don't have to work the overnight shift tonight, so I'll be ready to take care of you."

"Can you help take care of me right now?" she purred. "Because I'm in my favorite little secret place thinking about you, baby."

He chuckled. "Yeah, I think I can help you out with that. Gone and take them panties off."

Chapter 4

"Ma, I'ma need the rest of the money by next Friday, or I'm not gonna be able to go to class," Nikki communicated to her mother.

"How much is it this semester, Nikki?" Taunya huffed in exasperation. "I'll be right back." She glanced over at Dee-Dee before walking down the hall toward a door leading to a patio outside. She pulled a pack of cigarettes from her smock pocket, tapped it against the side of her hand, slid one from the pack, and inserted it between her lips. She quickly patted her pockets, feeling for her lighter, then cursed, realizing she didn't have it with her.

Nikki quoted a figure that nearly made Taunya's knees buckle. She sighed as her eyes scanned the moving cars below. "Did you at least try to find some scholarships?"

"I looked, Ma, but I didn't qualify for none of them."

Taunya began thinking of where she could come up with a lump sum of money in a matter of days. There would be this week's tips but other than that, there were no additional resources. "What are you doing with that work-study money?"

"I be needing that to pay my bills with."

"What bills?"

"I got my cell phone, and I be needing other stuff."

"Stuff like what, Nikki? That money is supposed to go toward school, not shopping sprees," Taunya snapped.

"Like tampons and stuff, Ma," Nikki replied, smacking her lips.

"Oh. Well." Taunya paused momentarily. "All right, well, let me make a few phone calls and call you back. You got food?"

"Yeah, I'm fine with that. I just need the rest of this tuition paid."

"Okay, it will get taken care of somehow. I'll call you back before the week is out," Taunya assured her daughter.

"All right, Ma, love you."

"Love you too, baby."

Taunya chewed on the flesh of the inside of her mouth, trying to figure out what to do. She hated being in this predicament. It seemed that every time she tried to move ahead, something would pop up to remind her of the past she was trying to leave behind, a past that had helped her stay afloat many days when there was just no light at the end of the tunnel.

Before she could talk herself out of it, she dialed another number.

"G-Spot," a rough male voice called out with no thought of customer service.

"Hey. Let me speak to T.J.," Taunya rushed from her lips.

"Yo, T.J., get the phone!" The sound of the receiver clanging against the bar exploded in Taunya's ear.

"This T.J., what's good?" the club owner said.

"Hey, T.J., it's Taunya," she cooed, not wanting to give the impression that she was hard up for cash, although they both knew that just by the fact that she was calling, the shortage of money was her dilemma.

"What's shaking, baby? What's up, you need a spot?" T.J. always made it easy for Taunya, sparing her the shame of having to ask to dance at his club.

"Yeah. My baby need books. You got something for this weekend?"

"Fo' sho, but you know I gotta check you out and make sure you still tight." Taunya knew all too well the price of calling T.J. He would let her keep nearly all the cash she'd earn over the weekend, but he'd expect to be paid up front in a totally different way. She was glad that he didn't have much stamina and the sexual transaction between them would more than likely take less than five minutes.

"Oh, I keeps it tight now, ain't no doubt about that," Taunya reassured him. She made sure to exercise regularly to keep herself in top shape just in case times like these arose. "What time can I come by?"

"Come on by this evening and let a brotha check you out so I can put you on."

"I'll be there." She snapped her phone closed, then stared up into the sky, already dreading what would take place that night and over the weekend. "Gotta do what I gotta do, and this ain't gone be forever, so I'ma work with what I got, 'cause when all else fail, I can shake my tail," she said to herself before going back inside the building and returning to work.

* * *

T.J. hung up the phone and looked over at his partner. "That was Taunya's old ass. She tryna get on for the weekend."

"Word?"

T.J. nodded his head as he chuckled. "She know she getting too old for this bull, man. But if she wanna come up in here and shake that ass, I gotta spot for her. She need to teach these stiff, nondancing chicken heads we got in here now a thing or two. She might be old, but that girl can work a pole . . . that one out there and this one right here," he snickered, grabbing his crotch and slapping his partner a high five with the other. "Make sure she get in when she show up tonight."

Chapter 5

"Ms. Cox, can I speak with you for a few minutes?" Even with her nerves on edge, Genesis was determined to find out what were the specific reasons that she wasn't considered for a second interview.

"Sure." Deidra motioned her toward her desk while flipping a stack of papers upside down. "What can I help you with today?"

"I just wanted to find out from you what I can do in the future to be more successful in my venture to move ahead with the company."

"Well, to be honest with you, Genesis, your work performance is stellar, and I see that you've been seen many times as the go-to person for training new housekeepers, which clearly speaks of your leadership abilities. At the same time, I'm concerned that you have no formal education." Deidra pursed her lips and interlaced her fingers tightly. "Without that critical piece, I am just not certain that you have the acumen needed to be successful in a management role." Her raised eyebrows gave finality to her words, and while Genesis searched her mind for a response, she could not articulate an argument to counter Deidra's feedback. "I would recommend that you look at continuing your education, even if you have to take one class at a time. As a matter of fact . . ." She paused as she pulled open her file cabinet drawer. "The company does offer tuition reimbursement. I'm not really familiar with the details," she lied, knowing that the benefit was only for full-time management employees. "Here, look over this brochure and see if you can get enrolled in a few classes next semester. It may take you a little while to finish, but that time will go by quicker than you'll realize." She slid the brochure across her desk, just as her cell phone rang from her purse. Hurriedly reaching down to retrieve it, she dismissed Genesis. "I need to take that. Good luck to you."

"What a way to start the weekend," Genesis mumbled. Dejected, she meandered to the parking lot to her car that had finally been repaired, pulling the folded paper from her smock pocket. She read it three more times, then crumpled the decline letter into a tight ball and tossed it into a trash can. Looking for a shoulder to cry on, she dialed Alton's number.

"I didn't get it," she said once he answered.

"I'm sorry to hear that. Did they tell you why?"

"Yeah, because I don't have a degree," she replied, almost whining.

"But you've been working there long enough to know the place like the back of your hand."

"I know but I guess that's just not enough." Genesis sighed as she plopped down in the driver's seat.

"You want me to come make you feel better?" he

uttered softly. He could hear the smile in her voice when she responded.

"You know I do."

"I'll be round there in a little bit."

With that bit of motivation, Genesis sped home and hopped in the shower, scenting her body with a wild berry body wash. As she toweled off, she took inventory of her body in a full-length mirror, pleased with what she saw. Her breasts were still firm although she was approaching thirty, her belly flat, and her behind round. She turned her back to the mirror and looked over her shoulder as she attempted to do the booty shake featured in Beyoncé's *Crazy in Love* video. It had only been a little over a month since she'd been seeing Alton, but when she thought of him, she identified with the lyrics of that song.

She lotioned her body and dusted on a shimmering powder across her shoulders, then slipped into a baby-blue chemise. Just as she finished pulling a few tendrils of hair out of her ponytail, a tap on her door signaled Alton's arrival.

His eyes widened when she opened the door, absorbing all they could take in. "Girl, they need to turn you down for a job more often!" he commented before wrapping his arms around her waist. She giggled as he planted kisses on her neck. "You feeling all right, or you need me to put a Band-Aid where it hurts?" He kicked his foot back to close the door, then reached behind him with one hand to turn the dead bolt.

"I think I need a Band-Aid," she murmured.

"Where at?"

"Right here." She placed her hand over her heart while she pushed her lips out into a pout.

He slid his hands up her gown, cupped her behind,

lifted her from the floor, and carried her toward the bedroom. Using his teeth, Alton slid the spaghetti strap of her chemise off her shoulder and took her left breast into his mouth. "Let me see if I can make it feel better," he mumbled.

Alton wrapped his arms around Genesis's waist as she stood at the kitchen sink washing the breakfast dishes. She'd gotten up early and prepared home-made waffles topped with whipped cream and honey butter, served with slices of apple sausage from Trader Joe's.

"Girl, you know how to put it on a brotha," he commented between nibbles he placed on her neck. Grinning, Genesis tilted her head, allowing him full access. "Last night you whipped some stuff out I ain't never seen before," he whispered in her ear, pulling her hips backward toward him while he thrust forward. "Then this morning you serve me breakfast in bed." He cupped her breasts, then ran his hands down her sides and rested them on her hips. "I like how you work out your frustrations." Giggling she turned to face him and he immediately absorbed her lips into his own. He pulled away after three wet kisses and smoothed her hair down with his hand. "I gotta go, baby. I need to get my hair cut and have the oil changed in my car." He pecked her nose. "What are you doing today?"

Genesis shrugged as she turned to face the sink again, but nestled into his arms and chest at the same time. "I think I'll research some college Web sites, see what's out there." While she had found temporary comfort in Alton's arms, she still felt the sting of rejection, which would become more pronounced as Monday morning's obligation to report to work drew nearer. "If anything is going to change for me, it's up to me, right?"

"That's right, baby, 'cause ain't nobody gonna give you nothing but a hard way to go."

She dried her hands on a dish towel and saw Alton to the door.

"I'll call you later, baby, okay? And keep your head up. Things gone work out for you."

"Yeah, I know." She nodded. She pecked his lips in a good-bye and pushed her door closed.

"It's time to live up to my name and give myself a new beginning," Genesis said to herself, heading to her spare bedroom that was set up like a den to log on to her computer. She spent half of her Saturday reviewing college Web sites and crunching tuition numbers. Smiling faces greeted her on every page, and the more she searched, the younger the faces seemed to be, although most schools had continuing education programs for older students. She tapped her pencil on the desk as, considering the costs and time requirements, her frustrations grew. While she would probably qualify for financial aid, the price for books was still quite hefty, not to mention the time it would take her to complete a degree program. Going part-time would make it affordable, but who wanted to wait another six to eight years to get a real job? *I'll be almost thirty-six years old by then,* she thought, counting semesters and credit hours.

She shook her head, discouraged by how dim the reality of her starting and completing college seemed, but continued visiting Web sites. Just as she had decided to give up for the day, a pop-up caught her full attention. A few mouse clicks later, she had arrived at a Web site of a company that offered replicated degrees from the university of her choosing.

Can't get ahead because you don't have a degree?

Perhaps you couldn't afford the high costs of a college education, or maybe you hated school altogether, but now you are finding out that you just can't seem to get ahead in the professional world without a degree in your hand. We've got the solution. We can produce the very finest of degrees and college transcripts to look like the real thing!

Your diploma, whether it's a college degree, high school diploma, bachelor's degree, college transcript—whatever you require—will be custom-designed by our design team to look like an exact replica of the original document you want to match. We take great pride in the most minute details—so you don't have to! It's the attention to detail that counts. Our products have been subjected to the highest level of scrutiny and proven their value time and time again. You will be amazed what our authentic replica documents can do for you!

For additional authenticity, our diplomas are printed on high-quality parchment paper to match the original documents. We also use security paper on each of our transcripts in order to match the original. Our work is as true to the original as possible, and we are proud to lead the way in industry standards in our field.

Weighing the costs in her mind, Genesis didn't take long to decide that this was her ticket up. For about the same price of taking just one class at a community college, she could have an authentic-looking degree with her name on it and show the world that she was indeed a force to be reckoned with.

She made a list of schools that weren't too prestigious, but seemed credible, then visited each institution's Web site to see which looked like it would be a good fit for her, studying the school's population, cultural mix, and degree programs. She finally made her choice of North Carolina Central University, a school that she didn't think would raise too many eyebrows. She picked a graduation year of six years prior, which would have been the year she would have actually graduated had she gone to college, selected magna cum laude as how she completed her studies, then chose a degree in business management with a minor in marketing and finance.

Her fingers punched in the numbers from her check card to complete her order, and as she clicked on ENTER, she bit into her lip and partially smiled. In less than a week she would have a document that would state to the world that she was a college graduate. "Let's see how much difference this piece of paper actually makes."

Chapter 6

With her daughter's tuition in mind, Taunya went through a stretching routine, then slathered herself in baby oil getting ready for her next set. She'd already danced three songs and had collected dollar bills hand over fist, which she'd stuffed into her duffel bag and locked away. Using a spray bottle, she pumped a fine mist of water all over her body to simulate sweat, then ran to the sink to wet her hair, causing it to form into long wavy tendrils.

Topless, she stepped onto the stage in her silver satin thong, a pair of thigh-high stockings, and four-inch heels. Taunya once again blocked out the faces of her audience as she began her routine, thrusting, gyrating, and rotating her hips to D'Angelo's "Brown Sugar." It was obvious to her googley-eyed paying on-lookers that Taunya wasn't as young as the other women dancing there, but they crowded the stage amazed by her incredible flexibility and agility. Turning her back and dropping to the floor, she felt a number of hands grope her body as money was placed between the narrow piece of elastic and her slick skin. She rose to standing, then slid slowly into a Chinese split with her head thrown back, her eyes shut tight, and her hands lost in her hair. Once her body eased onto the floor, she rolled her pelvis back and forth, giving some man the imaginary ride of a lifetime. Hands covered her legs as the men stuffed money wherever they could, even between the sole of her feet and the instep of her heels. As the song began to come to an end, Taunya rolled forward to her stomach and attempted to close her legs, but a tall white gentleman had a hold of her ankle. Not panicked in the least, she caught his eye and winked. He winked back, pressed a five-hundred-dollar bill to his lips, then ran his hand up from her ankle to her behind and stuffed the money there, never breaking eye contact.

"You want some of this brown sugar, Daddy?" she whispered. He only bit into his lower lip as Taunya, keeping her eyes on him, finished her routine and exited the stage.

"That fool crazy enough to spend five-hundred-dollars on something he cain't do nothing but wish he could get, I'm fool enough to take it," she said, pulling bills out from varied places and compiling them in her hand.

In minutes she was in her sweats and tennis shoes with her bag slung over her shoulder and on her way to give T.J. his percentage of what she'd collected.

"Thanks, T.J.," she said, stuffing a wad of money into his hand.

"Anytime, doll baby. And you right, you sho' keeps it tight." He chuckled. "You ain't never lied about that."

On her way home, Taunya stopped at 7-Eleven and

bought a money order for half the amount Nikki needed for school, made it out to James Madison University, stuffed it in an envelope she'd brought with her, and dropped it in a nearby mailbox. Every muscle in her body ached as she headed downtown toward home. She forced herself to pack away the familiar feelings of self-degradation that came from flaunting her body in front of the lustful eyes of strange men. It was something she'd never gotten used to, no matter how many times she'd done it. Nonetheless, she was relieved that her baby would be able to continue her education and find a good job and would never have to stoop as low as to sell her body and soul for a dollar bill.

Alton wrapped his arms around Genesis's shoulders as they made their way through the movie theater parking lot. They'd caught an early show of *The Pursuit of Happyness*, and were now headed out for lunch.

"What do you have a taste for?" Alton nibbled on her cheek before opening her car door.

"A big fat juicy cheeseburger with a pile of greasy fries drowned in ketchup." Genesis patted her belly, although it couldn't have been more flat. "This tank is empty."

"I don't know how when you gobbled up all the popcorn," Alton teased. He shut her door, eased into his own seat, then leaned over the armrest and kissed her lips before sliding the keys into the ignition and pulling off. He rested his right hand on Genesis's thigh while the other maneuvered his car into flowing traffic. "Let's ride up to Williamsburg and eat at Cities Grill."

"As long as they serve cheeseburgers, that's fine with me."

Before they pulled onto the freeway, Alton made a U-turn and then a right into a small subdivision of newly constructed homes.

"Where are we going?"

"To look at some houses. I've been meaning to stop through here but I always forget."

"Are you thinking about buying?"

"It probably won't be for another year, but there's no harm in looking, is there? Plus I need to know what my baby likes so I can see how much money I need to save up," he added, shaking her leg slightly. "You might be a high-maintenance wifey."

Wifey? Where did that come from? Genesis crinkled her brows and looked at Alton with a confused grin.

"Oh yeah, you's a keeper." He winked. She gave no response to Alton's last comment other than a dismissive shrug and giggle, trying not to read too much into Alton's words that clearly hinted of a future together. At the same time, she had increased his value by ten points.

"No, no harm in looking," she replied instead. "Actually I could use some decorating ideas." For a few minutes, Genesis thought of each room in her home, and how it was in dire need of updating.

They were greeted by the sales representative, who sat behind the desk in the model home's converted two-car garage space. After gathering some basic information, she welcomed the couple to tour the home. Genesis gasped, oohed, and ahhed at many of the home's features and upgrades. A fully mirrored wall in the dining room gave the illusion of increased space and beautifully accented the polished white oak furnishing. Place settings for eight gleamed on the table, as if Thanksgiving dinner would be served in the next half hour. A spacious kitchen with an island was gallantly dressed in granite and marble, and featured chic stainless steel appliances. A first-floor bedroom flanked the kitchen, decorated in a navy blue and tan nautical motif.

"This would be the guest bedroom," Alton stated, as he peered into a closet that stretched the length of the wall. "They have their own bathroom too," he added, opening another door and stepping into a full bath.

"This is really nice." Genesis lit up the stairs and called to Alton as soon as she stepped through the double-doored entranceway of the master suite, "Baby, you've got to see this."

Alton took the steps two at a time and in a flash stood behind Genesis, wrapping his arms at her waist. "This is the biggest bedroom I've ever seen," she squealed, imagining how wonderful it would be to live there.

"I would love to wake up here every morning with you in my arms." He kissed the tiny spot behind her left ear, then lowered his lips to her neck. Clumsily he trod forward, pushing her toward the king-sized bed. "Mmmm," he moaned, beginning to press his hips forward into her behind.

"Boy, stop it," she whispered, attempting to pull away. "You so nasty."

"You like nasty. At least that's what you said last night," he teased. "Come on, let's pretend this is our room." Alton slid his hands down her legs and quickly gathered her skirt, bringing its hemline up to her waist. He caressed the smooth skin on her thighs and behind. "You got on a thong too? We 'bout to leave a wet spot on their bed." He slightly pulled her hips toward him, but Genesis wriggled from his grasp.

"You need to cut it out." A few quick steps put her in a cozy alcove in the corner of the room featuring a chaise longue and a small table and lamp. "This corner would be perfect for reading or just having some quiet time, wouldn't it?"

Alton huffed in defeat before walking over and collapsing on the chaise.

"Yeah. I'd lie right here and be like, bring me my paper, woman!" He tugged on her arm, causing her to fall into his lap, and immediately began planting wet kisses on her neck." Genesis giggled as she first struggled to free herself, then for a moment became settled in his embrace, kissing him passionately. Beginning to feel her own temperature rise, she slowly pulled away.

"Come on, let's look at the rest of the house so we can get home," she whispered.

The tour of the remainder of the model home took less than five minutes, three of them spent standing in the master bathroom shower while erotic visions rushed through both their minds.

"You like this house?" Alton's words were muffled as his lips were enveloping Genesis's into his own.

"Are you going to get it for me?"

"I'll get you anything you want." He pulled her tighter against him. "You just keep taking care of me, girl . . ." He kissed her once more. "And I'ma always take care of you."

Genesis pulled away and slipped from his arms, allowing her hand to linger behind her only for a split second to give his lower extremity a promising squeeze.

* * *

"I'm going to start looking for another job," Genesis shared as she stabbed her fork into a small house salad.

"Really? Where at?" Alton was having a difficult time listening to Genesis and keeping up with the game that was displayed on three of the bar and grill's large televisions. Mostly all Genesis said had to be repeated.

"I don't know exactly. I'm just going to start looking for places where I can apply my talents and grow professionally." There was a pause of silence until Alton realized it was his turn to respond.

"Huh? Uh . . . that's good, baby. Make the shot, man!" he yelled toward the screen. Once the basketball sank through the netting, he sighed in relief, then looked over at Genesis.

"What did I just say?" she quizzed.

"You said, uh . . . that you was gonna start applying at a coupla places . . . and, uh . . ." Genesis's expression of pressed lips and raised brows signified that he'd do better just to confess that she hadn't had his full attention. "I'm sorry, sweetie, I just wanted to catch that part. Go 'head with what you were saying."

"It's nothing," she dismissed. "I'm just tired of cleaning toilets for a living, so I'm going to try to find something I like a little better."

"You'll find something." He lifted a fry from her plate, then bit into a buffalo wing from his own platter. "You can do whatever you put your mind to. And what you can't do, I can do for you."

A man that's got my back. I like that. Note to self, award a few extra points, Genesis thought as Alton leaned in and pecked her cheek.

Chapter 7

Genesis used her fingernail to break through the clear tape that sealed a small flat box holding the key to her new future. With nervous fingers, she opened an oversized white envelope and pulled out a degree certificate printed with her name in handsome calligraphic lettering. Even though the degree wasn't hard-earned by spending nights on end with her head in books, it was hard-earned due to the long hours she'd put in at the hotel scrubbing toilets and changing sheets. And while the total cost couldn't even begin to compare to the real costs of college, Genesis felt justified by the money she'd sacrificed to get the document, which looked to be as real as the ground she stood on.

"Girl, it came," she announced to Taunya, beaming.

"For real? How does it look?"

"It looks pretty genuine to me," Genesis replied, flipping the document to the backside, looking for any indication that would give away its lack of authenticity.

"Well, congratulations. Now what are you gonna do with it?"

"Start applying for some real jobs and make some real money." Genesis had already researched and made a list of hotels that were looking for management employees, and was simply waiting on the arrival of her degree to actually post for them. "But first I'm going to get this bad boy framed, so I can hang it on the wall whenever I get an office somewhere. Much as this thing cost, I need to put it in a vault!"

"You right about that. Well, when you get your new job, call me, girl, so I can get up outta that hotel. They killin' me in there. I wish Nikki would have found that Web site before she went enrolling at James Madison University. I'd be a whole lot richer right now," Taunya joked although actually she was quite proud of the fact that her daughter was in college earning her degree.

"I'm on my way to the bookstore. You wanna ride?"

"No, go 'head. My dogs hurt too bad. I'll see you tomorrow at work."

Genesis ended the call, packed her document away, then headed out for Barnes & Noble in search of resources that would help her strengthen the wording of her resume. Browsing through several titles with a notepad and a copy of her resume, she sat for two hours jotting edits in the margins and on the backside of the paper, realizing how simplistic her resume had previously been. Her fingertips massaged her temples, trying to ease away the onset of a headache.

"Study long, study wrong," a voice said from above her head.

Genesis let her eyes float upward from the floor, taking in a pair of soft leather loafers, cuffed khaki pants, a loose-fitting white oxford rolled at the sleeves, and a handsome brown face with incredibly piercing eyes. His hair was cut close to his scalp and brushed until small waves had formed at his crown. In her mind, Genesis flipped to an empty page of her journal and gave him ten points. His lips parted slightly, revealing a small fraction of his less than perfect teeth. *Two-point deduction*, she immediately thought, *but he's still cute.*

"Study light, study right," he finished. "Do you mind if I use this chair?" His hand rested on the back of the vacant seat, but his eyes were locked into Genesis's. "We have a pretty large discussion group over there and there's not another chair available anywhere."

In a flash she remembered how she was dressed and was somewhat embarrassed that she was still in her work clothes with the exception of her smock. How many times had Taunya told her about leaving the house looking "any ol' kinda way"?

"You never know where Mr. One Hundred is going to pop up," she'd say.

"Wherever he shows up, he has to take me how I am, so if he can't deal with me looking like a wolf, then he don't deserve to have me looking like a queen," Genesis would argue back.

"You keep on thinking like that and see you don't be lonely for a long time."

In this instance, Genesis wished she had listened to Taunya for a change. She dusted a spot of powdery cleanser off her leg. Wishing she had put on something a little more appealing, Genesis cleared her throat and unconsciously ran a single hand over her hair. "Um, sure."

"Thanks," he said, lifting the chair, then turning to walk toward his group. He positioned the chair so that he faced Genesis although he was several feet away. Once he sat at his table, he seemed to dive right into the discussion, clearly articulating his words accompanied by the movement of his hands. Genesis caught herself several times unfocused on her own task but looking up at the brother, somewhat smitten by his aura. She tagged a few more points onto his score, impressed by his intelligence, indicated by his rich vocabulary. She hadn't even had to look away to make her staring inconspicuous, because he never looked her way.

Realizing that she was too distracted to finish what she'd come there to do, she began gathering her things and rose from her table. When she took one last glance in his direction, their eyes caught, and he acknowledged her with a quick wink complemented with a half smile. Genesis blushed, dropping her eyes bashfully, pretending to search for something in her purse. When she glanced up again, he was back in his discussion.

"Too bad I don't have a name," she whispered before losing herself in several rows of books. She picked Bebe Moore Campbell's *72 Hour Hold* and settled in an armchair to indulge herself in the printed words.

"You still here, huh?" Genesis looked up into the man's face again. "I'm Ric." This time he extended his hand.

"Genesis." She smiled back.

"Genesis . . . a church girl, huh?"

"I don't know about all that. I could stand to go regularly, I guess." She shrugged, smiling.

"Really? Well, maybe you can come with me and my

son one Sunday." Ricardo squatted to the floor, resting his elbows on his knees, and laced his fingers.

Right away the smile began to fade from Genesis's face. *A son? Oh nooo*, she thought. "Well, I'm actually seeing somebody right now," she said truthfully, thinking about how well things were developing between her and Alton. *And I don't do kids and baby mama drama*, she kept to herself. *That is supernegative point value.* She began gathering her things again and lifted herself from the chair, taking the novel she'd been perusing to the front counter. "Take care," she ended cordially.

Unable to get Ricardo out of her mind, Genesis wondered if she should have given him more of a chance. He was smart, handsome, and witty from what she could tell, but the fact that he had a child was a piece that could not be ignored or accepted.

Chapter 8

Milton Lewis perused the table of Danishes, croissants, muffins, fresh fruits, and juices, piling his selection of foods onto a saucer. He balanced the plate atop his leather portfolio, while he poured himself a cup of black coffee. As he walked leisurely into the conference room, he scrolled down his list of things he had to accomplish to include making a trip to the courthouse to attend a foreclosure auction right at one o'clock. He wanted to make a bid on a three-bedroom brick home located in Azalea Gardens, an older and well-established neighborhood in Hampton. He took a seat at a round table, opened his portfolio, and began to review his notes. The property was situated in a no-outlet area, which meant very little traffic; it was very close to Hampton High School, home of the Hampton Crabbers who year after year were named the state champions in football; it was close to the bus line; it had a convenience store at the neighborhood's entrance; and it was centrally located to the city's other attraction areas. He already had a chance to view the seventeen-hundred-square-foot home, which had been meticulously kept, but for one reason or another the owners, a married couple with two kids, had stopped paying the mortgage. He punched a few numbers into a calculator, figuring out what he thought he could rent the property for if he won the bid, which he planned to do.

Entering into his thirteenth year as a real estate broker had afforded him a lifestyle that many could only dream about. He owned rental properties all over the peninsula and south side, all of them well kept and maintained, and most with rent-paying families in them.

Milton was a man who believed in the principle of sharpening the saw; he did what he could to keep his skills current and stay on top of his business game, sometimes traveling to attend various seminars and presentations that would help him increase his net worth. His watch showed that he had ten minutes before the sales training he'd registered for would begin. He rose from his seat and went out into the hallway to visit the men's room. He turned into a hallway leading to the hotel's rooms, then immediately turned around, convinced that he was headed in the wrong direction.

"Excuse me, where is your lavatory?"

Taunya turned around to answer him. Acknowledgment, though unspoken, was evident in both their eyes; they recognized each other. "Oh, you just passed it, it's right there around the corner," she directed while batting her lashes, taking in his debonair appearance. A black knit sweater beneath a gray suit accented his well-cared-for physique and perfectly complemented the silver and gray strands of his neatly cut

hair, mustache, and goatee. In Taunya's mind, he
could pass for Richard Gere's brother.

"Thank you." He winked before turning in the opposite direction. When he exited the bathroom, he
ran into Taunya again as she stood nearby polishing a
water fountain. Taunya had loosened a button of her
shirt, allowing a bit of cleavage to peek out, and
smeared on a bit of gloss. It didn't matter to her that
the man was white, and visibly older—she knew he had
cash; he even smelled like money. "Have a good day,"
he said purely out of cordiality more so than out of sincerity since their eyes had met again. Honestly, he
couldn't have cared less what kind of day Taunya had.

She had no clue as to what event was being held in
the hotel's conference rooms, but quickly thought of
something to say to keep him in her presence. "Are
you participating in one of the workshops here?" she
asked to stall him and hopefully begin to work her
mojo, disregarding his wedding band.

"Uh, actually, yes." He stopped to acknowledge her,
sliding his hands into the pockets of his trousers. He
raised an eyebrow, searching for her motive. "Are you
interested in real estate investing?"

"Not exactly," she answered, resting a single finger
on her puckered lips, then slid it slowly down to her
breast. She watched as his eyes seemed to instinctively
follow. "I am actually looking for a home and thought
you might be a real estate agent or something, and
could help me."

Milton cleared his throat, feeling a slight and unexpected throb in his loins, then reached into the inside
of his jacket to retrieve a business card. "I, uh . . .
might have a few properties you'd be interested in.
What is it that you are looking for?"

Taunya shrugged her shoulders nonchalantly. "I don't know . . . it depends on what you have to offer," she said with apparent seduction in her tone, quickly lowering, then raising her eyes as she bit her lower lip. "I kinda have to see it, but basically, someplace that will offer me many pleasant and cozy evenings at home. You know fall is setting in. I'll need to be kept warm on a chilly night."

"I think I have something that fits that description."

"I bet you do." Taunya slid her finger across his extended hand before she took his card and tucked it into her bossom. Her touch had sent a shock wave to his manhood, which was slowly rising to attention. She glanced conspicuously at his pants, then gave a sly smile. "I'll call you to set up an appointment." At that she sashayed past him and on to her waiting rooms around the corner and Milton darted into the bathroom to adjust himself before returning to his training.

He stood in the bathroom stroking himself; his body had betrayed and embarrassed him. He'd never been attracted to black women before seeing Taunya. Not that he thought them unattractive; he'd just never had one turn him on in the snap of a finger. Maybe it was because it had been a while since he and Karilyn had experienced the intimacy he longed for. Sure, they had sex once or twice a week, but he found that he wasn't nearly as satisfied as he'd once been when he married her twenty-one years earlier, or even five years ago. She had somehow along the way lost her spice, not to mention her flexibility and stamina. Age was setting in for the both of them, but he made sure to do what he could to hold on to his youth, while Karilyn seemed to accept that she wasn't getting any younger and couldn't return to the days of their erotic yesteryears.

Getting a hold of himself, he exited the bathroom once again, glanced in both directions, hoping to catch a glimpse of Taunya, but at the same time hoping he wouldn't run into her again.

"Let's see if she calls," he said to himself.

Chapter 9

"Vanessa, get Genesis Taylor on the phone for me please." Marvin Waldron leaned back in his chair and thumbed through Genesis's application package once more, giving careful attention to her offer letter, reading aloud her salary and a list of benefits to include first-day medical, dental, and vision, 401K, HECRA/DECRA, three weeks of vacation her first year, personal and sick days, and tuition reimbursement.

His phone rang back, indicating that Genesis was on the line. He cleared his throat before picking up the receiver. "Ms. Taylor?"

"Yes, it is," Genesis answered a little more anxiously than she'd intended.

"This is Mr. Waldron from the Regal Towers Hotel's corporate office. Is now an okay time to chat with you, or should I schedule a more convenient time to ring you back?"

"Oh, now is fine." Genesis quickly swiped her key card into the sliding lock of the unoccupied room she'd just finished servicing. Too nervous to sit down, she paced back and forth between to the two queen-sized beds.

"Great! Well, after very careful consideration, we were able to come to a hiring decision for our general manager position for the Williamsburg location." He paused for three seconds purely for effect. "I'm calling today to extend to you an offer for that position, if you are still interested in the role."

"I sure am." Genesis's smile could not be contained although she tried not to let it be heard so clearly in her voice, wanting to give the impression of diplomacy.

"That's good news. We were lucky to find you with your strong skill set and background. Let me review for you the details of the offer, and I will overnight your employment package confirming everything in writing. You should receive it via FedEx tomorrow."

Genesis took a seat at the desk in the room and quickly took notes on a small notepad bearing the hotel's name and information. Her hands trembled as he called out a salary that, as it processed in her mind, she could have sworn that she heard the sound of a cash register.

After confirming her start date, Genesis ended the call, then stood, only to fall backward on the recently made bed. "Yes!" She lay there for a few minutes simply daydreaming of starting an actual professional career in a white-collar world. She pretended for a few minutes that she was Sanaa Latham's character from *Something New*, walking into boardrooms to meet with clients, taking a firm stance on issues and gaining respect based on the accuracy of her forecasts of the business and sound decision making.

She stood to her feet once more and went to the mirror above the desk. Leaning forward, she looked

NINETY-NINE AND A HALF JUST WON'T DO 63

herself in her eyes with her most serious face. "Mr. Waldron, I cannot sit back and allow these four vendors to continue to provide us with substandard service, and although I have submitted formal complaints on several occasions, resolution of this issue yet remains to be seen. Unfortunately, they leave me no other recourse but to reconsider our contractual agreements and deliberate on the proposals that have come across my desk that will meet our current business needs." She paused for a second to speak as Mr. Waldron. "Genesis, you present a strong argument. Clearly you've done your research and I support your decision." She nodded at herself, smiling, bringing her imaginary discussion to an end.

She pulled her phone from her smock pocket and sent Taunya a text message.

I got the job!!! Drinks on me tonight!

A few seconds later she received Taunya's reply.

Congrats! I'm all up for free drinks! What floor are you on?

Genesis replied with her floor number, and minutes later Tauyna met her at the elevator tower. As soon as the doors parted, she threw her arms around her friend. "Congratulations! When do you start?"

"I'll put in my two weeks here before I leave," Genesis responded.

"You better than me, 'cause I wouldn't put in nothing. Girl, I would be clocking out right now if I was you. After you done sat up here and worked all these years and they wouldn't even think about promoting you? Shooooo! They wouldn't be seeing nothing but my backside right about now."

"I don't mind putting in a notice. You never know when you might have to go back somewhere."

Ain't that the truth? Taunya thought, reflecting on how she'd spent the past few weekends. "Well, I'm happy for you. What are you going to be doing again?"

"I'll be the general manager in Williamsburg," Genesis said, beaming.

"A GM? My girl!" Taunya congratulated her.

Before her shift was over, Genesis placed a letter of resignation on Deidra's desk.

Chapter 10

When Taunya arrived at the Silver Diner, Milton had already gotten a table close enough to the back where he wouldn't be easily spotted from the entranceway, but sat so that he could see the entrance reflected from a piece of framed artwork. Watching as she talked to the hostess, he neatened a stack of papers he'd pulled from his briefcase in preparation of showing her a few properties, convincing himself that housing was what she was really after. Scanning the restaurant's patrons searching for Milton, lifting her hand up, indicating that she was looking for someone tall, she bobbed her head with a smile as the hostess pointed her in Milton's direction.

Milton rose to his feet as she approached the table, extending his hand for a business shake, taking in the curve of her breasts stuffed into a formfitting white V-neck T-shirt, beneath a cropped denim blazer. A pair of low-rise jeans hugged her hips and thighs, and black stiletto boots added three and a half inches to her height. Neither his mind nor his body could deny the fact that she was sexy.

"Ms. Johnson," he greeted. "Glad you could make it."

"I'm glad I could too. I'm ready to move from where I'm at."

"I'm sure I can help you."

Rather than taking a seat across from Milton at the table for four, she moved to sit beside him. "You don't mind if I sit on this side, do you? That way we don't have to flip papers across the table."

"Oh," he responded with slight surprise. "Uh, sure." Milton rearranged the papers he'd brought and quickly pulled out her chair. As she took her seat, he noted the black thong that peeked over the waistline of her jeans. He cleared his throat and sat.

"So, what do you have for me?" She smiled as she reached for a menu. "Are you going to get something to eat?"

"I am a little hungry." Taunya leaned toward Milton, sliding the menu between them, allowing him to look on with her rather than get his own. The fragrance of a soft vanilla musk filled his nostrils as he read over a few menu choices. He willed his loins to submission, trying to refocus his thoughts on possibly gaining a new tenant.

"This sounds good." Taunya pointed to a platter of barbecue chicken cilantro quesadillas described on the menu just as their server approached the table. They decided to split an appetizer and ordered a couple of sodas. "All right, let's get down to business," Taunya suggested, rubbing her hands together.

"Okay, well, first, let's talk a little more about what you are looking for." Taunya went through a brief description of her ideal home, although she was perfectly content with the small three-bedroom apartment she currently occupied in Dickerson Court, a subsidized housing project. The rent was based on her income and family size, and was barely fifty dollars a month. The neighbors weren't always the best, and police cars often drove through the neighborhood, but it was convenient to the bus line, near the grocery store, and had been the place she'd called home since she was eighteen with a one-year-old daughter on her hip. She had pretty much become an icon in her community. There was something she felt Milton could do for her, but take her from the comforts of her lifestyle was not one of them.

"It's just hard trying to find somewhere decent with the little bit of money I make at the hotel and then having a daughter in college, you know?" she asked, although she was sure Milton had never seen a day of lack in his entire life.

"You have a daughter in college?" The shocked look on Milton's face was a boost to her ego, although she knew that she looked far younger than her thirty-eight years. She made sure to drink plenty of water and take care of her skin and body, which kept her looking in her mid to late twenties.

"Yeah, my baby is in her third year at James Madison, and the tuition is just through the roof," she exclaimed, punctuating her thoughts with appropriate hand gestures. "I mean, I pay my rent on time, but I don't know if I can afford to move into the place of my dreams, so let me just ask you this. Do you take Section 8 tenants?"

Milton squirmed in his seat; he did have two properties that were being occupied by families supported by the Section 8 program, but he had always shunned it, and trod lightly regarding it, because he'd both seen and heard the horror stories of the tenants not having respect for the property, bringing even the nicest home to its knees in damages. He'd seen holes knocked in walls, carpets utterly ruined, broken fixtures, busted windows, stolen appliances, and a whole gamut of things that factored into his decision to primarily rent to tenants who could well afford to pay rent on their own. But Taunya looked well kept; her hair was neatly styled, her clothing fashionable, her nails were natural at a length that was becoming to her hands, rather than artificial and claw length, painted in a multitude of colors and embellished with clusters of crystals and rhinestones. She did work steady at the hotel, he reasoned; and he knew she was capable of making a little extra cash on the side.

He nodded. "I do consider Section 8. But I'll be honest with you. It's not something that I typically do but I think we might be able to work something out. Of course I'll need some basic information from you to fully consider your application." He reached into his bag for an application and a pen. "Why don't you go ahead and fill this out, so I can have what I need to get started?"

Taunya leaned forward to work on completing the application so that he would have her information for his personal use more than anything else. She smiled inwardly, watching him in her peripheral vision; he leaned back and let his eyes dart down the back of her pants . . . just like she wanted him to. She let him fill his eyes for several seconds, then pretended to stretch, rotating her torso and arching her back, letting out a mock yawn. "Whew! Excuse me. I don't know where that came from." The server headed toward them with their order. "Oh, here's our food, and just in time too," she said, repositioning herself in her seat, tugging her shirt down over her jeans to feign modesty. After all, she had accomplished what she needed to; she had planted the seed. She handed Milton the application, which he placed in a manila folder, and slid it across the table.

Over mouthfuls of shredded chicken and cheese, Milton asked questions about her tenure on her job and the makeup of her family, finding out that she had two teenaged sons at home. That fact alone made him more leery about renting to her, thinking two teen sons would surely tear a house up, but she had bragged so about their grades and extracurricular school activities, he figured they couldn't be but so rough and rowdy. By the time they rose from the table to leave he considered his newly acquired property from the auction, but then decided to offer her a short-term lease on one of his less valued properties that had long been paid for yet had remained vacant for the better part of a year. He reasoned that he would start her at six months, which would be enough of an opportunity for him to see if she would take care of the place and pay on time, although he wouldn't charge her anywhere near what he knew he could rent it for. But he hoped there would be some other benefit to him outside of guaranteed rent payments from the state.

He showed her a property listing of a fifteen-hundred-square-foot single-family split-level home, making mention of its four bedrooms and two full baths. The house offered the privacy of having the master bedroom downstairs with its own bathroom, while the other bedrooms were on the upper level. Where Taunya lived now, she could practically stand in the entranceway of her bedroom and reach inside her boys' room to knock either of them upside the head. And there were many mornings when her kids got cussed out for taking too long in the single bathroom they shared. Taunya found herself seriously considering the possibilities of actually living in a house instead of an apartment.

"This is nice," she commented, glancing over the listing's photos. "How much would you want for this place?" They negotiated on a rental amount that would fit into her budget.

"Of course the deal has to work for the both of us," he said, giving her a suggestively knowing eye, but at the same time, measuring his words carefully just in case he was misreading her provocative body language. "Do you want to go look at this house today?" he asked as they strolled outside toward their vehicles.

"Sure. I'll follow you there."

Milton wasn't sure exactly what he could expect once they arrived at the house, or even what he wanted to happen. Suppose she got in the house and stripped naked to seal the deal. Suppose there was no deal at all and she was using her sexual prowess to get what she needed, without giving him anything. "Get a hold of yourself, Milton, you're a married man, for Pete's sake." He switched on the radio, trying to clear his mind of thoughts of infidelity, and thinking of ways he could spice things up between himself and Karilyn. *Maybe we can take a trip somewhere*, he thought, fully knowing that a trip would do nothing for Karilyn's sunbaked withering skin, her sagging breasts and stretch-marked stomach. Karilyn had been good to him down through the years; he had to admit that to himself. And every now and then even sex had its sparked moments where they would giggle like teenagers, playing chase around the house. Yet, visually, Karilyn just didn't do it for him anymore even though she was the same age as Taunya. She would never even think about putting on a thong. Just like that, his thoughts circled back around to Taunya and what she would feel like lying beneath him or straddled across his lap. He wondered if there was any truth to the phrase "the blacker the berry, the sweeter the juice."

By the time he arrived at the property, his imagination had led him to a full erection. He sat in the car momentarily, listening to voice mail messages and trying to give himself an opportunity to deflate, but when Taunya walked up to the car and bent forward to peek in the window at him, the view of her cleavage only sent more of a charge to his lower extremities. He held up a finger, asking her to give him a moment, then adjusted himself in his pants while Taunya strolled around the property's perimeter. A few minutes later, he exited his BMW, covering his midsection with his portfolio in an attempt to appear at ease, but Taunya took note.

She hid her excitement as Milton walked her from room to room, casually bumping against him and stooping and bending whenever she could. She wasn't going to sell herself so cheap, however.

"So, what do you think? Is this in line with what you were looking for?"

She shrugged nonchalantly. "It's nice but I need to think about it." She turned and headed for the front door, leaving Milton momentarily stunned.

"Well, hold on a sec," he said, stopping her. She smiled to herself, but erased it before turning to face him with raised brows. "I mean, what is that, uh . . ." He shrugged himself, as his free hand motioned around the living room prompting her to elaborate. ". . . you don't like?" he finished.

"Well, I am just thinking that if I take it, it will actually cost me significantly more, because I will have to pay additional utilities than what I have right now," she stated matter-of-factly. "I mean, there's lights, water, sanitation, gas . . . I just don't know that I can afford it."

"I understand." Milton nodded, semidisappointed. He locked the house and shook hands with Taunya on the doorstep.

"I do appreciate you showing it to me, though," she said before turning to walk to her car, adding extra movement to her hips. Milton watched, unable to peel his eyes away.

Later that evening, after watching his round-figured wife emerge from the shower and pull on a large pair of briefs, a white matronly bra, and a long oversized sleep shirt, Milton went into his home office, picked up the phone, and called Taunya, agreeing to include her utilities in her rent.

Chapter 11

With a box tucked under her arm, Genesis strolled through the parking garage of Regal Towers, located in historic Williamsburg, to the elevator. She slid her key card into the slot, gaining access to the seventeenth floor, which was where the administrative offices were. In a few seconds of smooth gliding, the doors opened to a still dark floor. While she wasn't expected to be in the office for another two hours, her excitement of starting a new role, along with her desire to be proactive, had her reporting in at 6:00 a.m. rather than 8:00. The sun was just making its entrance into the morning, its rays reaching through the east side of the building, which was made entirely of glass. Genesis walked over to the window and stood, silently watching the sun fully rise into the sky. She whispered a prayer of thanksgiving.

She turned on her new black pumps and sauntered down the hallway toward the mahogany door with her name posted on the wall just outside its frame. She ran her fingers over the engraved letters with a grin on her face. Using her key card once more, she opened the door to her office. It too had a glass wall that faced the east side, and the sun flooded the large room endowed with oak and chrome furnishings. A small table surrounded by four chairs provided an area for discussions and additional workspace. Her desk was flanked by a huge bookcase, where several company manuals occupied a few of the shelves, along with a TV/VCR/DVD combo.

From the box she'd brought in with her, Genesis lifted a photo of herself and her grandmother taken at a wedding reception and placed it on one of the vacant shelves. Next she pulled out her matted and framed degree and placed it beside the photo. Taking a step back, she admired the font in which her name was printed across the certificate's center, then let her eyes float over to the photo. Genesis frowned. The gleam that had been in Anna Marie's eyes in the photo now seemed to be gone, and maybe it was her imagination, but her smile seemed a little less happy . . . it almost seemed as if she was scowling at her. Genesis dismissed the thought and began placing other office trinkets on her desk, including a small CD player, and a case full of CDs. Thumbing through the minicollection, she stopped when she got to Fantasia's project, feeling inspired by the woman's story of rising from the projects to fame.

She inserted the CD, pressed PLAY, and sang a few lyrics while she logged on to her computer to check e-mail, although she really wasn't expecting to have anything, since it was just her first day. Much to her surprise, once she clicked on the SEND/RECEIVE icon, her in-box was suddenly flooded with messages that demanded her attention. Immediately, she plopped her day timer on her desk and began drafting a to-do list and printing some of the e-mails to leave on her desk as reminders. It hadn't taken much time for Genesis to realize that her whole day would be consumed with paperwork. "If Fantasia can write a book without even knowing how to read, then I know I can do this job," Genesis said as an affirmation to herself.

Genesis turned to grab a stack of papers from her printer when Karilyn Lewis popped her head in the door.

"Good morning, boss," the jubilant white woman chirped. She pushed her rounded glasses up on her nose and smiled with yellowing teeth. "You're up and at 'em pretty early." She held a small bouquet of flowers nestled in a coffee mug with a yellow smiley face balloon attached to it.

"Good morning," Genesis replied, spinning in her chair to face her. "Just trying to get a jump start on my day."

"I brought you this," she said, presenting the floral arrangement, "to welcome you on your first day. I thought I would beat you here and at least have coffee waiting for you when you arrived, but I guess I should have made it in a little earlier, huh?" Karilyn chuckled.

"Thank you, Karilyn," Genesis said sincerely as she accepted the token and set it on one of the bookcase shelves. "That was so unnecessary, but so thoughtful of you. And it's okay about the coffee." Genesis's nose crinkled slightly. "I much more prefer tea."

"Well, why didn't you say so? I can handle that, be right back." She turned on her soft-soled flats headed for the minikitchen.

"Karilyn, Karilyn," Genesis blurted, standing to her feet and lifting a hand to motion her assistant's stop. "Really, I can get it, but I would like your help on a few other things." She tapped a stack of papers against her desk to neaten them. "Will you have some time today to review some things with me?"

"No problem!" Karilyn agreed readily. "Just give me a few minutes to get settled and I'll be right in. Also, go ahead and make your lunch selection so I can call it in early this morning."

"Excuse me?"

"You know—lunch? The meal after breakfast and before dinner? I left the menu selection card on your desk. All you have to do is circle your choice for the day, and I'll do the rest." Genesis was too embarrassed to ask if she would have to pay for it. She thought quickly of how she could uncover that information without looking stupid. Before she could think of anything, Karilyn answered the question. "Maybe one day I'll get to sit in your seat and have the company pick up lunch for me every day!" She smiled again as she smoothed her hands over her black polyester skirt. "Be right back."

"Can you close the door behind you please?" Genesis asked. Once Karilyn was gone a smile spread across Genesis's face. "So this is what it feels like to be the boss," she said, looking around at the office furnishings, then running her fingers lightly across the items on her desk.

She pulled open the top drawer of her desk, grabbed a set of highlighters, and began going through the stack of papers she'd printed off, bringing visual attention to the important details. By the time Karilyn came back with a mug of steaming tea, Genesis had at least an hour's worth of things to discuss with her. She spent the greater part of the morning asking questions and reviewing processes, then right before lunch, walked the hotel's floor greeting and introducing herself to employees as she came across them. Some acted as if they couldn't have cared less about who she was and what she did. Some were pleasant and cordially congratulated her, and others showed excitement and pure elation.

"It's about time they put some color in that office!" was the comment of a woman who went by the name of Eedy. "Chile, I seen a whole lotta faces come through that office and ain't one of 'em look like this here." She rubbed the back of her own hand, referring to the rich brown hue of her skin. "They always tryna pretend like we ain't qualified for these type of jobs, but you show 'em what you got now, baby," Eedy said through a mouthful of wobbly dentures.

Genesis swallowed hard, reminded of her lack of qualification, but just as quickly convinced herself that her experiences alone were just as good as an education. She shook Eedy's hand, thanked her for her hard work, and moved on to the other floors.

By the time her day came to a close, her mind and body were exhausted, but as she plopped into the driver's seat of her car, she felt exhilarated and empowered by a successful first day on the job. To celebrate, she ran herself a bubble bath, set some candles on the toilet seat and lit them, then moved her portable stereo into the bathroom, resting it across the sink. She slid in a copy of India.Arie's CD and played "Private Party" for herself.

Chapter 12

"So, when do you actually move in?" Genesis asked, walking around Taunya's new home. Milton had just handed Taunya the keys that morning so the house was still empty. Genesis grinned to make Taunya believe that she was happy for her, but inside she felt disparagement; how was Taunya able to pay for a place like this? Genesis found herself jealous of the larger square footage, two-car garage, and a huge covered deck out back. *Since when did scrubbing toilets pay this much?* Jokingly, she tossed her suspicions at her friend. "Who do I have to sleep with to get a hookup like this?"

Taunya planted her hands on her hips, taking immediate offense. "What? Since you saving for a house, you think you the only one that can have something? You the only person that can move up in the world? Everybody else got to be turning tricks?" she rapidly fired.

"I'm sorry, deg! I was just playing, calm down." Genesis turned away from Taunya, opening and exploring the space of a hall closet. *We both know you a ho, though,* she thought.

"I work just like you work," Taunya added, trying to cover up the fact that Genesis had stepped on her toes in the worst way. When Milton had met Taunya at the house that morning to give her the keys, she had thanked him and ensured that her rent wouldn't go up by climbing up on the kitchen counter, spreading her legs apart, and letting him slam into her for six minutes. She gasped, moaned, and cooed in his ear, inflating his ego, while she ran her hands through his hair. As he pulled out of her nearly ready to collapse, Taunya gave him an open invitation to come back.

"You hold on to a key, right?" she whispered.

"Yeah," he replied, pulling his pants up from around his ankles.

"I hope you know how to use it." She jumped down from the counter and pulled her skirt down. "I might have a few things here that may need your attention at odd hours of the night, and I want to make sure you'll be able to access the property."

Milton smiled, fully understanding her implication. "Yeah. I do. I'll take care of anything that needs, uh . . . a little fixing."

None of that was Genesis's business, and Taunya resented that she would even suggest it although she hit the nail right on the head. "Well, I can start moving in right away, so I'll be ready to have a housewarming party in a few weeks. How's your job coming along?" she asked, switching the focus off her.

"Oh, it's going really well," she said, still touring the house. "I have a pretty good staff, and my assistant is awesome. Now, don't get me wrong, it has its challenges, but I'm loving it."

"I bet you are with that new SUV sitting outside."

With the money Genesis now earned, she was finally able to scrap her old Geo Metro and had recently purchased a Nissan Murano. She felt like a million bucks driving it off the lot, sitting up high over traffic, coasting on a ride so smooth, she wasn't fully convinced that the tires kept in contact with the street.

"Yeah, that's my baby." She winked.

"Can't do nothing with money."

"Seems like you're keeping up pretty well to me. This place is beautiful, Taunya," she commented, still wondering how it was that she was able to afford it in the first place. There had to be a sugar daddy somewhere in the mix. Genesis was sure of it.

Chapter 13

Nine months later

Diane Jackson led Genesis around the luxury condo located in Newport News's Port Warwick, pointing out its features. "It's right at sixteen hundred square feet, so there's plenty of room," she stated. Although she pointed out other features and building amenities, Genesis had long tuned her out. She was in her own world, changing the colors of the white walls to a warming sand with eggshell-white trim. She'd pick a mocha-colored couch and add some greenery to give the place life. Her home would be far different than the flowered couch protected by homemade multicolored afghans. Rather than have a shrine of family photos on the wall, Genesis would mount a plasma TV. The antiquated floor model sans remote she currently owned would have no place there.

French double doors led to a spacious balcony that overlooked lush, well-kept grounds featuring a beautiful gazebo. She stepped outside and allowed her ears to be filled with the sound of a few chirping birds; it was an incredible change from the racket of undisciplined children running up and down the street and blasts of bass from the trunks of passing cars. She envisioned a cushioned outdoor chaise with some hanging lights bringing her many nights of natural peace.

The walk-in closets of all three bedrooms featured built-in shelving, sets of drawers, and several hanging bars at varied heights. Her current closets were barely two feet deep and four feet wide and were literally stuffed from top to bottom and wall to wall, making it a challenge for her to hang or pull out anything.

Closing the door of a small room, which hid her washer and dryer, she finally turned to Diane and spoke. "I think I've found a new home. Where do I sign?"

"Where is Alton?" Genesis looked out her front window again, expecting to see Alton drive up any second. She glanced down at her watch and let out a frustrated sigh, having moved alone everything she could. Leaning against the wall, she yanked her cell phone from the clip at the waist of her jeans and dialed his number for the seventh time.

"Hello?" a voice called out.

Perplexed at the sound of a woman's voice other than Alton's, Genesis paused momentarily while her thoughts bounced back and forth between asking for him and simply hanging up. She decided on the latter. *Who the heck was that?* she wondered as she checked the number that had been tracked in her phone to make sure she hadn't misdialed. Seeing that she hadn't, she felt a flurry of thoughts rushing through her head as she paused, with one hand on her hip while her eyes intently studied the phone for answers. *Maybe he lost his phone, or . . . or . . . the woman sounded white, though.*

Before she could work through her thoughts, her cell rang back with a number she didn't recognize.

"Genesis speaking," she answered, a habit she had developed since taking on her new job and realizing that her boss or any other member of management frequently called and expected to reach her at any time of the day or night.

"Genesis?" the woman's voice quizzed. "Genesis Taylor?"

"Yes, it is. Who's calling please?"

"It's Deidra, Deidra Cox from the Omni," she said more in a question tone than a statement. "I interviewed you a while back for a manager position."

"Yes, I remember. How can I help you?" she asked pleasantly although she immediately remembered the sting of Deidra's rejection letter.

"Actually, I'm returning your call. You just called my fiancé's phone?"

"Excuse me?"

"You just called 555-9247, right? That's my fiancé Alton's number."

"Oh . . . ummm . . ." Genesis was shocked and had no words.

"I didn't realize you two knew each other. What a coincidence, huh?" Deidra giggled. "Honey, I didn't know you knew Genesis. She used to work with me at the Omni."

"I knew what? What you mean—like the Bible?" Genesis heard Alton ask in the background.

"Actually, Deidra, it really is a coincidence because I had dialed the wrong number trying to call my mom. I had no idea that I'd end up talking to you. Her number is 555-9244," she lied, maintaining her demeanor, not willing to expose how angry and embarrassed she was. "Well, it was nice talking with you. Take care," she finished before pressing the END button.

She stared at the phone in total disbelief, shaking her head.

"What's wrong with you?" Taunya asked, scooting a large box from the hallway into the living room.

"That dirty mother—"

"Shutcho mouth!" Taunya ended laughing until she saw the hurt look on Genesis's face. "What happened?" she questioned more seriously. "Alton can't make it?"

"As a matter of fact, he can't!" Genesis folded her lips inside her mouth and stared straight ahead at the wall fighting back tears. "And do you want to know why? Because he's with his fiancée!"

"What? Fiancée?"

"And guess who it is?" She turned from the wall to look directly at Taunya. "Deidra . . . Cox."

"White, coochie-tickling Deidra Cox?" By this time Taunya's hands were on her hips.

"Coochie tickling? Deidra's bisexual?" Genesis gasped.

"I don't know about all that, but I caught her in the bathroom playing with herself," Taunya spilled.

"Taunya, stop lying!" Genesis exclaimed, scrunching her nose.

"I kid you not. I had to clean the offices one day because Yvonne had called in sick, and I guess Deidra forgot to lock the door when she went to the bathroom because I walked right in and caught her in there with her skirt hiked up and one foot up on the handicap railing and her draws down around the other ankle, just a-going at it." Taunya flicked her index finger back and forth quickly. "Girl, I scared her so bad, she dropped her cell phone in the toilet and turned red as a firecracker! Talking 'bout she had a yeast infection."

In an instant, Genesis's anger had done a 180-degree turnaround as she held her sides, doubled over in laughter.

"The next time she saw me, she couldn't even look me in my face. I asked her, did you get rid of that little itch you had?" Taunya chuckled.

"Well, apparently, she wasn't the only one taking care of her itch."

"I told you that boy wasn't worth a two-headed nickel in the back of a dark alley. And there you were just giving him points and giving him points." Taunya circled her hand in the air to emphasize her words.

"All right, all right. If you hate to say I told you so, don't say it." Genesis plopped down on the couch, trying to come up with a plan B to move her furniture.

"How many points was he up to anyway?"

"It don't even matter, 'cause right now, he doesn't have a single one."

The following weekend, Genesis slid the last box of odds and ends into the back of her SUV, then trekked inside the house once more to take a final walk-through. Her mind was flooded with memories as she entered each room for the last time. In her grand-mother's room, she chuckled as she recalled the time that, terrified there was a monster dwelling under her bed, she was comforted by her grandmother with the verses from the ninety-first Psalm. "Thou shalt not be afraid of the terror by night nor the arrow that flieth by day," Genesis whispered to herself, quoting the words that were now engraved in her mind.

She peered into her own bedroom, which had become seemingly enlarged now that it was empty, its walls stark naked, void of anything else but scars left from nails and tacks.

The living room reminded her of quiet evenings spent at home seated on the floor between her grandmother's knees, having her hair brushed while they competed with each other to solve *Wheel of Fortune* puzzles.

Genesis could visualize and nearly smell a plate of crisp fried chicken, a casserole dish of lima beans, and buttery squares of hot corn bread sitting on the table that was once positioned in the middle of the floor of the small eat-in kitchen. That table had hosted many a coming-of-age discussion between Anna Marie and her granddaughter. It was at that table and over varied meals that Genesis learned of the nature of a woman's developing and ever-changing body, the fly-by-night lifestyle of her mother, and the reality that there was no money for college.

She pulled the front door closed behind her and slid her key into the lock, not noticing the car that pulled up to the curb in front of the house. The driver leaned over to the passenger side, cranked the window down, and called out to her.

"This your house?" Genesis turned quickly and squinted her eyes at the figure hidden under the shadows of the car's interior.

"Yeah," she said nonchalantly, turning back to lock up.

"How much you rentin' it for?" He motioned his head to the FOR RENT sign that had been planted firmly in the yard.

"You have to call the management company," she said, also motioning to the sign, pointing toward the realty management company's number. *I am not about to do any business negotiating out here on the sidewalk*, she thought, beginning her stride to her vehicle.

"You mind if I take a look right quick—I mean since you right here?" he asked. Genesis paused for a few seconds, giving it a bit of thought. "I can look at it by myself. You don't have to walk me through or nothing."

"I do need to hurry up and rent this place," she whispered out loud, before giving her response. "Sure." She shrugged as if it were no big deal. She trotted back onto the porch to unlock and open the door, while the driver put his car in park and stepped out onto the street. When Genesis turned around, she took in all six feet of his vaguely familiar medium build. He was dressed in a pair of faded blue uniform pants, with a matching blue-and-white-striped shirt that had clearly seen better days. Even so, the creases down his legs, the shirt neatly tucked into his pants, and the black belt that circled his waist gave indication that he took pride in his appearance. Atop his head hiding his facial features was a ball cap, bearing a company logo that Genesis did not recognize. His eyes were covered by a pair of dark shades. His feet were covered in heavy black boots that she could imagine let out a pungent odor at the end of the day once they were removed.

He pulled a pen and a business card from his shirt pocket, jotted down the number from the sign, then strolled up the sidewalk that led to the porch. "How are you doing?" he asked, extending his hand for a shake, but then quickly withdrew, taking note of the dirt embedded in the creases of his fingertips and beneath his nails. "You gotta excuse me, I just got off work and haven't had a chance to wash my hands yet." He dusted his hands against each other as if it would make them cleaner.

"It's quite all right," Genesis replied, careful not to share her name. "Go ahead and take a look, I'll wait out here." She waved a dismissive hand and turned her back quickly, not wanting him to think there was any interest.

I know she ain't trying to act funny with those raggedy sweatpants on, he thought. He nodded. "Thanks." Trying to disregard her less than friendly behavior, he bounded up the four steps, swung the screen door open, and went into the house, but turned back right around to look out the living room window, catching a view of Genesis from behind. "She is fine, though," he said, taking note of the smooth skin exposed at her waist by the T-shirt Genesis had knotted in the back, and the rounded curve of her backside. He turned away before his imagination and thoughts could run away with the moment, bringing his attention back to viewing the house.

He made a quick assessment of the kitchen and living room; the house didn't have much to offer in the way of special features, but that was the least of Ricardo's concerns. He didn't need a lot and had no one to impress. His goal was simply to provide a home for himself and, more importantly, his son. A boy needed his own home. A home where he could play freely rather than being subconsciously preoccupied with not breaking anything or being in someone's way. A boy needed his own room. A room that would house his favorite toys and a real bed instead of the folded comforter that served as a mattress and a throw pillow from the sofa on which he rested his head each night.

Even though Ricardo's current living conditions were not the best, he was yet grateful. Sleeping on the floor of his mother's overcrowded house every night was better than sleeping in a cell on any single day of the year.

"I'm pregnant!" Sarita Knight screamed loud enough for every person on the entire North Carolina Central University campus to hear. The weight of her words forced him to take a seat on the steps of Chidely Hall. He shoved his hands into the pockets of his jacket while his mind reeled at the thought of a baby. How could he have let this happen? After all the sex education classes and many methods of birth control available, there was no excuse in the world for an unplanned pregnancy.

Although she continued in her tirade punctuated with profanity, Ricardo heard almost none of it. Her first two words seemed to be stuck between rewind and play and resounded loudly in his head. He thought back to the night that had most likely brought him to this point. Ironically, it had been one of the most passionate nights of his life. While he and Sarita had consummated a sexual relationship months prior, that night she unleashed a level of passion that she'd never before revealed.

Sarita had opened the door to her apartment,

which had the erotic glow of a thousand candles, clad
in nothing but a small triangle of fabric connected to
a thin pink string that circled her hips. In an instant a
fire was ignited in his loins that refused to be extin-
guished . . . even by the fact that no condom was present. Between heated wet kisses, and struggling
between his weakening self-control and Sarita's long
legs wrapped around his waist, he expressed this
dilemma to her. With his hands full of her rounded
backside, she forced his head downward to her
breasts, encouraging the softness of his mouth to en-
velop her nipples, all the while whispering in his ear.
His lustful desires overrode his judgment, trusting
Sarita's promise to take a "day after" pill, something
he had never even heard of. In less than a minute of
contemplation, he pressed her back into the front
door, stripped from the waist down, and sank deep
within her walls.

When the sun made its appearance the next morning, his stamina had been far spent and he could
barely find the strength in his legs to walk across
campus to his dorm room. He was grateful that his
first two classes had been canceled due to a heavy
snow, because he could think of nothing else other
than getting more of what Sarita had given all night
long.

A slap to the side of his head brought him back to
the reality of Sarita's ranting. "Your ass better come
up with some money, 'cause I ain't havin' no damn
baby!" At that, she stormed off to her car, jumped
inside, and sped away.

Ricardo had sat there for nearly thirty minutes
longer despite what felt like a sudden drop in the temperature. He wasn't a supporter of abortion; in his

heart he believed it was murderous. But at the same time, he wasn't ready to trade his schooling and his future for soiled diapers, soured bottles, and pricey formula. For a fleeting moment, the thought of letting Sarita raise a baby on her own ran through his mind, but he could never turn his back on a child he'd created. He couldn't imagine taking on the responsibility of raising a child in the midst of books, papers, thesis papers, and dissertations. But who was to say that the baby was even his in the first place? Neither of them had really committed to a relationship, not with words anyway. As far as he knew, she could have been sexing a whole string of guys. As much as he wanted to make it easier for himself by believing that, his conscience discarded it, internally confirming that the child had come from his loins.

Her demand for money played back in his head. How much did an abortion cost anyway? Suppose Sarita was just running a scam? She hadn't shown him a positive test result or some sort of official documentation from a doctor's office. Ricardo had heard of girls falsifying pregnancies and collecting money in order to buy schoolbooks, pay tuition, and fund shopping trips, sometimes tricking three and four guys at a time. If it weren't a trick, where in the world would he get the money? Money was something that he had become accustomed to doing without in most cases, and doing with very little in all others. It was his brains and skill of his hands and feet on the basketball court that had earned him a full scholarship, which had been his only ticket out of a poverty-stricken life. His experiences in growing up in a single-parent home with four other kids taught him how to make do with what was available, or simply go without. Unfortunately, this wasn't a "make do" situation.

By the end of a full week of replacing sleep with arguments between himself and Sarita, he'd reluctantly made arrangements to make a quick hustle by delivering a package. The transaction would be quick and simple, he'd have the money to give to Sarita, and he'd be able to move on with his studies and his life. He struggled with the thought, though, feeling that he would be just as guilty of snatching a life as she would. To clear his conscience of the guilt of innocent blood being shed, he would tell Sarita that the decision of what she would do with the six hundred dollars was totally up to her, whether she decided to stock up on diapers and bibs, purchase a crib . . . or make a silent trip to a clinic.

What should have been a fifteen-minute walk to a side street turned into a three-year stint behind bars when Ricardo delivered the package to an undercover police officer who had been tipped off that there would be some trafficking that evening. In the same amount of time it would have taken Ricardo to run down the court and dunk a ball, his future was gone. He didn't even bother to call his mother with his allotted one phone call; he knew there would be no money for bail, but even more so he wasn't ready to hear the disappointment he knew would be in her voice once he told her he'd been locked up for possession of a controlled substance. He'd only been three and a half semesters away from achieving a degree in architectural science, and had already begun to target possible employers and research his salary potential. A salary that would pull his family out of the curse of public housing and poverty. He just couldn't find it within himself to call her, so instead, three months later, with his face turned to the wall and tears brimming his lower lids, he sent the news scripted on paper and delivered with a postage stamp. Four months later, in a handwriting suggesting anger, frustration, and at the same time unconditional love, his mother wrote back informing him that Sarita had delivered a baby boy, taken a trip out her house, and practically left the baby on the doorstep.

No sooner had Ricardo been released after serving three years of his five-year sentence than he made his way home, wrapped his son in his arms, and changed his name from Dhani Knight to Dhani Knight-Stewart.

Now as he looked around the small bedroom, he thought it couldn't be a more perfect place for Dhani to come home to every night. He envisioned a set of bunk beds on the far wall dressed in Spider-Man bed-clothes, and toys scattered about on the floor. After including a dresser, there would be just enough room for a small table and chair to serve as a desk and an activity station to keep Dhani's young mind developing toward brilliance. Ricardo walked over to the window, which gave a full view of the backyard, providing lots of room for football tosses, pitching and catching practice, and maybe even a dog.

Ricardo turned to leave the room but was stopped by a business card that lay on the floor upside down. He picked it up and flipped it between his fingers to be greeted by a professional photo of a smiling Genesis printed with the Regal Towers logo, her title, and her business contact information. "Genesis Taylor, huh?" He slid the card into his front pocket, patted twice, then moved to the next room.

Genesis stood outside leaning against her SUV chatting with Taunya on her cell phone.

"What is taking that man so long?" she exclaimed, looking toward the front door.

"Let the man look at the house and stop rushing him. You need to be in there with him trying to make a love connection," Taunya suggested.

"No, thanks, he has on those big old work boots. He looks like his feet stink and that has negative point value." Genesis crinkled her nose, imagining the smell that she was sure emanated from Ricardo's shoes nightly.

"Keyword, work!" Taunya emphasized. "At least the brother looks like he got a job," she continued, stressing the word "looks."

"Yeah, well, looks can be deceiving," Genesis countered. "He is kinda cute, though," she added. She still hadn't recognized him from the bookstore.

"So why don't you get the man's number and—"

"Ooh, here he comes. Hold on a second." Genesis lowered the phone away from her face, preparing to ask Ricardo what he thought.

"A'ight, thanks," he said before she could utter a single syllable. "I'll give the place a call." At that he got in his car and pulled away.

"Ooo-kay," Genesis said more to herself before bringing her cell back up to meet her ear. "Okay, he's gone."

"Damn, girl! You didn't even tell the man thanks for stopping by? I'ma have to give you some lessons on how to catch a man," Taunya huffed.

Genesis rolled her eyes. "He didn't give me a chance to say anything. He came flying out of the house and got in his car and left."

"'Cause you let him leave."

"Anyway . . . are you still coming over tonight?" Taunya had promised to help Genesis get more settled into her new home, although she didn't really see what Genesis needed help with. She had sold just about every piece of furniture that she could, and donated the other furnishings to Goodwill. There were several things that Genesis just simply threw away, disgusted with the evident brown speckling of roaches.

"What am I going to be over there doing? You didn't take nothing but one box of plates and a laundry basket full of towels over there."

"I had some things delivered last week that I've not even had the time to take out of the boxes yet. Plus I need help putting up my blinds." Genesis slid into the driver's seat, started her SUV, and backed out of the driveway.

"You gone cook?" Taunya asked. "'Cause I don't work for free."

"Now, you know good and well I don't do no cooking. How about some Chinese?"

"How in the world did you get raised by your grandma and cain't bake a biscuit?"

"I didn't say I can't cook, I said I don't cook. There is a difference, you know," Genesis chuckled.

"Long as it ain't balogna, I guess I'll be all right," Taunya said, sucking her teeth.

"I'll see you later, then." Genesis ended the call just as she approached the corner. She took a look in her rearview mirror, catching the side view of the house.

"Good-bye, Ivy Avenue."

Chapter 14

"Ms. Taylor, we found a suitable tenant for your property, and wanted to review the application with you, so if you could please return this call at your convenience, I'd greatly appreciate it," Diane's voice sang on voice mail.

"Finally!" Genesis thought she would never get the house rented, and at this point, paying two mortgages had become more than taxing. "Whoever it is, tell them they can move in right away," she said aloud to herself.

Settling down into her sofa, she eased her feet out of the pumps that had confined them all day, then thought about everything that had to be done in the next couple of days. For some reason, the hotel was having a difficult time retaining employees, and it was affecting Genesis's bonus pay. In addition to that, several patrons who were assigned to the fifth floor had complained that their rooms had not been properly cleaned prior to their arrival. At least five complimentary upgrades had been processed, which she would have to give an account for. She was definitely paying the cost to be the boss.

Lifting the phone from the cradle, she pushed in Diane's cell number, eager to get the rental squared away. Diane answered after three rings.

"Hi, Genesis, I'm glad you called. I have a tenant app for you to look over, single male with one child."

"Where does he work?"

"He does maintenance at Oxford Trail Townhomes and Apartments."

"How long has he been working there?"

"About a year now, so he definitely meets the criteria in terms of employment tenure. His income is just slightly below the minimum, though. He needs to make about a hundred dollars more a month."

"Mmm," Genesis said, thinking. "A hundred dollars is not that big of a deal," she responded, more concerned about the ongoing double mortgage payments. "Did you meet this person? What kind of feel did you get from him?"

"He seemed like a pretty nice guy. Sincere, respectful, had a cute little boy with him." Before Diane could add on to her statement, Genesis's other line chimed out.

"Hold on just a second." She switched over momentarily, then reconnected to Diane. "Go ahead and rent it out to him, I guess. I need to take this call."

"Okay. I'll follow up with you later once we have a signed lease."

"Great, thanks, Diane." Genesis clicked back over where Karilyn was waiting on the other line.

"I'm sorry to call you at home, Genesis, but there were some last-minute changes to your flight arrangements," Karilyn said apologetically.

"Oh, don't worry about it, you're fine."

"Okay, well, Ray sent out an e-mail to let everyone know that the Leadership Summit had to be pushed back by a week due to a change in the corporate quarterly business review. It's taking the big boys a little longer than they anticipated to get to all of the locations, so they're having to push it back."

"Hold on a second, Karilyn, let me grab my day timer." Genesis returned a few minutes later and recorded the new dates of an upcoming business trip she was to take in a few weeks.

"So your flight will leave out at six that morning out of Norfolk, you will catch a connector in Dallas, then land in Sacramento around one, Pacific standard time."

"Sounds good!"

"You'll be nice and pooped by the time you get there, but you do have a meet and greet scheduled for that evening. You may be able to catch a couple of hours of sleep before it starts, though," Karilyn chattered. "So I think you're all set!"

"Thanks, Karilyn, I really appreciate you taking care of it for me."

"No problem."

Genesis ended the call and smiled at the thought of her actually taking an all-expenses-paid business trip. Although she would be working, she was more than excited as she had hardly been out of her own state before, and had never even had a reason to go to the airport, let alone catch a plane. In her mind, she felt like she was going on vacation.

She imagined herself running through the airport with a wheeled suitcase in tow and a laptop bag slung across her shoulder, then hailing a cab at the curb as she had seen done many times on TV. She planned on ordering room service, swimming in the hotel's pool, and relaxing with a good book during her downtime there.

"Lifestyles of the rich and famous," she said out loud, proud of herself and what she'd accomplished in the past year.

Chapter 15

Taunya pulled a large pan of lasagna out of the oven, set it on the stovetop, and covered it with foil. The boys would be home soon and would be as hungry as monsters. She checked the freezer once more, making sure there were all kinds of microwavable snacks and foods available for them that would last throughout the week, although she had cooked three full-course meals and stored them in sealed containers for the boys to simply warm them up.

She quickly wrote a note to her sons stating at what time she would be home on Saturday evening, posted it with a magnet to the refrigerator's front, then headed out the door to her new Mazda Tribute, compliments of Milton. The shiny black vehicle had been a birthday present a few months prior, after she had complained for weeks that her Hyundai had become unreliable. Although the SUV wasn't brand-new, it was brand-new to Taunya and drove like a dream in comparison to what she had before.

This was their first getaway, and she had looked forward to it ever since he'd presented her with the tickets more than a month ago. They would be spending the week in Nevada's Sin City at a time-share property he owned.

To be as inconspicuous as possible, they decided to meet at the airport rather than arrive in the same vehicle, and interact as strangers who happened to be seated together on the plane, just in case anyone spotted Milton. They would save their indiscretions for when they landed. As planned, they met up at Norfolk International Airport, where she casually sat a few seats from him in the terminal. Dressed as she was in a pair of black stiletto boots, stretch denim jeans, and a pink baby T-shirt, Milton was immediately turned on by her youthful appearance. All Karilyn seemed to wear were too long polyester skirts or stretch knit pants paired with oversized knit tops with flowers around the neck, or kittens on the front. He eyed her perky round breasts as he folded a newspaper and placed it on his lap to hide his erection.

"American Airlines would like to welcome all first-class passengers at this time. If you are seated in rows one through three, we would like to welcome you aboard," the ticketing agent's voice sounded over the PA system. They both rose, giving no visible attention to each other, then approached their seats located at 2A and 2B. Taunya sat by the window and slid her knockoff Luis Vuitton bag beneath the seat in front of her, while Milton folded his sports jacket and laid it in the overhead compartment. Once he sat he whispered to her.

"You are a sexy woman."

Taunya blushed at his comment. "Excuse me, do you know me to be talking to me like that?"

"I sure would like to get to know you," he said,

playing along. "What kind of panties do you have on today?"

"The kind you like most, the ones with nothing in the middle."

Milton shifted in his seat in excitement. "I sure hope I can make it through this flight, or we just might have to induct ourselves in the mile high club."

"Both of us can't fit in that bathroom, Milt. But if I wasn't afraid of getting kicked off this plane, I'd jump on your lap right now and make your friendly skies a little more friendly," she said, raising her eyebrows.

"Can I get you something to drink, ma'am?" a bald flamboyantly gay flight attendant asked, batting his eyes.

"Umm, I'd like a rum and Coke please," she ordered.

"And for you, sir?"

"Anything you got that's cold. It's getting a little warm on this plane," Milton responded, chuckling and running his index finger inside the collar of his crisp white oxford.

"Will a Coke be all right?" Dante tilted his head toward Milton and raised his sculpted brows.

"Actually, a rum and Coke sounds pretty good. I'll have what she's having."

"Be right back," Dante said, then turned toward the front of the cabin.

"Oh yeah, I think I'm going to have what you've got," Milton said suggestively, resisting the urge to fondle Taunya's breasts. "Who is it that sings that Brown Sugar song again?" he said under his breath. "I want somma your brown sugar," he attempted to sing. Taunya laughed as Milton winked at her, then laid his head against the headrest and momentarily shut his eyes, all the while wearing a wide grin on his face.

* * *

Karilyn hummed as she pushed the vacuum from room to room, finishing up her Sunday afternoon cleaning routine. It had gotten off to a late start, delayed by her taking her husband to the airport. He'd be out of town for the entire week, and Karilyn looked forward to having some quiet time to herself, not that Milton was much of a bother. She loved her husband and would do anything for him. He was an excellent provider and would rather that she stay home and tend to the house, prepare his meals, and keep the flower bed looking nice, but Karilyn couldn't stand to sit at home twiddling her thumbs when the chores were done. Cleaning, although it was work, always seemed to bring a sense of calm over her, allowing her the time to think and focus on the prior week's happenings.

Work was going well for Karilyn. So far, she had really enjoyed reporting to and working for Genesis. Initially, she'd had her doubts about reporting to a younger woman . . . who happened to be black at that. *Not that I'm prejudiced,* she told herself; *it's just a new experience for me.* She'd been impressed with Genesis's quick acclimation to her position and her professionalism. Rarely did Genesis wear her standard uniform blues anymore, which she had done every day when she started, but over the past several months Genesis had traded them for her own business skirt and pantsuits and snazzy heels. She was quick on her feet, treated her employees fairly, and gave everyone a sense of value. Karilyn could honestly say that so far, Genesis had been the best boss she'd had since working at the hotel. With Boss's Day coming up in a few weeks, Karilyn made a mental note to start looking around for a nice gift for Genesis.

She pushed the vacuum down the hall, turned into Milton's office, plugged the vacuum in again, and turned it on. Generally, she left that room solely to him because things just seemed to be in such a clutter, but Milton swore that he knew where everything was, and would get confused if Karilyn started "cleaning up" there. She looked at the mess of papers and folders scattered across his desk and shook her head. "As long as it works for him," she said aloud, winding the cord around her hand and elbow before hanging it on the vacuum. She reached over his desk to retrieve a trio of coffee mugs that had collected there over the week. As she pulled her arm back, she knocked over a stack of folders.

She huffed, but continued walking toward the kitchen to put the mugs in the sink, then returned a few minutes later to pick up the array of papers that now lay on the floor. While Milton wasn't the most organized businessman, he normally did a good job at labeling his folders with his clients' names, making it easier for her to figure out which papers went where. Any loose receipts would have to be resorted when he returned home, but for the most part she would be able to reassemble the folders with ease.

As she lifted and replaced one document after another, she came across Taunya Johnson's application. Nothing about it stood out in her mind as it was filled out in the same fashion as Milton's other tenants'. She thumbed through the folders until she spotted one labeled JOHNSON T., then opened it to replace the application. It was then that her heart began to skip beats. Inside her folder was a red envelope that looked to hold a greeting card, addressed to Milton and sent to his post office box. Karilyn quickly flipped the envelope on its reverse side, opened the flap, and pulled out a red and white card with gold accents, whose front read *Mmm, mmm good!* On the inside was a handwritten message that read *That's what you are to me!* Karilyn was most appalled by a professionally taken photo that had been included of Taunya standing in a G-string with her arms folded across her naked breasts. Her hair hung down over her face, revealing nothing other than her right eye. With Taunya's fair pigment and the altered lighting in the photo, Karilyn couldn't tell that she was a black woman.

Her hands began to tremble as tears trickled down Karilyn's face. She felt a wide array of emotions run through her in an instant, shock, hurt, anger, and even envy and jealousy, as she stared at Taunya's obviously well cared for body. *He is whoring around with this woman?* she asked herself in disbelief. Maybe the woman was trying to lure him. But why would he keep this card? she questioned. She lifted Taunya's file and went through every document there, finding utility bill records and varied other receipts. All of the utilities were in his name and had also been sent to his post office box. Her eyes scanned over the printed information and soon located the property address, 229 Wellington Court. Without hesitation she took a seat at Milton's computer, pointed the Web browser to MapQuest, and punched in the address. With a copy of the directions from her home in Toano to the address in the file in a shaky hand, she tried to think if she was vaguely familiar with the area, having been through there only a few times to cross the Hampton Roads Bridge Tunnel. And even then, Milton had done the driving; Karilyn hardly ventured outside her subdivision except to go to work or to run a few local errands. But with this new information in her hand, she quickly made the decision to be daring enough to drive to Hampton alone.

Standing to her feet, she thumbed through the remaining documents in Taunya's folder. Her hand flew to her heart as she turned to the backside of Taunya's application and reviewed her references. At the top of the list she found the name Genesis Taylor.

Genesis stepped hurriedly through the airport, looking forward to her week although it would be crammed with meetings and training sessions. She retrieved her luggage from the carousel, then stepped outside to the center island to catch the shuttle to the rental car lot. Feeling accomplished, she signed her name, picked up keys, and in minutes, pulled out onto California's I-5 headed into Stockton.

It was her first trip to California, a state she'd only visited vicariously through Joan, Toni, Lynn, and Mya of *Girlfriends*. As she drove the forty-five minutes from Sacramento International Airport to Stockton, she was both surprised and disappointed to see miles and miles of farmland, cows, goats, and vineyards. "Am I in California or North Carolina?" she asked herself, switching on the radio and scanning for an R & B station.

Usher's "Confessions" blared through the speakers as she cruised alongside a truck toting red bell peppers, then another transporting several horses. *So much for seeing the rich and famous*. Pulling off the freeway on March Lane, she was glad to see familiar signs of city life, to include Starbucks, and other chain restaurants and stores. She whipped the rented Pontiac into the hotel's lot, retrieved her luggage, and walked inside to check in. When the automatic doors slid open, she was met by the warmest brown eyes she'd seen in a long time.

In a rich Nigerian accent, he greeted her as she walked up. "Welcome to the Regal Towers, Stockton."

Taken aback by his incredibly dark, smooth skin and gleaming smile, she was momentarily speechless. She stuttered as she caught herself staring.

"Uh . . . thanks. Reservation for Taylor please." She dug in her purse for her driver's license while the gentleman typed her last name into the computer in front of him.

"Oh, you're here for the leadership conference," he said. "Which location do you manage?"

"Williamsburg," she said, presenting him with her corporate American Express card in an attempt to showboat.

"Oh, I won't need that. All of the expenses are covered by the hotel."

Genesis tried to hide her embarrassment. Of course the expenses would be covered. *What was I thinking?* "Oh yeah, I just get so used to being asked for a card to cover incidentals I wasn't thinking."

"No problem." He slid her a room key. "You are in room 712, which is a king suite. The elevators are right behind you, and we can have a valet take your things up for you. If you need anything else, please feel free to let me know. I'm Aungie Okeyo."

"Aungie," she repeated, loving the sound of his name. She nodded her head, expressing impression and approval.

"I will actually be in those meetings as well. I manage this location," he added with a wink.

"Great. I look forward to seeing you then. Maybe you can save me a seat at your table," she flirted, then switched away. Just before she stepped onto the elevator, she glanced behind her to see if Aungie had watched her walk off. She was pleased to find that his eyes were directly on her. She wiggled her fingers in a good-bye wave as the elevator doors slid shut, then fanned herself with the small folder that held her key card. "Whew, he's fine! Maybe I can strike up a little romance while I'm here."

There would be a meet and greet social hour later that evening, giving Genesis plenty of time to unwind from her flight, hang her clothes, take a dip in the hotel's pool, and shower before rubbing elbows with her peers. She inspected her garments, trying to decide what she'd wear, now that some instant chemistry had been kicked off between her and Aungie. She had brought a couple of dresses that were more on the conservative side, and she wished, for once, she had a little bit of spice that would allow her to show some cleavage or some thigh. Deciding to skip the pool, Genesis headed out to the shopping center she'd passed right off the Eight Mile Road exit. Maybe she'd be able to pick up something there. She would need shoes too as she'd only brought her everyday work pumps, a pair of low-heeled dress slides, and a pair of sneakers.

She headed out for a little shopping and returned two hours later with a black strapless formfitting dress paired with a burgundy shrug and black-heeled sandals.

She liked the way she looked in it: flirty, casual, and sexy. She had also picked up a little extra makeup, ready to try a few of Taunya's suggestions that she spruce herself up a little.

She took the elevator back to the first floor and tipped down the hall to the hotel's conference room. Pinning a name badge to her clothes, she tried not to be conspicuous as her eyes immediately scanned the room for Aungie's dark skin and piercing eyes. Not finding them, she searched for anyone else there she would be able to connect with, or maybe had already met. Before she could approach anyone, a thin white woman with bleached blond hair bounced toward her with an extended hand.

"Hi! I'm Cheryl," she introduced, making two syllables of her name rather than one. "And you are?" She backed away for a single step to read Genesis's badge. "Genesis?" she asked. "How unique." Her voice squeaked like a mouse.

"Thank you. Nice to meet you, Cheryl."

Cheryl frowned as her eyes quickly assessed Genesis's makeup. "Your makeup is just a bit smudged," she whispered. "You might want to go to the ladies' room."

"Is it?" *I just checked my makeup. I looked fine*, she thought. "Okay, thanks."

Once Genesis looked at herself in the bathroom lighting, she was horrified. Her foundation was two shades too light and was as thick as a pancake. The lip color she'd purchased to match her sweater made her look like she was ready to perform under the big tent, and in an attempt to make her lashes look long and full, she'd overapplied her mascara and it was clumped together in balls. "See, that's why I don't wear this mess." She rushed to the elevator tower to return to her room and wash her face. As she rounded the corner, in her haste she ran into Aungie.

"Where's the fire?" he asked, then began to chuckle looking at her face. Genesis could feel her face warming.

"Excuse me." She pushed off him and darted down the hall, turning one heel over, nearly breaking her ankle. "Ow!" she yelped, but not loud enough to be overheard by Aungie. She hobbled into the elevator, then to her room, jerked out of her shrug, and began washing her face. In her careless haste, water splashed on the front of her clothes, leaving several wet circles on her dress. She mumbled a couple of choice words, now looking at her face looking plainer than ever and her wet clothes. "That's what I get for trying to be something I'm not." She went to the closet and re-assessed the clothes she brought with her, then selected a basic black pantsuit with a white spaghetti strap shell. Quickly, she redressed, simply lined her eyes with a brown pencil, then covered her lips with a touch of clear gloss. She gathered her hair into her fists, twisted a few times, and secured the twist with a hair clip. Still feeling a bit of pain from turning her foot over, she decided on her slides rather than the shoes she'd just bought, throwing them back into a bag to be returned prior to her leaving the area.

Approving her appearance in the mirror, although she didn't look as striking as she wanted to, she had to admit that she was a whole lot more comfortable and confident. At any rate, it was an improvement from the jeans and sweatshirt she'd arrived in.

Genesis made a casual entrance back into the ballroom and began to socialize with the many faces there, trying to work her way around the room to Aungie. *Stop acting so desperate,* she reprimanded herself, taking notice of the way her eyes kept circling the room in search of him. Nibbling on cubes of fresh melons and strawberries from an appetizer spread, she decided to stand in one spot and let the man come to her if he was at all interested. It didn't take long for him to ease up beside her.

"So, are you enjoying yourself?" he said, bending to whisper in her ear.

Sipping from a glass, she nodded and smiled pleasantly.

"I see you changed clothes."

"Yeah, the outfit I had on was a little bit uncomfortable."

"But you looked amazing in it. I think you should go put it back on." Genesis began to blush. "It showed off your figure, and those shoes were sexy as hell."

"You need to quit it," she giggled in response.

"I'm serious. I'm just a man that doesn't mind expressing my appreciation for beautiful things."

"Well, thank you, Aungie."

"So, what are you doing later on?"

"I hadn't planned on doing anything more than relaxing in my room a little bit. I brought my laptop to get some work done, and make sure everything is still running smoothly back at work."

"I can't blame you for that." He bit into a piece of shrimp before he continued. "A couple of friends of mine are having a little get-together down in Sacramento tomorrow night. I would love for you to join us."

"What kind of get-together is it?" she asked, not wanting to seem too anxious.

He shrugged. "Umm . . . we just get together and hang out a little bit, you know, hold intelligent conversations, eat a little food. There is no special occasion, other than friends getting together."

"Let me think about it and let you know tomorrow after our sessions. Is that okay?"

"Sure. That will be fine."

At the end of the evening, Augie escorted Genesis to the elevator, sharing with her how much he looked forward to the next evening.

"Likewise," she said, having made the decision to live a little and see the city, as long as she drove. *He won't be taking me to never-never land to never be seen or heard from again.*

Karilyn started the engine of the champagne-colored Lexus SUV and slowly backed out of her garage and driveway, still shaken from what she'd found but motivated by her determination. Her large dark Coach shades hid most of her face, and she'd covered her head with one of her husband's golf hats although she was sure no one would recognize her once she got to where she was going.

She eased the vehicle onto 64 eastbound and scanned her directions to be reminded of which exit ramp to take. After she'd driven in silence for nearly forty-five minutes, her mind was still muddled and her thinking unclear. *What are you going to do with that gun?* she asked herself, shooting her eyes to the glove compartment as she waited nervously at a stoplight on Mercury Boulevard. She had placed Milton's nine millimeter there right before she'd left the house. *You don't have the guts to kill anyone,* she said internally, feeling like a character from *Desperate Housewives. And who would you shoot? Are you going to shoot him or her?* "Think,

Karilyn, think!" she said out loud, trying to come to her senses. "You are not going to kill anybody!"

But even with that spoken affirmation, there was a part of her that wanted to hold the cold steel and pull its trigger in revenge.

Slowly she pulled onto Wellington Court and began searching for the house number. Cruising from house to house, she almost brought the car to a stop as she approached 229. She thought better of it when she took note of what looked like two full-grown men standing in the front yard tossing a football. Taunya's boys were just teenagers, well-mannered young men. However, with both standing over six feet and muscles bulging from their involvement with high school sports, in Karilyn's mind, they looked like two giants who wouldn't think twice of brutally beating and strangling a white woman.

The boys barely gave attention to her as she passed by, yet she wished she had placed the gun under her seat rather than putting it so far out of reach. Instinctively, her fingers clicked on the control to lock her doors, although the SUV had an automatic locking feature once put in gear. Her foot hit the pedal harder and more quickly than she intended, causing her to slam backward in her seat while the vehicle skidded off several feet. She whipped out of the neighborhood in unwarranted panic, willing her heart to slow its racing.

Making a left onto Queen Street, she kept straight, unsure of exactly where she was going. She fumbled with her directions, trying to locate where she was and at the same time be conscious of traffic. Before she knew it she had come to the end of the road at Jefferson Avenue, which brought out a sigh of relief,

knowing that Jefferson Avenue would become Merri-
mac Trail once it reached Williamsburg, and she
knew her way home from there. Yet she unknowingly
turned in the wrong direction and headed toward
downtown Newport News. As she passed more and
more unfamiliar sights, she became increasingly nervous, which triggered a hot flash. In an instant, she
felt like she was both suffocating and burning in hell.
Scared but needing to breathe, she let down her
front window halfway, but kept her fingers on the
control to put it up again if anyone approached her
vehicle.

Just as Karilyn was about to turn around, she noticed a sign directing her to keep straight to get to an
on-ramp. Keeping her eyes peeled for the ramp, she
mumbled a prayer through her lips as she slowed for
a stoplight. Without turning her head, she let her eyes
follow a couple to her right, who seemed to be argu-
ing over some lost money. She slowly eased to her
right, extending her hand toward the glove compartment to retrieve her gun. Before she could pull the
latch, a voice to her left startled her.

"Yo, what you need, Ma?" A black man who looked
to be letting his hair lock on its own tapped twice on
the window. He was dressed in an army-green jacket,
which was two sizes too big for him. Karilyn batted her
eyes quickly in fear, grasping for her heart. Immediately, the man backed away, holding his hands up to
expose both palms. "I'm sorr', I wa'n't tryna scare
you, miss. What you looking for, though? You need
something? 'Cause I got it."

Terrified, Karilyn sped off and pulled onto the
ramp a few blocks later.

Chapter 16

Milton left his phone off for the entire week. After hearing Karilyn's voice, shaky with tears, he just didn't feel like facing the music until he had to. He could easily lie and say he couldn't pick up a signal where he was. Besides, he needed the time to think of what he could say to his wife about this picture she had found. His initial thought was to say that he didn't know who Taunya was, or what Karilyn was talking about, but wasn't sure that would fly since she was living in one of his rental properties. He hoped that he could convince her that he had no idea why a tenant would send him such a card and photo, and that she had come on to him several times, to the point where he was seriously considering evicting her. He'd then add on that the only reason why he hadn't done it yet was that that particular property had stayed vacant for so long, it would be sacrificing income to have her leave, although Taunya was no longer paying a single dime in rent.

But for now, he planned on doing nothing else but enjoying Taunya's company to the fullest. He loved the dazzled look in her eyes as they entered their resort whose entire ground floor was a casino, with the exception of the check-in desk, restaurant, and gift shop.

"Ooh, I can't wait to get down here and make me some money!" she squealed. "What do you play?" she asked, looping her free arm into his.

"I will probably hit the blackjack and poker tables, I don't know." He shrugged, still thinking about selling a story to Karilyn.

"I want to see a couple of shows while we are here too." She pulled her bag onto the elevator and leaned back against the wall.

He stood beside her and dropped an arm over her shoulder. "Of course. Whatever you want to do."

Taunya smiled up at him, then puckered for a kiss. He pecked her lips, then kissed her more intensely, and she let out a low moan. "I know what I want to do before I do anything else, though." He reached down to her behind and suggestively raised his eyebrows.

Taunya giggled like a schoolgirl and pressed up against him. "I bet I know what that is."

As soon as they got in their room, Taunya did begin making some money, but she didn't have to invest any cash to do it. She dipped into the bathroom with a little more than a handful of material and a cosmetic bag that she'd pulled out of her suitcase. Stripping out of her flight clothes, she rushed through a shower, then put on her barely-there thong and sliver of a bra that left her nipples exposed.

"Sweetie, can you run out and get some ice for me real quick?" she yelled to Milton through the closed door, wanting him to leave the room so she could get her thigh-high boots out of her luggage.

"Ice? You need it right now?"

"Yeah, I bumped my head when I was getting in the car. I need to put something on it."

"Let me see it."

Taunya huffed. "Can you please just go get the ice first? I'll be out in a minute."

"All right." Seconds later, once she heard the door slam behind him, she scurried out of the bathroom, jerked the boots up her legs, then turned off the lights and the television in the room, leaving nothing but the multicolored glow of the lights from the strip to illuminate her private stage. She rushed to her bag and flipped through the CD case she'd brought with her on the flight and found an old Tupac project, *All Eyez On Me*. Slipping it into the player, she advanced to track fourteen, "What'z Ya Phone #," a rapped remix of a Prince old-school hit. Propping a foot up on the seat of a chair, she waited for Milton to return.

He nearly fell over backward and was instantly aroused when he returned to the room seeing her dark silhouette against the Vegas skyline and hearing Tupac rap about explicit sex.

"I hope you brought some cash, because I have a special show just for you." Taunya invited him to take a seat, crooking her finger.

Returning Karilyn's call would have to wait.

Genesis slid into a comfortable pair of jeans, a tan off-the-shoulder sweater, and a pair of brown low-heeled pumps. Aungie promised that the evening would be casual and there was no need to dress up.

With his directions in hand, she headed downstairs for her drive to Sacramento.

Comfortably seated in her rental car, she slid John Legend's latest project into the CD player and pulled on to I-5. Swaying to "Maxine" as she neared her exit, she dialed the number Aungie had given her, letting him know she would be there shortly.

"Great! We're just getting started here, so that's perfect," he said, semiyelling over the background noise of old-school R & B hits and people talking. "Listen, I'm going to drive out to the main road to meet you. There are a few curves back here in the neighborhood that can get a little confusing," he offered. "Just stop in that shopping center once you pull off the exit, and I'll be right there."

Less than ten minutes later, Aungie pulled up beside Genesis in a black Lincoln Navigator.

Wow! Are they paying you like that? she thought as she eased her window down.

"You ready?" he said, looking down from where he sat. Genesis gave him a smile with a thumbs-up, then pulled off, following him to an elaborate gated estate. All types of luxury vehicles were parked around the circular driveway.

"If this is his house, I'm going to have to renegotiate my salary," she said out loud. "He gets fifty points for the house alone. And if his parents are rich and he has some kind of inheritance—that will make up the other fifty!" Had Taunya been there, they would have high-fived each other on that note.

They entered the house together, and Aungie started slapping hands with guests who had arrived since he'd been gone. He turned and introduced Genesis to a few of them, letting them know she was in town for the week. Genesis shook hands and nodded graciously although she was taken by surprise by the lustful looks in the eyes of both the men and the women. She eyed the rest of crowd, who, as Aungie had described, were sitting around chatting idly with a drink in hand or a small plate of food.

"You want something to drink?" he asked, taking her hand and leading her toward a wet bar.

"Umm, sure," Genesis accepted. Aungie mixed her an apple martini and handed her the glass.

"Mmm," she moaned, sipping her drink. "This is good." She leaned against the bar, standing next to Aungie, absorbing and assessing the action in the room, feeling like she was in a photo shoot for a Kool cigarette campaign.

"So, what do you think of the city?" he asked, leaning back on his elbows.

"It's okay." She nodded. "I didn't know there was so much farmland here."

"Oh yeah. Well, you know California is known for its great wine, and the grapes have to be grown somewhere." He noticed that the alcohol Genesis consumed was kicking in, causing her to become more relaxed. "You need another drink?"

"No, I'm good. You're not trying to get me drunk, are you?"

Aungie let out a hearty Nigerian laugh. "Of course not, you have to drive back home tonight. Unless you want me to drive you," he chuckled, testing the waters.

"Oh no, you said it right the first time, I have to drive back," she quickly replied. Aungie released another laugh.

"Is this your house?"

He nodded. "Mm-hmm."

"It's beautiful! Are you sure we work for the same company?"

"Come on back here with me," he said, leading her to another part of the house. They walked down a marbled corridor that led to a large beautifully lit furnished patio surrounded by trees. The patio was occupied by a second crowd who were also laughing and talking. Aungie pulled Genesis over to an empty leather sofa and dropped his arm around her shoulder. Genesis's eyes stretched as she observed a couple sitting across from them taking turns heaving smoke from a flexible hose connected to a tall vase-looking contraption. They giggled, snickered, and talked between puffs while Genesis tried not to stare. As she looked around the room, she took note of others clustered together around both larger and smaller contraptions, all inhaling from either their own or a shared tube.

It's time for me to go, she thought although she kept her words to herself and didn't move right away. "What is going on in here?" she finally questioned.

"What do you mean? We are just having fun."

"Yeah, but what's going on?" She waved her hand around the room, prompting Aungie for some level of explanation. "Is this illegal?"

Aungie threw his head back in laughter again. This time, Genesis found it to be irritating. "No, it is not illegal . . . well, most of it anyway. Do they look like they are getting high to you? Look at their eyes."

Genesis looked for the familiar glazed-over look she had seen many times on the faces of some of her neighbors and others who strolled through her old neighborhood. She had to admit, none of the individuals quite looked like what she'd seen before. They all looked sane and sober.

"They are just smoking tobamel," Aungie said.

"Toe-who?"

"Tobamel. It is like tobacco leaves mixed with fruit or honey. Do you want to try it?"

"What is that thing they are puffing in? They can't smoke it like a cigarette? Not that that would be any better."

"It is called a hookah pipe. Really it's nothing to it. Come. Let's try it."

"No, thank you." She paused for several minutes feeling highly uncomfortable and incredibly vulnerable. "So, they aren't getting high?" she asked again.

"Most of them, no. There are a couple of them that bring their own hashish if they want to get high, as you put it."

"And where are they?" Before Aungie could answer, Genesis was stunned by a loud series of grunts and moans that suggested sex. Whipping her head around to her right, she witnessed a couple pressed up against the wall fully engaged in intercourse. The man had the woman's leg lifted into the crook of his bent arm, her dress high around her waist, while he shamelessly thrust forward several times. In complete shock, Genesis stood to her feet. "You know what? It's time for me to go. Thanks for inviting me," she blurted as she rushed to the doorway, passing the couple who, still going at it, seemed to be oblivious of the presence of other people.

As quickly as her feet would carry her, Genesis walked through the crowd and out the front door. She was both offended and glad that Aungie had not followed her outside. Without looking back, she hopped in her vehicle and sped off, luckily remembering which turns would lead her back out to the main road.

She spent the remainder of the summit avoiding Aungie at all costs, although he'd tried several times to chat with her. House or no house, his points were gone.

Chapter 17

Karilyn arrived at work early, measuring her steps down the hall toward Genesis's office. She had cried so many tears in the past week, her eyes were as puffy as marshmallows and as red as a fire engine. In the week that Genesis had been out of the office, Karilyn's automatic hatred for Taunya spilled over into her feelings about her boss. She no longer saw Genesis as a capable young woman who treated her employees fairly and with dignity and respect. All she recognized now was the fact that Genesis was black and was friends with the slut that was screwing her husband.

"I'm old enough to be that . . ." She struggled within herself to refrain from using the N word, but since no one was around to hear her, she said what she felt and thought. ". . . that nigger's mother. Who does she think she is to give orders?" she mumbled. "And then that whorish friend of hers, flaunting herself around like a shameless hussy."

She dug through her purse and retrieved an unauthorized copy of the key to Genesis's office, slid it in the lock, and let herself in. Silently, she began rambling through files and drawers, looking for anything that she could use to ultimately get rid of Genesis. She looked around at the varied things on Genesis's desk, picked up the photo of Anna Marie, mumbled more racial slurs, then set it down again.

After snooping through files and folders for several minutes, Karilyn slipped the payroll reports into her bag, looked around Genesis's office for anything else she could sabotage, and rested her eyes on Genesis's degree certificate. She lifted it up from the shelf where it sat behind the coffee mug she had given Genesis on her first day of work.

"North Carolina Central University? What kind of fly-by-night school is that?" Karilyn mumbled, taking a good look at Genesis's framed certificate. "I bet that school isn't even accredited." She put the frame back in its place, grabbed a sticky note, and jotted down the school's name to research later. Not seeing anything else she could get her hands on, she left the office, closing the door behind her.

Taunya walked to the office, ready to pick Genesis up for lunch. She stopped at Karilyn's desk. "I'm here to see Ms. Taylor please," she said, flinging a head full of microbraids behind her.

Karilyn smiled as pleasantly as she always did. "May I tell her your name please?" Karilyn's heart nearly stopped when Taunya gave her first and last name. Her smile slowly faded although she held back the scowl that fought to come forth. Taunya sat in a chair against the wall, crossing one thick leg over the other. She was dressed in a lycra-knit black miniskirt, paired with a red lace see-through blouse, and four-inch red stilettos that laced up her legs. Tears burned in Karilyn's eyes as she dialed Genesis's extension, announced Taunya's arrival, then excused herself, fleeing for the ladies' room.

She turned on the water to cover the sound of her sobs before locking herself in the handicap stall. *How could he do this to me? He's cheating on me with her? A black woman?* Totally flabbergasted, she leaned against the wall, struggling to stay on her feet rather than sliding down the wall to the floor. *Maybe there is more than one Taunya Johnson in the city,* she thought, trying to be optimistic, feeling that Milton's infidelity with an African-American woman was a double slap in the face.

Hearing the water being turned off by another restroom visitor, she silenced her moans and waited in the stall until she was sure there was no one else in the bathroom. With trembling hands, she exited the stall and trudged toward the sink to splash water on her face, still sniffling. Just as she pulled a paper towel from the dispenser to pat both the water and the tears, Genesis and Taunya burst into the bathroom, catching Karilyn by surprise.

"Woo, I gotta pee!" Taunya said, bustling to the first stall.

Right away Genesis took note of Karilyn's fallen countenance and beet-red face and eyes. "Karilyn, are you okay?" Her crinkled brows expressed her sincere concern as she moved closer to Karilyn's side.

"Yeah, yeah, I'm fine," she lied, turning her back to Genesis to reach for another paper towel. "I kinda got a double whammy, I guess. I had an eyelash in my eye, and at the same time, I started having a hot flash." She pasted an uneasy smile on her face as she dabbed at her eyes.

"Are you sure?" Genesis quizzed, unconvinced.

"Yes, it's nothing, trust me." Karilyn dismissed her with a quick wave of her hand as she heard the toilet flush. She hurried for the door, wanting to be out of the bathroom before Taunya came out of the stall. "Go ahead and enjoy your lunch. I'll be fine."

Leaving the bathroom, she took a detour to the elevators, pushed the button, and sighed in relief as one set of doors immediately slid open. She hopped inside and pressed the key that would take her to the very top floor. Rushing through the exit doors out onto the rooftop, Karilyn gasped for air, unable to hold back her tears.

"How could he do this to me?" she repeated out loud in a whisper. "I've been a good wife to that man, and this is the thanks I get?" She walked to the wall and peered down toward the ground below, for a fleeting moment thinking of hurling herself over the side. Before the thought could fully process in her head, an overpowering desire for revenge consumed her soul. "For you, Milton, for being the lying, cheating, backstabbing bastard that you are. For you, Taunya, for having the audacity to take my Milton away from me. And for you, Genesis, for just being friends with that whore and helping her to cover it up!" she spat into the air.

Karilyn stayed on the rooftop for twenty more minutes trying to make sure she had all of her tears out of the way. She gained her composure more quickly remembering the degree in Genesis's office. Genesis wouldn't be back for at least another thirty minutes, which would give Karilyn time to do a little research on the school and place a call to their alumni records office.

Back at her desk, Karilyn cleared her throat in preparation to speak to the records clerk. "Good afternoon, this is Patricia Hines calling from Regal Tower Hotels in Virginia, how are you?" she asked, lying in her sweetest voice.

"Fine, and yourself?" the voice flatly replied.

"Great, great," she sang. "I have an applicant who is seeking a management position here with our hotel, and I am performing a background check this morning." She paused slightly. "I just need to confirm the attendance and completion of an alumni student." Karilyn submitted Genesis's name, received a time frame when she would be hearing back from the school, then ended the call.

Chapter 18

Although she hadn't seen him in a week, Karilyn jumped on Milton no sooner than he'd come in the door that evening, practically dragging him to his office where she'd laid Taunya Johnson's file out with the photo on top.

"I barely even know that woman," Milton said in his normal tone of voice as he took the folder from Karilyn's hand and nonchalantly tossed it on his desk. "What else happened while I was gone besides you rummaging through my office making yourself upset over nothing?" He took a seat at his desk and logged in to his business e-mail account, unable to bring his eyes to meet Karilyn's.

"What do you mean you barely know her? She's living in one of your properties! I know how carefully you screen your applicants, Milton," she fumed. "You know everything about that woman."

"Really, I don't. John Hammerstein took care of that particular applicant while I was away in Colorado. By the time I got back here, he'd interviewed her, verified her employment and references, and given her the key."

"So why isn't she thanking John Hammerstein? Why is she sending you the cards and photos?" Karilyn fought to hold her ground, but Milton's explanation, which sounded like it could be true, began to make her doubt herself.

"He probably ran out of business cards or something and gave her one of mine or something, I don't know!" he spat, attempting to manipulate his wife by showing exasperation. "I mean, I come home after a long week of grueling business meetings, boring dinners, and cutthroat negotiations and this is what I have to deal with?" Milton clicked out of his e-mail, jumped to his feet, and grabbed his keys. "Maybe I should go back to where I just came from. At least I could go to bed surrounded by peace and quiet rather than a slew of railing accusations!" He stormed toward the door with Karilyn on his heels.

"Milton, wait! I wasn't accusing you, I was just asking! How else was I to react when I saw—" The slamming of the door leading from the kitchen to the garage cut Karilyn's sentence in half. She stood in the kitchen in shock and in tears, listening to the sound of his car starting, then the sound of the garage door opening and closing again. Her entire body seemed to be paralyzed replaying what had just happened; even her eyes were affixed to a clock on the wall although they were blurred by her tears. Instead of getting to the bottom of things, she had run her husband away.

Karilyn watched the second hand make a full rotation around the clock's face five times before her trance was broken by the sound of the garage opening again. Her eyes darted around the kitchen looking for something to wipe her face with. She quickly grabbed the dish towel from off the counter, wiped her face dry, then opened the refrigerator pretending to look for something. She grabbed a bottle of water, ran it across her forehead, then twisted the cap off and took a swig as Milton entered. Saying nothing, he tossed his keys on the counter and walked toward his wife. Gingerly he took the bottle from her hands and wrapped his arms around her.

"Sweetie, I'm sorry," he whispered. "I overreacted just now and you didn't deserve that."

Falling into his chest, Karilyn began to sob loudly. "Honey, I'm sorry . . . I—"

"Shhh," he coaxed. "I know what it looks like, but I promise you, I don't know that woman." He pulled back and stared straight into his wife's teary blue eyes. "I've never even met her. I don't know why she sent that card and photo, and we can burn it right now, okay?" Before Karilyn could respond, he relaxed his arms, walked steadfastly to his office, and returned with the card and photo. Silently he went to the stove, turned on the front burner, and lit the corners of both pieces of paraphernalia. As the flames grew, he placed them in the kitchen sink, then went back and embraced his wife, watching bits of black residue float in the air. He was satisfied with himself as he felt her body surrender to his. He had seen Taunya's naked body enough times to have her engraved in his memory.

While he consoled his wife, he became both aroused and frustrated thinking about Taunya. She hadn't answered her cell phone when he'd called just minutes ago, or else he would be on the highway headed for the pleasures of her body. She probably needed to spend time with her boys anyway. He'd cleared the call from his phone, circled his car back around, and come back home to Karilyn.

"I was planning on sleeping by myself tonight while you slept in the guest room," Karilyn said with a crooked smile on her face, feeling the rise of his manhood through his pants. "But I changed my mind . . . let's go to bed," she said, leading Milton toward the bedroom.

Chapter 19

"We still have about ten minutes before people should start to arrive," Karilyn stated, as she busied herself in the kitchen, pulling a tray of miniquiches from the oven, then inserting another, all the while studying Taunya's behaviors. *Keep your friends close and your enemies closer,* she reminded herself. She didn't let on that she knew who she was, or what type of woman she was. *Nasty black whore,* she thought, reminded of the photo that her husband had burned. *What kind of a woman mails naked pictures of herself to a man!* She finished preparing the meat and cheese wraps, and set both appetizers on the table with various other finger foods. "Those sure look yummy, Taunya," she said with a phony smile pasted on her face.

"Oh, they are, and they're easy to make," Taunya commented. She was busy filling small plastic cups with gelled cubes of spiked Jell-O, occasionally popping one into her mouth. "What else do you need us to do?" she asked Genesis while placing the cups in the refrigerator.

"I think we're all done," Genesis said, taking a seat

NINETY-NINE AND A HALF JUST WON'T DO 133

on the couch after lighting a few scented candles. "I really should have had a painting party instead of a housewarming party." Her eyes scanned the stark-white walls of her living room. "Maybe I will get a few Home Depot gift cards to cover the cost of paint."

"I'm going to run out to my car and get your gift." Karilyn winked. "You're gonna love it!" She slipped her feet into a pair of worn mules and scurried out the door.

"How do you deal with her happy-go-lucky behind all day every day?" Taunya asked, rolling her eyes.

"Leave my assistant alone please," Genesis defended although she couldn't help but chuckle. "That woman is worth her weight in gold to me at work."

"Hmph. Well, that is saying a lot considering how big she is. You got that white woman all up in your house and in your business," she said hypocritically.

"Cut it out and be nice." Genesis tossed a pillow from the sofa at her friend on her way to the door, responding to the chiming doorbell. A couple of older ladies from her former neighborhood came in with their arms filled with boxes. "Come on in and make yourselves comfortable," she welcomed.

"Oh, Genesis! Your grandmama would be so proud of you." Millie Edwards's eyes bucked as she looked around the condo in awe. "This sho' is nice! Looka there, Pearline," she said, pointing toward the three-sided fireplace.

"What they call that, shug?" Pearline Payne asked, squinting her eyes at the smoked glass that encased the hearth. Before Genesis could respond, Pearline went to her next question. "Where your baffroom at?"

"It's right this way." She led the woman down the hall.

"Lawd, I better gone back here with her. She be done messed around and peed all on your flo'," Millie said, following Pearline.

"I'm a grown woman," Pearline snapped. "I know howda pull my draws down and use the toilet! Now, if you was a man, I'd let you come on in here," she chuckled. "'Cause Pearline still got it, honey!" she finished, moving her hips as best she could in a slow-motion wiggle.

Both Taunya and Genesis broke out in laughter while Millie rolled her eyes. "Now, that's the real Mama Payne right there," Taunya commented, referring to the character from Martin Lawrence's sitcom *Martin.*

"Go 'head and sit down, Miss Millie." Genesis waved, heading to the door again, letting Karilyn in, escorted by Dee-Dee and Simone from the Omni. They both let go of the huge rug they were helping Karilyn carry just long enough to greet Genesis.

"Hey!" they both chimed excitedly, throwing their arms around Genesis and embracing her in a tight hug.

"It's so good to see you two! I'm glad you could make it!" Looking over Simone's shoulder, Genesis saw a familiar figure step off the elevator and start toward her. "Go ahead inside," she directed. "I'll be right back." She pulled her door closed and took a defiant stance, crossing her arms over her chest. "Can I help you?" Genesis asked angrily, staring directly into Alton's eyes.

"I heard you were having a little get-together and, uh . . ." He paused momentarily as if he couldn't decide what he wanted to say. "I wanted to bring you a little something to help you celebrate." He presented a squared envelope from Kirkland's, which held a hundred-dollar gift card.

"You didn't bring your fiancée with you? Where is she?" Genesis hadn't moved an inch.

"Pfff! I ain't messing with her no more," he replied, sucking his teeth. "That wa'n't never nothing anyway."

"Yeah? It was enough for you to put a ring on her finger."

"Man, she bought that, I ain't buy that for her." Alton began to chuckle. "That girl proposed to me," he stated, patting his hand against his chest.

"Even so, you were seeing her while you were seeing me. You were screwing her while you were screwing me. You were making a fool of her, just like you were making a fool of me."

"I mean, we were just kicking it, though," he attempted in his defense.

"Kicking it, huh? That's what you call it?" She stepped closer to Alton.

"Yeah, I mean, we never said we were serious about each other. We were just . . ." With lifted brows his eyes darted around randomly. "Just kicking it."

Genesis nodded slowly as if she was coming to a clear understanding. "Well, this is what I call kicking it." In an unexpected and sudden move, she kicked Alton squarely in the crotch. The gift card flew from his hand as he buckled to the floor holding his manhood, yelping in pain. He blurted obscenities at her as she casually strolled to pick up the gift card. Leaving him curled in the fetal position by her doorstep, she turned away, twisted the knob of her front door, and stepped inside. "And, uh . . . if you aren't able to get up in the next two minutes, security will be glad to assist you to your car.

Thanks for the gift, I appreciate you stopping by." She winked before slamming the door.

"What was that about?" Millie asked, peering out of the window and watching Alton hobble to his car. "All-uh sudden I heard all this hollerin' and carryin' on—what in the world?"

"It was nothing," Genesis dismissed with a flick of her hand. "I was just dropping that zero so I can be free for my hero. When are we going to start eating?" she asked with a smile.

"We was waitin' on you, chile," Pearline said, boosting herself up from a chair. "Lawd knows I ain't ate all day." She led the way to the table. "Now, what that young man do ta you for you to have him hollerin' like that?" she asked, starting to meddle.

"He just ain't the one," Genesis replied, not about to open her personal life to the group of women.

"But what make you say that? Hol' on a minute, 'fore you answer that." She held up a finger commanding that everyone become silent. "Lawd, thank you for blessing Anna Marie's baby with this beautiful home. We know she looking down on her smilin'. Now, Lawd, we ask that you bless this good food, make it nourishing for our bodies while you nourish our souls, and bless the hands that prepared it. In Jesus' name, amen. Now, what that boy do?" she continued without skipping a beat, causing the women to break out in laughter.

"He couldn't make up his mind on what he wanted," Genesis said reluctantly.

"So he was creepin', then," Millie interpreted. Genesis sighed. "Chile, I don't blame you. I can't deal with no cheatin' man."

Picking up a plate, Karilyn cut her eyes over to

Taunya, but kept her face straight. She added a few wingettes, a spoonful of potato salad, and a few cubes of cheese. "Yes, infidelity is a tough one," she added, hoping that Taunya would speak up.

"Y'all girls married?" Pearline asked. Only Karilyn and Dee-Dee confirmed. The other ladies expressed their singleness in different ways. Some reflected happily single, while a few others wore a look that said they were desperate for a band around their ring fingers. "Well, it's two things I cain't put up wit . . . that's cheatin' and beatin'. Either one of them and I'll put that joker in an early grave!"

"How long you been married, baby?" Millie asked Karilyn.

"Twenty-one years," she shared. She smiled at Millie momentarily but kept her eyes on Taunya, still taking note of her actions.

"So you know a little bit about what it takes to be and stay married, then."

"Oh, we've definitely had our share of ups and downs," Karilyn chuckled in response. "And we've had some things we've had to work through."

"But you've hung in there, huh?" Dee-Dee asked. "I've only been married a few months, and I am still wondering what in the world I was thinking."

"Well, honey, if you got a good man, you best learn howda keep 'im," Millie advised. "Y'all got babies?"

"He got two by some heifer across town." Dee-Dee rolled her eyes and pressed her lips together tightly.

"Don't you disrespect that woman like that," Pearline admonished her. "He ain't cheat on you to get them kids, did he? You knew he had kids 'fore your married 'im, didn't you?"

"Yes, ma'am, but—"

"Do she disrespect you?"

"Well, no. I guess not."

"Is he being a father to his babies?"

"Oh yeah, he takes good care of his kids."

"So what you putting your mouth on her for? Let that woman raise that man's kids. And don't you mistreat them babies tryna get at her, you hear me?"

"Yes, ma'am," Dee-Dee answered meekly, taking her plate back to her seat.

"A man that takes care of his kids is worf somethin' now. You better learn how to honor that man," Pearline finished.

"I know that's right, Miss Pearline, 'cause them no-good men I got knocked up by ain't nowhere to be found," Taunya interjected. "But you know what, I don't even want no man that ain't got kids now, 'cause I ain't poppin' not a nan-nother one outta here," she stated, pointing to her crotch. "When I open these legs up, I want something going up in there, not coming out!"

"Taunya!" Genesis shrieked. "Girl, have some respect!"

"Ooh, girl, I wa'n't thinking," she said as her hand flew up to her mouth.

"You wasn't thinking or you been drinking?" Simone giggled.

"She did eat quite a few of those Jell-O things," Genesis stated.

Karilyn headed to the kitchen to get the napkins she'd forgotten to lay out. "Does anyone need anything while I'm up?" she offered.

"Yeah, you mind passing me the salt and pepper?" Taunya asked.

"No problem." Karilyn delivered the shakers and

watched as Taunya sprinkled a great deal of both seasonings over her plate.

"So, what you call a good man, Miss Pearline?" Simone asked. "And how can I get me one of them? You know what I'm saying?" She slapped hands with the young lady beside her.

"Ask Genesis," Taunya cut in. "She got a whole great big black book of men." Genesis shot her eyes in Taunya's direction. "She write down every little thing they do," she added.

"Don't pay Taunya no mind." She glared at Taunya, elbowing her in the side. "Go 'head, Miss Pearline, because none of the guys I've dated have amounted to much of anything. I need some pointers myself."

"Well, first you gotta know yourself," Pearline suggested. "If you don't know who you are, you'll find yourself in all kinda mess. Y'all gone hafta let me eat now. I told y'all I ain't ate all day." The ladies burst into more laughter at Pearline's frankness.

Several separate conversations broke out amongst the group as the women consumed their food and enjoyed each other's company. Genesis wiggled down between Taunya and Dee-Dee.

"We really haven't had a chance to catch up in two weeks. You never did finish telling me about your trip." Genesis swatted Taunya on the leg. She forked some fruit in her mouth, and raised her eyebrows, listening for a response.

"All I can say is I wanna go back! Girl, that man spoiled me some kinda terrible!" Taunya bragged. "We ate at some restaurant that spins at the top over the city. I can't remember the name of it, Around the World or something like that. And you talkin' about shopping? Girl, look what Lewis bought me."

She held her wrist forward, showing off a stunning tennis bracelet.

Karilyn's heart leapt, hearing the mention of her husband's name. She leaned forward to look at the jewelry that dangled from Taunya's arm. "Oh my goodness, it's beautiful!" she said. "Where did you two go?"

"Vegas," Taunya openly volunteered. "We had a ball."

Karilyn's blood began to come to a slow boil as Taunya confirmed what she'd suspected. She tried to keep a smile on her face, but it became more and more of a challenge as her lips began to tremble. Lucky for her, no one seemed to notice. She nibbled more on her food, but was struggling to keep her composure. Quietly she rose from her seat and went to the bathroom. She willed herself to hold back the tears this time, letting anger rise to the top over hurt and sadness.

"Okay." She bobbed her head up and down, looking at her reflection, but her words were expressly for Taunya and Milton. "You want to lie and cheat, Milton, you want to take this whore on trips and buy her jewelry? You want to lie up with my husband? Okay. I hope you heard what that woman said . . . cheating will put you in an early grave." She flushed the toilet, although she hadn't used it, washed her hands, and returned to the living room.

"So, Vegas, huh?" she started in, beaming at Taunya, encouraging her to talk. By the end of the night, Taunya had consumed far too many Jell-O shooters and glasses of wine, and was singing like a canary, sharing all kinds of details about the man she was seeing, and Karilyn absorbed every bit of it. She purposely stayed late under the guise of wanting to help Genesis clean up, but in reality, she dared not miss a single word that Taunya would utter.

Karilyn left Genesis's house knowing everything she needed to know about the woman who was sleeping with her husband.

Chapter 20

"Hello?" Karilyn said into the receiver in Milton's office.

"Good morning, Karilyn," John Hammerstein answered in surprise. "Old Milton finally convinced you to be his secretary, huh?" he chuckled.

"Not exactly," she said cheerfully. "I just happened to be in here doing my normal cleaning so I thought I'd answer the phone."

"Well, where's that husband of yours? I got some important news for him. I tried to reach him on his cell but couldn't get through. I'm surprised he hasn't returned my messages."

"He's playing a few holes of golf, but you know what, John, he can't keep up with his own head these days. He misplaced his phone yesterday and hasn't found it yet." Karilyn giggled out loud as she smiled to herself. She had called the cellular company and had his voice mail password changed and asked that the account be noted that only she could make changes to it. Since she had initially opened the account and kept it in her name only, although eventually Milton did get a second line, the customer service agent didn't even question her. While Milton had slept the night before, she took his phone, turned it off, and hid it amongst her Christmas ornaments in the attic. She secretly laughed as he practically tore the house apart searching for it once he woke up.

"Well, I know you aren't on the payroll, but do you mind taking a message for me?" John asked.

"Not at all, hold on just a sec." Karilyn pretended to grab a pencil to take down the name and phone number of an investor that Milton had spent many hours laboring with in negotiations.

"He's ready to write the check, so tell Milton to give him a call right away."

"Sure thing." Karilyn repeated the message back to John to assure him that she'd captured the details. "I'll get it to him," she sang, then ended the call, pressing her finger on the hook.

No sooner had she hung up than she erased the message from her memory.

She released the hook, dialed Milton's cell number, entered the new pass code, and played all his messages. John had called three times leaving the same message he'd just left with her. The investor called, expressing his readiness to close the deal, and then there was one explicit call from Taunya inviting him over for dinner with her as the featured dessert. The message made Karilyn's stomach turn, but at the same time fueled her revenge.

Chapter 21

Karilyn pushed her graying locks of hair from her face with a headband as she sat in the office chair tapping on the keyboard, trying to figure out Genesis's password. She had been trying to track her keystrokes for weeks, catching a single letter here and there. With enough observation, she thought she had captured all of the keys used in her password, and had a whole notebook full of possibilities. The system would only allow four log-in attempts before it locked the user out of the system, causing an administrator to be called, so Karilyn had to limit her attempts to two a day, allowing Genesis enough room to fat-finger her password at least once without being prevented from logging in. She crossed her two combinations for the day off her list, then slid the small notepad into her purse.

"Good morning, Karilyn," Genesis greeted, fumbling with her laptop bag, purse, and keys.

"Well, well, well," Karilyn responded, giving her a knowing look. "Good morning to you, missy."

Genesis crinkled her brows. "What is all that about?"

"You tell me." Karilyn rose from her chair and followed Genesis to her office door, which was already open.

"What is my door doing o—" Before Genesis could complete her sentence, she gasped at the sight of a large fragrant arrangement of flowers centered on her discussion table. "Where'd these come from?" She set her bags on the tabletop and reached through the spray of baby's breath to retrieve the card.

"Oh, don't pretend that you don't know! I had one of the facility's guys open your door just to set your flowers in. I didn't think you would mind. When they were out on my desk, people thought they were mine and kept sticking their noses in them," Karilyn explained, giggling.

Genesis read the card.

Study long, study wrong, study light, study right.
Study for hours, get beautiful flowers. . . .
I'd like to see you tonight . . . Barnes and Noble—7 p.m.

A grin slowly spread across Genesis's face as she thought back to the evening that the gentleman had asked for the chair. *How does he know where I work?* It had been several months back, so she couldn't clearly picture what he looked like. She did remember that he was smart and handsome, though.

"Ah . . . there's the Cheshire Cat grin. So, who is he?" Karilyn probed.

Genesis shrugged and she bent slightly to fill her

nostrils with the scent of tiger lilies. "I don't know," she said semitruthfully.

Karilyn gave her a sly grin. "Oh, you can't fool me, missy, not with that big smile on your face. You just don't wanna tell me."

"No, seriously, I don't know." Genesis picked up her bag and purse and transferred them to her desk. "What is going on here this morning?" she said, switching the focus away from the flowers. She took a seat at her desk and quickly logged in to her computer.

"Not much. A few girls called in, the paychecks arrived . . . I was busy going through the customer comment cards right when you came in." Karilyn fanned her face with her hand. "Whew, I feel a hot flash coming on." Her face began turning bright red as her other hand pulled at the front of her blouse in an effort to send cool air to her chest. "Anyway, let me get back to doing those. Did you need anything from me?"

"No, I'm good," Genesis replied, still smiling, re-reading the card.

"Okay, well, I'll be at my desk if you need anything." Karilyn disappeared, leaving a gloating Genesis to herself. She took a seat at her desk and one at a time, trying to alter her handwriting and the ink color, completed ten customer comment cards, listing a slew of complaints on each one of them.

I've stayed at your hotel several times, and I have never been treated so terribly in all my life than during my last stay. I was berated at the front desk when I had to get a replacement room key. When I asked to speak to the manager to seek resolution, I was told that I was speaking to the manager. The woman's name was Genesis Taylor. I

am very disappointed in what you have selected to rep-
resent your name and company. I will never stay at
Regal Towers again!

Knowing that a portion of Genesis's pay was based on overall customer ratings, Karilyn had been adding cards to the package that went to corporate every week for a month now, making sure to extract a few cards with positive ratings.

She smiled as she sealed the large envelope addressed to the corporate office along with the altered payroll records. She made sure to inflate Eedy Williams's work hours to make it look as if Genesis was intentionally overpaying the woman, and skimmed hours off the top of others. She planned to accuse Genesis of doing special favors for her black employees.

"I can hardly remember the man's name," Genesis said to Taunya with her phone wedged between her face and shoulder. She took a seat and logged in to her computer. "And here I am excited about a bookstore date." She'd been so distracted by the flower delivery, she hadn't noticed that the items on her desk had been shifted and slightly rearranged.

"So, are you going to go?"

"I don't know. After what happened in California with ol' boy inviting me to the get-drunk, get-high, or get-laid party—I have to keep my guard up."

"Girl, you should have gone ahead and got laid and got you a few dollars. You said the brother was rich."

Genesis wanted to reply with "everybody ain't like you," but knew that Taunya would take offense. Instead she said, "Money isn't everything. I mean, those people were standing up against the wall hucking and bucking like nobody was there," she exclaimed. "Now, why would I want to be with a man like that?"

"I personally like to huck and buck," she snickered.

I need to go to the restroom to freshen my makeup. Genesis found her way to the customer service counter and approached a young lady with flat mousy hair. "Excuse me, where is the restroom?"

"Keep straight down this way and make a left once you hit the humor section and then you should see it."

Genesis smiled and thanked the girl. *Poor thing, someone needs to take her to get some Pantene.* She flung her hair over her shoulder, proud of its length and body since she had found a professional to religiously wash, condition, and style it. She thought for a second about the days when she was forced to do her own hair, standing in front of the bathroom mirror with a boxed perm and wide-toothed comb. *Glad I don't have to do that anymore.*

Once Genesis found the restroom, she lined her lips with a dark brown pencil and glided lipstick across her lips. She began to have second thoughts about meeting Ricardo, feeling foolish and desperate. *What am I doing? I can't believe I am out here meeting someone. This was stupid. I'm going home.* Genesis dashed out the restroom and headed for the door. She had almost made it out, but Ricardo had spotted her.

"I thought I missed you. I'm Ric." He introduced himself again, thinking she'd recognize him from him viewing her house.

"Genesis," she said in response. "But you knew that already, huh? Since you sent flowers to my job and all."

"Yeah, I guess I did." He folded his lips inside his mouth and slightly rubbed his mustache as he looked at Genesis from head to toe. She had changed out of her work clothes and was wearing a denim cropped jacket with a long brown sequined knit top, denim gauchos, and high-heeled brown sandals with freshly manicured toes. "You look nice." Genesis smiled without commenting while Ricardo studied her face. He frowned just a bit and said, "I was hoping you would come, but you looked like you were trying to make a mad dash for the door. You weren't getting ready to ditch me, were you?"

"To be honest with you, this does feel a little awkward," she admitted. "Thanks for the flowers, though. They are beautiful."

"You're beautiful."

"So, how did you know where I worked?" she asked, crinkling her brows.

"I just did a little homework."

"What kind of homework?"

"I happened to come across your business card and recognized your picture."

"I see. So, now that you have my attention, what do you want?" she teased.

"Oh, I had your attention from day one." He stuffed his hands into the pockets of his jeans and rocked back and forth on his heels and toes. "I saw you watching me that night."

"Excuse me?" Genesis said through a snicker. "You're kind of arrogant, I see."

"No, not at all, but I do know that I had your attention. Say it ain't so," he challenged with humor.

"You were talking so loud, everybody in the store was probably looking at you."

"See, you hurt my feelings now. I thought I was special." Genesis smiled in appreciation of his sense of humor. Even though she was becoming more comfortable, she had to ask herself again, what in the world was she doing there standing in front of this fine six-foot, pecan-brown, casually but very nicely dressed man? She thanked God that he didn't have his pants sagging off his behind. She glanced down at his long feet inside a pair of of black Jordan's. *Umph, brother got to be packing.* She closed her eyes and inhaled slowly and asked, "What is that fragrance you're wearing?"

"Cool Water."

"It smells nice."

"Thanks." Ricardo tilted his head and took her gently by the hand. "I know you have your doubts about being here, but since you still are, let's at least get something to drink. That's not asking too much, is it?"

"No, I guess that will be all right." Genesis smiled as he let her pass in front of him headed for the café. She noticed two women sitting in a couple of cushioned chairs gawking at Ricardo. She spoke cordially to them and then said to herself, *Yeah, he is fine, isn't he? And he's with me.*

They each ordered a tall cup of gourmet coffee and a slice of cheesecake. "That will be fifteen ninety-three please," the aproned clerk stated. He gave her a twenty-dollar bill. Once he received his change they stood patiently waiting for their orders, awkwardly not knowing what to say to one another.

"Do you want to sit on the patio?" Genesis asked.

"That would be nice, but I can't."

Genesis frowned with confusion. "Why not?"

"There would be no one in here to watch my son."

Genesis looked him in the eye and folded her lips inside her mouth to keep from saying anything out of the way. *Your son? You ask me out and bring your son? Okay, you were headed to a good start, but that's an automatic twenty-five-point deduction. Why did you ask me to meet you knowing you didn't have a babysitter? You couldn't get somebody to watch him for just a couple of hours?*

"I hope my bringing him doesn't spoil things. Besides, I wanted him to meet you too."

She nodded her head slightly and said, "Mmm." *Meet me for what? Why would he want to do that? He doesn't even know me! That's another five points off.*

The café clerk set their orders on the counter for pickup and smiled. "Enjoy. Thanks again."

Ricardo lifted the tray and followed Genesis to a vacant table. He was about to say something as he set the tray down but was interrupted by a little hand tapping him on his hip.

"Dad, guess what? They have a Spider-Man book in the kids' section that have stickers inside it."

Ricardo corrected him, "That *has* stickers inside it." He dropped to a stoop to meet his son eye to eye. "Where are you manners?"

Dhani saw that his father was referring to the nice-looking woman who sat at the table. "I'm sorry, how are you doing?" He smiled with pearly straight white teeth. Dhani was wearing a light blue Ralph Lauren oxford, tucked neatly into a pair of tan khakis, complete with a brown belt and matching brown loafers.

Immediately, Genesis was impressed by his manners and also by how nicely groomed the lad was. *All he needs is a navy blue jacket and necktie and he could fill in for Alfonso Ribeiro to play Carlton Banks on* The Fresh

Prince of Bel-Air. Genesis laughed to herself. *Okay, Ricardo, you look like you take good care of your kid. You can have ten points back.* "I'm fine, thank you for asking."

"You're welcome." Dhani then focused his attention back to his father. "Dad, can you buy it for me?"

"I do have the ability to buy it, but the question is, will I buy it?"

"Will you buy it for me please?" Dhani asked with desperation in his eyes.

"Let me think about it. Did you want something to drink?" Ricardo asked.

"No, thank you. May I go back in the children's section while you think?"

"Yes, but stay in my view, okay?"

"Okay." Dhani ran back into the area where there were small tables and chairs, and toys lying everywhere.

Genesis sipped her cappuccino and said, "He's adorable. What is his name?"

"Dhani."

"Like Donnie Hathaway?"

"Actually it's spelled D-h-a-n-i. It's Hindu. It means rich man and giver."

"Wow. That's nice. Judging by the way you're teaching him to speak properly, he will be just that when he grows up, a rich man."

"Exactly. He doesn't know it yet but he is going to buy his own book."

Genesis laughed a little and asked, "Does he have a job?"

"Of course, he has to keep his bedroom clean and empty all the trash cans in the house into the kitchen trash can." He gave her a slight smile.

It was then that she began to recognize him. "Oh my goodness! You stopped by to see the house that day."

"You've finally put two and two together, huh? So you've been sitting here not knowing who you were talking to all this time."

"I'm sorry but actually I didn't. I just totally didn't recognize you. You had on a blue uniform or something that day with a ball cap pulled down really low on your head," she said, trying to justify her lack of recognition.

Ricardo smiled and shook his head. "I'm not mad at you. I was on the dingy side that day."

"So all is forgiven?" she asked.

"It all depends."

"It all depends on what?"

"It all depends on whether or not I can continue to see you."

She smiled and said, "Let's work through tonight first and let tomorrow take care of itself."

Chapter 22

"Girl, not only does he have a child, but he also rents my old house! Now, if that ain't a double negative, I don't know what is." Genesis had her cell phone glued to the side of her head as she pulled out of the bookstore's parking lot and headed home.

"Wow. Small world, huh? But you know, that is not such a bad thing, is it? He has his own place to live. He's not stuck up under his mama."

"Okay, but look where it is. Not that I'm looking down on it. I mean, I just moved out myself, but I'm trying to move up in the world, not circle back to the same place I just came back from." Genesis ran her fingers through her hair. "What do I want with someone who's still scrambling to make it? Why can't the man have something more than a baby accomplished?"

"You can't give the brother no points? Obviously he has good credit since he made it through the property management company's criteria. He providing a roof for his child, the man at least has a job that pays three times the rent. Girl, what more do you want?"

"He's a doggone maintenance man or something."

"And when has anything *ever* been wrong with that?" Taunya asked. "Every now and then, we all got something that need a little fixin'."

"I'm not looking for sex, Taunya. I'm looking for a professional, intelligent, clean-cut, six-figure-earning black man."

"See, that's your problem. You want too much. Why does he have to be professional? What's wrong with a blue-collar brother? Why he gotta be black? White men can jump, and so can Latinos, and Asians."

"I don't think I want too much. Why should I have to settle?"

"It's not that you have to settle, but I'm just curious as to where these new standards came from. Not saying that you should only look for riffraff, but you haven't *been* exclusively seeking professional brothers."

"Is there something wrong with me wanting somebody who matches me? Who brings something more to the table than a high school diploma, half of a paycheck, and a beat-up car that he can only afford to put five dollars' worth of gas in?"

"Mmph!" Taunya said.

"What does that mean?"

"It means it sounds like you done forgot where you came from."

"So, what are you saying, that it's wrong for me to want something more out of life? Just because that is where I came from, then I should never strive for more than what that quality of life has to offer? I'm supposed to eat pork and beans forever because I had to eat them growing up? That's asinine."

"It's not that it's wrong, Genesis, but what is right about you looking down your nose on other people?

Especially the ones who are trying to come up and who are trying to make better lives for themselves."

"I'm not looking down on them, I just choose to date someone who has already cleared those hurdles."

"You know what, that damn fake degree and this new job have really gone to your head," Taunya commented. "Next time you go to the bathroom, make sure you take a good whiff, 'cause you starting to think your stuff don't stink."

"Whatever," Genesis dismissed. "Let's change the subject please." Silence hung in the air for several seconds.

"Okay, please tell me that you are still going tonight."

Genesis let out a puff of air. She had forgotten all about her agreement to go to Black Fridays, a monthly after-hours mixer for African-American business professionals. "Girl, I don't feel like it tonight. I had a crazy day at work and just spent an hour on a date with a man and his child. I just want to soak in the tub and relax for the evening."

"I'm sorry, but I have to say this again. Ever since you got this new job, you been acting a little stank," Taunya retorted with a hint of attitude. "You ain't got time for nobody no more since you done moved up to the east side."

"It's not that, I'm just tired, that's all."

"Girl, come on! You promised! And you know you ain't doing nothing. Would you rather go there or come with me to the club?" Taunya tested, knowing that the club scene was the last place Genesis would want to be. "I mean, you the one said you in search of the professional black brother . . . where do you think they hang out at?"

"All right!" Genesis agreed reluctantly, sucking her teeth. "What time does it start again?"

"It started at six, but it's not over until eleven, so come on, I'm on my way right now."

In less than twenty minutes, Taunya pulled up in front of Genesis's home and blew the horn. Genesis barely had time to change clothes and put her shoes on. She had decided on a basic black pantsuit with a pin-striped camisole beneath it and a pair of high-heeled sandals. She grabbed her purse, checked inside for business cards, mints, and her cosmetic case, then ran out to meet Taunya.

"What in the world do you have on?" she asked, taking a seat in Taunya's Mazda and crinkling her nose at the pink miniskirt suit Taunya sported. A black tube top lay beneath her jacket, exposing plenty of both cleavage and belly.

Taunya immediately took offense. "Don't act grand, Sista Weezie," she said before pulling off. "I said we were going to Black Friday, not Bible Study."

Genesis was slightly taken aback, and quickly re-assessed her outfit. "What do you mean by that? I don't look like I am going to church. This is standard business wear."

"Yeah, I guess you would know all about that since you have a business degree and all," Taunya shot back, turning up the stereo and singing along with Mary J. Blige.

Whatever, Genesis thought.

She tried to dismiss it, but throughout the evening, her mind kept circling back to Taunya's comment. It was eating away at her insides.

Maybe the brother does deserve a chance.

Chapter 23

Karilyn circled the block a few times on the east end of Jefferson Avenue, slowing her vehicle each time she got to the place where she had been caught off guard a few months before. This time, her gun was nearby, under her elbow in the armrest compartment, and while she still was uncertain about whether she would actually use it, it gave her the security she needed to be where she was.

Finally, Karilyn spotted the same shabby green jacket emerging from behind a gray building with burgundy trim. Hunched over with a cigarette between his lips, the man took easy strides across an empty parking lot, which was badly in need of repair. He seemed to have glanced up at her, but didn't break his stride. She wasn't sure if she needed to make herself known or wait to be approached, but not wanting to let him get away, she quickly tapped twice on her horn. Her heart began to beat in triple time, as she watched him take a long drag from the cigarette, then bend to the ground to extinguish it against the gravel and place it behind his ear. He stuffed his hands in his pants pockets, spoke over his shoulder to a passerby, then strolled to her window.

"What's up, what you need?" He could tell from her nervousness that she was in unfamiliar territory, didn't know what she was doing, and wasn't working an undercover operation.

"Umm, I, uh . . ." she stammered, not knowing what to ask for. "I'm looking for something that can help me get rid of a problem."

"You want a long or a short ride?" He glanced to his left and right, looking for police cars. Karilyn stammered more, but somehow got across to him what she was looking to buy. "What you got?" he asked, rubbing his thumb and forefingers together, meaning money. Karilyn exposed a wad of cash, not knowing exactly what she needed to spend, but thinking she'd brought enough. "A'ight, look. Meet me back there in, like, fidteen minutes."

"No, here," Karilyn demanded, glancing in her rearview mirror, seeing nothing but dark silhouettes of trees and dilapidated houses. "Here or forget it."

"Man, po-po be out here, you gotta watch for that."

"Okay, there, then," she said, pointing to a McDonald's a few blocks up the street.

"A'ight," he agreed. "Gimme the loot," he instructed, motioning with his head, testing her.

"I thought you said to meet you in fifteen minutes."

"A'ight, Ma, chill. Fid-teen," he confirmed, then walked off.

Chapter 24

Going against her standards trying to prove to herself that she was the same person she'd always been, Genesis invited Ricardo and Dhani over to watch movies, although she still viewed his situation as a double negative—especially the child part. Genesis could imagine Ricardo being denied seeing his son once the mother found out Ricardo had a new woman in his life, or being confronted or stalked by some strange woman who wanted her "baby daddy" back. She just chose not to deal with that type of drama. But when she thought from different angles, she had to admit that Ricardo was a nice guy, seemed to be doing a great job with his son, he did indeed work, was intelligent, respectful, and had a list of other positive qualities that she liked—a lot.

She rented *The Cat in the Hat* and *Fantastic Four*, hoping that the latter wouldn't be too inappropriate for a younger viewer. Shuffling around the kitchen, Genesis quickly prepared some chicken quesadillas, poured some tortilla chips into a bowl with a side of mild salsa, and pulled two glasses and a plastic cup down from the cabinet to later fill with raspberry Kool-Aid.

Right on time, her doorbell rang. "Just a minute," she sang as she wiped her hands on a towel and trotted to the door. When she opened the door Dhani presented her with a single white rose. Ricardo stood behind him resting his hands on his son's shoulders.

"Hi, Miss Genesis, this is for you!" Dhani said, grinning from ear to ear.

"Oh, how sweet, thank you very much." She lifted her eyes to meet Ricardo's. "Good evening, come on in."

"Good evening to you," Ricardo responded, leaning in slightly for a minihug.

Genesis stepped to the side, allowing Dhani to pass before her, then blocked Ricardo from passing with a single hand pressed into his chest. "Wait a minute, Dhani paid his entrance fee, where is yours?" she asked, inhaling the scent of the rose.

Ricardo chuckled and offered an explanation. "See, what had happened was, what had happened, right, see, me and Dhani, right, we was, um . . . we was at the flower shop and, um . . ."

"Never mind," Genesis giggled. "Come on in, the food and the movie are ready."

"Thanks for having us over tonight."

Dhani was already rambling through the videos that Genesis had on her bookshelf by the TV. Genesis frowned as did Ricardo. *He ain't in here for a whole minute and already he got his hands all over my stuff! See, that is exactly why I can't deal with kids.* Genesis hid her thoughts behind a pasted-on smile, but Ricardo was quick to reprimand.

"Dhani," he called sternly, casually sliding his hands into the pockets of his slacks.

"Yes, sir," he replied, detecting by his father's tone that he'd done something that was unacceptable.

"I don't recall hearing Miss Genesis, or anybody else for that matter, give you permission to touch anything." He paused for a few seconds, which added emphasis to his statement. Right away Dhani placed a handful of DVDs back on the shelf. "Now, did I miss something, or are you just out of line?"

"I'm out of line," the child said softly. His father's look suggested he say more. "Sorry, Miss Genesis," he finished with remorseful eyes.

"Now sit down and wait until somebody invites you to enjoy their personal things."

Dhani wasted no time taking a seat on the couch and folding his hands in his lap.

Oh, snap, he got that boy in check! And didn't even raise his voice at that. Genesis cleared her throat slightly. "Ric, do you want to help me bring the food in from the kitchen so we can get the movie started?"

"Sure. No problem," he answered, letting his eyes linger on his son. A single lifted eyebrow spoke volumes to Dhani. He knew he had better not even think about moving from where he was.

"Or do you guys want popcorn first?"

"Why don't we spoil our dinner with popcorn first? What's a movie without popcorn, right, Dhani?"

"Right, Dad," Dhani responded, recovered from his scolding.

"Hon, start the DVD while I pop the popcorn right quick."

Ricardo smiled slyly.

"What?" Genesis questioned.

"You called me honey. I guess that means I'm sweet to you, huh?"

"I actually said 'hon,' which is different from honey, hon." She smiled back and said just above a whisper, "So don't flatter yourself."

Genesis placed a big bowl of hot buttered popcorn mixed with candy corn on the coffee table. Dhani's eyes lit up like a Christmas tree when he spotted the candy, but Ricardo frowned and asked, "What in the world?"

She laughed and said, "Try some, you might like it."

"I'll try some!" Dhani stuck his little hand in the bowl and crammed his mouth with the treat. "Mmmm, it's delicious. Eat some, Dad."

Ricardo looked apprehensively at the mixture. "I don't know. Maybe I better stick to the old-fashioned way."

Genesis smacked her lips. "Just try it," she blurted.

"Okay, but if I get sick I'm giving you my medical bills." He put some in his mouth and took his time chewing it. Then he raised his brows. "Mmm, not bad—not bad at all. Who would have thought to put this together?"

"Years ago one of my girlfriends had this for her movie night. I've been addicted ever since." She popped a handful into her mouth. "I thought I asked you to start the movie."

"We were waiting on you, but you were tied up in the kitchen concocting this special-made pop-candy corn."

"Well, I'm here now so push PLAY."

Genesis sat beside Ricardo with her legs folded beneath her and her arm across the back of the chair while Ricardo sat leaning forward digging in the popcorn bowl. Dhani sat Indian-style on the floor, looking away from the movie every few seconds to get another handful of the sweet and salty snack. Genesis noticed that Ricardo was more into the movie than his little boy. She pushed his leg gently. "You are really enjoying this, aren't you?"

"What, the movie, the popcorn, or being here with you?" he asked.

She blushed for a few seconds, then nodded her head toward the TV.

He lay back underneath her arm and replied, "Girl, please, kids' movies are what's up."

Unable to resist his charm, Genesis kissed him on the forehead, which led to him facing her and puckering his lips toward hers. They pecked lightly four times, each one slightly longer and moister than the last. "Mmm, don't mess around and make me find a babysitter this time at night."

She smiled and said, "Okay." They were staring into each other's eyes.

"Whoa! Did you see that?" Dhani yelled. They focused their attention back to the movie. "Can we look at that part again? It was hilarious!"

Genesis burst into laughter, hearing such a small boy use such a big word. "He is just too funny," she commented to his dad, as she started the scene over for Dhani. "Come help me warm up the food."

Ricardo rose to his feet and followed Genesis to the kitchen. "This is a really nice place you have. Are you renting?"

"No, I bought it some months ago when I moved from downtown."

"So you own two properties now. That's great. You know they say home ownership or property ownership is the first step in creating wealth."

"Really? I hadn't really thought about a wealth strategy when I bought this condo. I was just ready to move from where I was. I grew up in that house."

"There's nothing wrong with wanting to move up and forward. It's a blessing that you were able to do that. Some people live their entire lives and never own one property, and here you are, young and beautiful with two."

"It's definitely taken some discipline and sacrifice."

"As most things worth having do." Ricardo smiled as he nodded, referring more so to his desire for her, but she seemed not to pick up on his insinuation.

Together they set the table and then they all watched *Fantastic Four* from across the room. Before the movie ended, Dhani became bored.

"Excuse me, may I play games on your computer, Miss Genesis?"

"What kind of games?" *Whatever happened to Chutes and Ladders and Candy Land?*

"Games like on Sesame Street dot com, and Nick Jr. dot com. They have good games for kids."

"You're not going to start downloading stuff, are you?" Genesis asked, leading him to her den where her desktop was set up.

"No. My dad doesn't let me do any downloading without his permission."

"Okay. Let me turn on the computer for you," Genesis replied. "What do you know about playing games on a computer anyway?"

"My dad taught me ever since I was a baby. I was only four at the time."

"Oh, so you are not a baby anymore?"

"No, I am a big boy now." She laughed. "Miss Genesis, may I ask you something?"

"Sure, sweetie, what is it?"

"Do you like my dad?"

"I'm hearing my name mentioned too much in that corner. What are you guys talking about?" Ricardo quipped from the dining room table.

"Stop being so nosy." Genesis playfully rolled her eyes. "Yeah, I do like him. Why?"

"He likes you too. You should marry him someday. You'd be a cool mom."

Genesis laughed and asked, "Where is all this coming from? Who is teaching you these things?"

"My dad. He told me when a pretty little girl starts being nice to me don't hit her and just be nice back because that is her way of letting me know she likes me. And you are nice to me . . . but since you are too old for me I thought you would be just right for my dad."

Genesis laughed again and walked away. She sat beside Ricardo and asked, "Are you teaching your son about love at such an early age?"

"Why do you ask that?"

Before Genesis could respond Dhani dashed over to them. "Dad, Genesis is treating you nice. I think you should marry her." Then he ran back to the computer.

"That's why I'm asking."

Ricardo laughed and shook his head. "That son of mine."

Genesis playfully hit him on the leg. "That's not funny. It's cute, but not funny."

"Sweetheart, I have to train my son in the right way so when he gets older he will not depart from it." He dropped his arm around Genesis. "Besides, who can argue with the innocence of a child?"

* * *

Even though Ricardo wasn't even close to one hundred points, he had more solidly and truly earned points than all the other men Genesis had dated. So far he had shown himself to be everything she was looking for in a man except his having a child. At this point, child or no child, Genesis was falling for Ricardo and she believed in her heart he was doing the same for her.

Chapter 25

Ricardo had barely stepped foot inside his mother's house before Dhani rushed forward blurting a mouthful of words. Although he was tired, Ricardo lifted his son from the floor and swung him around to his back.

"Dad, don't forget—Antoine is having a birthday party tonight. I can still go?" he chirped, although Ricardo had given him permission at least three other times.

"I thought I already answered that. Didn't you ask me that same question yesterday and the day before and the day before that?"

"Yes."

"And what did I say?"

"You said I could go."

"Well, you are asking me again, so maybe you did something today that you should be punished for by not going to the party. Did you get on your grandma's nerves today?"

"Nooo," Dhani answered, giggling.

"Un-huh. Let me ask her. Ma!" Ricardo yelled through the house.

"I'm back here in the den."

"Hey, Ma." Ricardo bent down to kiss his mother on the cheek with Dhani still in tow.

"Hey, how was work?"

"Work wouldn't be work if it wasn't work," he sighed. "Ma, did this boy act right today?" He cut his eyes over his right shoulder at his son.

"Mmm . . . I guess he behaved."

"He did everything you told him to do?"

"Yeah, which wasn't much."

"He ate his vegetables, put his plate in the sink after he finished, took the trash out, and washed his hands?"

"Mm-hmm, he sure did," Juanita Stewart replied.

"How about read a book?"

"He did that too."

"Did he protect you from all bad guys and supervillains, beat up the monsters in the closet, and check under the bed for snakes? Because you know if he didn't do all that today, his job is not done," he teased as Dhani began to laugh.

"I guess he did, Ric, because I haven't seen any monsters, bad guys, or snakes today."

"Did he tell you that his real name is Superboy, or did he keep that a secret?"

"He must have kept that part a secret 'cause he didn't tell me that."

"Well, I guess he can go to this party tonight, then." Ricardo swung the boy down to the floor.

"May I have my allowance so I can get him a birthday gift? I want to get him those big Incredible Hulk punching hands that when you hit somebody it goes psssh, pow!" Dhani said, trying to describe the sounds of the toy as he punched his father in the stomach.

Ricardo doubled over, holding his belly and groaning. "Man, how did you get so strong?"

"Gi-Gi told you already. I ate all my vegetables."

"Oh yeah, I forgot that. Well, let's go ahead to the store, then get you packed up to go."

"Yay!"

As Ricardo drove to the store, his mind drifted to Genesis. He was totally taken by this woman who was so unlike average by his own standards. Not only was she beautiful, but she was also educated, successful, and holding it down on her own. She didn't seem to be looking for a man to do for her what she could do for herself. That turned him on.

Knowing that Dhani would be away from home that night, he had planned to cook dinner for Genesis. He looked forward to having her all to himself. That motivated him to rush through the store, purchase the gift Dhani had chosen, then pack him up and ship him off in record time. He had a lot to get done in just a couple of hours.

He called Genesis as he drove home. "Hey, sweetie, you busy?"

Her sighed response indicated to him that her day had been stressful. "I was sitting here reviewing a few reports. I had super payroll issues this week. Six people's checks were jacked up and four didn't get paid at all."

"Man! How did that happen?"

"That's exactly what I'm trying to figure out. All I know is I got my behind chewed out in a royal way."

"Want me to rub it for you?" Ricardo snickered.

"Nah, I'm all right."

"How long are you going to be working on it?"

"I don't know. I'm sick of looking at it right now."

"Well, I'll tell you what. You could use a little pampering, so how about you give it another thirty minutes. Then go ahead and put on something special because I'm taking you out to eat tonight."

It was exactly 7:00 p.m. when Ricardo pressed Genesis's doorbell. Seconds later, she stood before him looking absolutely breathtaking, clad in a wine-colored, beaded halter dress with silver stilettos. Her dress was accented with a small silver clutch, and a rhinestone necklace with the matching earrings and bracelet. She'd swept her hair into a simple yet elegant bun at the nape of her neck.

"You are absolutely gorgeous." He stood frozen in place, stunned by her beauty.

"Thank you." She blushed.

"You're too perfect to touch."

"You can at least hug me, though." Ricardo wrapped a single arm around her waist and pulled her to him, meeting her at the lips. "Mmm," she moaned seductively before slowly pulling away. "What are you hiding behind your back?" she asked, taking note of his crooked arm.

"May I have another kiss first?" He pressed his lips against hers again. Genesis had never been kissed so passionately before. She felt the hair on her arms standing up. Ricardo broke away and handed her an armful of pink and mauve gladiolas.

"Ric, they are so beautiful," she gasped.

"Not as beautiful as you." He stepped inside, kissed her once more, then led her to the couch in the living room. Normally Ricardo was relaxed, but tonight, Genesis sensed that he seemed a bit edgy.

"Are you okay?" she asked, looking sincerely into his eyes.

"I need to talk to you."

Genesis began to get a little nervous. *Flowers for no reason and he wants to talk? Hmm.* "Okay, well, let me go and put these in some water. I'll be back."

She came back with a large vase and settled the flowers in it on the coffee table. She noticed that he was watching her with sexy bedroom eyes. He pulled, held her close, and stared. "What's up with you tonight? Coming in here with beautiful flowers, looking as handsome as all get out, and as nervous as a three-legged cat at a dog track. What did I do to deserve this special attention?"

"You are just you. I enjoy being with you. It's like when I'm with you, you make everything seem so easy." He paused momentarily, thinking of his next words. "It's hard for a man with a child to find a special woman that both he and his child or children love. Dhani adores you as well. You should see his eyes light up every time I tell him we're coming to visit you." Ricardo looked away, shook his head slightly, and smiled. "He's something else."

"Yes, he is. He's special . . . like his father," she whispered. Genesis leaned in and joined her lips to Ricardo's and stroked the side of his face. His hands caressed her back as he pulled her toward him.

"Do you mean that?" he asked, studying her eyes one at a time.

"Yes, I do."

Ricardo suddenly pulled her up to her feet. "Come on, let's get going before I change my mind about dinner."

* * *

"I left my wallet in the house, be right back," Ricardo uttered, jumping out of the car. He came back two minutes later. "I'm not sure where I put it. Come on in the house for a minute, honey," he said, opening her car door and taking her hand. Genesis got out of the car and followed Ricardo to his front door. Once he opened the door she was taken completely by surprise by the rich soulful melodies of Gerald Levert in surround sound and saw the dim lighting of a pair of candles centered on the dining room table, formally set for two including glasses filled with red wine. The aroma of chicken marsala with wild mushrooms and rice permeated the air.

Genesis turned to Ricardo. "You are such a liar." She smiled.

"What did I lie about? I said I wanted to take you somewhere special to eat tonight. I didn't say what restaurant in particular."

Genesis wrapped her arms around his neck. "Do you know what?"

"What's that?"

"I think you are going to make me fall for you."

A slow smile spread across Ricardo's face. "I'm kinda hoping that you will." He led her to the table, pulled her chair out, and made sure that she was seated comfortably, then served Genesis as if she were a queen.

After eating dinner they made their way to the living room floor, where Ricardo wrapped his arms around her and began to dance. Slowly their temperatures began to rise as their movements became less hurried and more sensual. Inevitably their lips came together in a kiss that melted away all inhibitions. Even so, Genesis looked for the strength to pull away.

"Maybe I should get ready to go home," she said softly.

"Please don't. Stay with me tonight, baby." He kissed her again. "Please." After a few seconds, she nodded, becoming more relaxed in his arms, and allowed him to lead her to his bedroom, which he illuminated with candles. The bed was covered with rose petals scattered around a small gift bag.

"You were really prepared for me to stay, huh?" Genesis smiled yet felt a twinge of embarrassment that she'd been so predictable.

"No, not really, but sometimes dreams do come true. And when they do, you have to be ready to embrace them. Open your present." She opened the gift bag and pulled out a red chemise. "Please put it on for me," he said.

She smiled naughtily and began a slow and seductive striptease. Ricardo stepped back to enjoy her performance without touching her, clasping his hands together in a struggle to maintain control. She stood before him completely naked with the exception of her stilettos and jewelry, then whisked the pins from her hair and shook her head to allow her locks to cascade upon her shoulders. With no shame, she turned and posed, leaving nothing to Ricardo's imagination. In an instant, she shimmied into the chemise, covering every curve that had previously been on display. With a single hand and a light nudge, she encouraged Ricardo to lie back on the bed while she straddled him.

"Okay, you have been giving me things all night. Now it's my turn to give to you."

Two hours later, they lay entangled in his sheets gazing into each other's eyes. Ricardo stroked and smoothed her hair.

"You are amazing," he said.

"And so are you."

Chapter 26

"I'm pregnant."

"You're what?" Genesis shrieked in the phone.

"Please, Gen. Don't beat me up about this. I'm feeling bad enough as it is," Taunya huffed.

Genesis remained silent trying to think of what she could say without sounding judgemental or condemning. When the words didn't come soon enough, Taunya spoke up.

"Hello?"

"I'm here. I'm just . . . just a little surprised, that's all."

"Well, I'm a lot surprised. Girl, how do I look having a baby and I'm almost forty years old with a daughter in college?"

"Women your age have babies all the time. I'm sure you'll be fine." Ricardo sat at the opposite edge of the sofa massaging Genesis's feet with a warming skin oil.

"I'm not concerned about what other women do! This is not what I'm supposed to be doing!" Taunya sniffed, signaling that she was in tears. "And the daddy is white!"

Genesis jerked her feet away from Ricardo's grasp

and stood. "What! Wait a minute, wait a minute. White? When did you start that?"

"Start what?"

"Start messing with white guys!" Genesis blurted, going toward her bedroom to make the conversation a little more private. "Be right back," she mouthed to Ricardo.

"What do you mean? I've dated white men before . . . but that is not even the worst of it."

"Okay . . ." Genesis trailed.

Taunya sighed first, then took an opposing deep breath. "He's married." She used the sleeve of her sweatshirt to wipe a stream of snot from her nose.

Genesis refrained from giving an immediate response and instead pushed a long breath from her puckered lips. "Is he married-married, or like split up and not divorced yet married?" she asked, crossing her fingers in hopes that he was at least no longer with his wife.

"He's still with his wife," Taunya responded shamefully. Silence hung in the air for several seconds.

"So what are you going to do? Have you told him yet? Are you still seeing him?"

"No, I haven't told him. And I don't know if I should." Taunya rubbed her belly as she talked although she had not yet begun to round out.

"What do you mean you don't know if you should? Of course you should. Why wouldn't you?"

"Did you hear the part that he is still married, Genesis? He's not going to leave his wife for me, I already know that."

"Even if he doesn't, don't you think he has a right to know that he's fathered a child?" The pain of not knowing her own father suddenly overcame her.

"Every father should know at the very least that he had a kid somewhere. It's up to him to decide if he is going to have a relationship or not, but at least he knows. There are too many kids out there who have no clue of who their daddy is because the mothers ran away from the issue." Genesis's voice changed octaves as she became more emotional. "That's not fair to the child or to the father," she said adamantly.

"As unfair as it may be, that decision is mine! Not yours, not his, mine!" Taunya snapped, offended by Genesis's comments.

"That's just crazy and selfish," Genesis mumbled. "So I guess your solution to this whole thing is to just conveniently get rid of it, huh?" She regretted the words as soon as they carelessly tumbled from her lips. Seconds later a tritone rang out.

"If you'd like to make a call, please hang up and . . ." She planted both hands on her hips and stared up at the ceiling debating if she should call Taunya back or not. Her lips twisted as she thought about what would happen; either Taunya would ignore the call staring right at the caller ID, or she would answer with a ready-made string of four-letter words. She dialed the first four digits, concluding that she should at least try to apologize, but then hung up to give the gesture more thought. She lay back on her bed, replaying their brief conversation over and over again in her head. She hadn't meant to offend, but what right did Taunya have to hold the truth away from the father of her unborn child? How could she just make a decision to not let the father be a part of his or her life? So what if he was married and white?

Tears began to trickle from the corners of her eyes and made paths to her ears, as she relived her own pain of missing a male figure in her life. Other than the name Moses Nelson, she had never known her dad—but did her daddy even know about her or had he been the victim of her mother's underhanded trickery? Although many years had passed, her third grade memory of Renee Cason calling her a bastard was as vivid as if it had happened only the day before.

"My daddy said that he is going to bring me a dozen roses tomorrow for the Daddy's Girl Dance," she bragged, biting into a slice of school lunch pizza. "And he is going to wear a tuxedo and let me pretend like I'm Cinderella going to the ball!" Renee's eyes gleamed with excitement. "Is your daddy coming?" She slurped chocolate milk through her straw without taking a moment to breathe.

"No." Genesis looked down and stirred her spoon in a pool of diced peaches. "He, um . . . he has to work," she lied. Maybe she wasn't lying. Maybe her daddy did have a job and would be working.

"For real? Where does he work?" Renee jerked her head to swing her bangs out of her face momentarily.

Having not thought that far ahead, Genesis quickly replied, "I really don't want to talk about it."

"I bet you don't even have a daddy, because my mommy said that a lot of black kids don't have daddies and that makes them bastards." Renee smacked her lips, finishing off her pizza, then tore away the paper from her ice cream sandwich. "I bet you are a bastard, huh, Genesis?"

Genesis had never heard the word "bastard" used in that sense; in her world, it had always followed the word "black," and seemed synonymous with another B word that, if she ever thought about saying it, her grandmother would slap the pure taste out of her mouth. Although she was shocked at Renee's words, in seconds Genesis created a career for her unknown father.

"No! I have a daddy. He is in the military and right now he is oversees at Desert Storm defending our country!" Anna Marie's insistence that Genesis watch the nightly news had paid off. At the time Genesis wasn't even fully sure what Desert Storm was, but she knew enough to know that it was an honorable service for a man to be there and that every day she would hear someone ask for prayers for the safe return of troops, whatever that was.

As if she could see right through her fabricated story, Renee turned to a redheaded, freckle-faced boy to her left and blurted, "Brian, did you know Genesis was a bastard?"

"I am not!" Genesis defended, standing to her feet.

"Yes, you are, because you don't have a daddy," Renee taunted.

"How do you know her dad's not dead?" Brian asked. "My dad died when I was two," he added. "And it's cruel to pick on somebody when their parent died."

Why didn't I think of that? Genesis asked herself, noticing the immediate sympathetic look Renee gave Brian. Even so, Renee didn't let that stop her.

"Well, her daddy isn't dead because she said he is in the military, but I think she's making it up. I think she's a bastard," Renee said matter-of-factly.

"Girls are stupid," Brian concluded, picking up his tray and leaving the table.

As Renee swung back to Genesis to continue her mockery, she was met squarely in the face by Genesis's lunch tray. Before she could even realize what had happened, Genesis had pushed her to the floor, straddled her, and begun landing blows.

"I do have a daddy!" she insisted over and over, shouting over Renee's screams.

When the dust settled, both girls faced a five-day suspension and Genesis got a whipping and a three-hour lecture from Anna Marie.

As Genesis reflected on that day, she realized that the name calling, the suspension, the whipping, and the lecture combined weren't as painful as never knowing her father.

Her soft sobbing had masked the sound of Ricardo's footsteps approaching the bedroom.

"You all right, babe?" he asked, startling her. He took note of her tears as she jumped and swiped her eyes with the back of her hand.

"Oh. Yeah, I'm fine. I didn't hear you come in here."

"What are the tears for?" He took a seat on the bed and studied her face for clues.

"It's nothing. Really. I'm fine." Her voice trembled as she inhaled to pull herself together. Ricardo wrapped his arms around her as she broke into louder sobs on his shoulder. He stroked her head soothingly until she slowly pulled away. "Ric, I . . . I misjudged you when we met and I am so sorry for that." She stared at a spot on the floor, unable to bring her eyes up to meet his.

"What are you talking about?" he asked as he nudged her chin upward.

"When you first told me you had a son . . ." She paused and shook her head while twisting her lips, now ashamed of how narrow-minded she'd been. "That was something that I looked down on. I mean, a man with kids was a man who didn't meet my standards." Biting down on her lower lip, she searched her mind for more words. "But when I see how much you love Dhani and how you're there for him and he is as much a part of you as you yourself . . . I just have so much respect for who you are."

"Well, sweetie, he is my son, and you're right, he is a part of who I am. But that still doesn't tell me why you're sitting here in tears." He wiped at her face with the hem of his T-shirt. "You know you're too pretty to cry."

"I was just talking to a friend of mine who is thinking about not letting her baby's father be a part of the baby's life. I'm just so touched when I see the relationship you have with Dhani and it makes me love you even more."

A smile crept across Ricardo's face. "Did you just say that you love me?"

Genesis hesitated before she confirmed with a whispered "yes," complemented with a smile of her own.

Ricardo wrapped his arms around her again in a bear hug. "I love you too."

Chapter 27

With her laptop fired up and a cup of tea, Genesis sat on the sofa, bent toward the coffee table and surrounded by numerous time-off requests. She sighed in frustration, wanting to honor them all, but couldn't feasibly do so with the upcoming Labor Day holiday. Her fingers worked back and forth over the computer's keys, plugging in data into her Excel spreadsheet, calculating hours and trying to stay within budget constraints. Ricardo emerged from the hallway, dressed only in a pair of loose-fitting basketball shorts.

"You're still going at it, huh?" he asked, padding past her and into the kitchen.

"Mmm-hmm." She had barely given attention to what he said as she flipped between workbooks studying names and numbers.

"You need to take a break and clear your mind." He opened the refrigerator, poured himself a glass of juice, then grabbed a bowl from the dishwasher to prepare himself some instant oatmeal although it was well into the afternoon. "Did you eat anything?"

Genesis shook her head, not even looking up. "You hungry?"

Folding her hands together and finally looking in Ricardo's direction, she spoke calmly. "Baby, I'm fine. I just need some time. I have to get this schedule done by tomorrow." Her tone suggested that he say nothing else to her while she worked, but he gave no attention to it.

"How are you going to work on your day off? I mean, what's the purpose of being off if you are gonna sit at home and be on that computer all day? You may as well have gone to work. At least you'd be getting paid for it." Genesis sighed audibly while he placed the bowl of oats into the microwave, then came and plopped down on the sofa beside her. "How long you gonna be?"

"Honey, please!" she said, throwing her head back and looking up at the ceiling. "Please let me finish what I'm doing."

"I'm not going to let you do anything," he responded playfully, leaning over to nuzzle her neck. He grabbed her hands, confining her ability to type.

"Stop, Ricardo!" she said, becoming more and more frustrated with his antics. He didn't know what it was like to be under the pressure of a deadline. He didn't understand how the numbers had to all work together in both work and payroll hours. *Must be nice to only have to be concerned with raking leaves and replacing lightbulbs, then clocking out when the clock strikes three,* she thought. "Can you please let me finish what I'm doing?"

"Nope," he answered, running his tongue in small circles on her neck. "Kiss me," he said softly, raising his face so that their lips met. Genesis gave him a hurried peck, but that didn't discourage Ricardo. He puckered his lips toward hers, allowing them to gently meet in slow successions. After the third one, Genesis stopped resisting and returned the passion by parting her lips and letting his tongue explore her own.

"Mmm," she moaned, pulling her hands away from his, then running one of them across his jawline and over his chin. Nothing else had to be said; Ricardo had primed her. He began a trail of kisses over her bare shoulders while his hands caressed the firmness of her breasts through the tube top she wore. He tenderly fingered and twisted her nipples, making them erect, before he pulled her top down around her belly, then suckled them both, his warm hands now resting on her back. The microwave chimed from the kitchen, calling Ricardo back to his breakfast. Slowly he began to pull away, not really interested in the oatmeal, but wanting to evoke a desirous response from Genesis. Just as he anticipated, she gently pushed his head back to her breasts, encouraging him to continue.

"Mmm-hmm," he murmured knowingly. "See, this is what you need right here," he said through a mouthful of flesh. She leaned backward, laying her head on the sofa's armrest, allowing Ricardo free reign of her body. Still lapping at her breasts, he tugged at the string that circled the waist of her knit shorts, loosening them just enough to slide his hand inside. Genesis arched her back and circled her hips, grinding against his hand. With his fingers he tickled her womanhood, pleased with the moans that escaped her lips. He removed her shorts completely, then lowered his head to her dark triangle. She inhaled abruptly as first his lips met her flesh, then his tongue, then his entire mouth, not stopping until she signaled complete satisfaction through a series of un-inhibited tremors and labored breathing.

He kissed his way up her body, then slid inside her with skill and ease, burying his face in her neck. Unable to control herself, she wrapped her arms around him and thrust against him, meeting him stroke for stroke in a rhythmic cadence that led them both to calling out each other's names. Ricardo rested atop her, still kissing at her breasts, while she ran her fingers across his back and shoulders.

"You were right, baby," Genesis barely whispered. "I did need that . . . but now I also need a shower," she finished, nudging him to sit up. He stood to his feet, grabbed her hand, and helped her to stand, then circled his arms around her and looked into her eyes.

"I love you, Genesis," he said sincerely.

A slow smile spread across her face as she pulled him closer to her. Those words had never sounded so good before. "I love you too . . . Ricardo." Her head tilted upward to kiss his lips; then she turned toward the hallway and started for her bedroom, leading Ricardo by the hand. Together they showered, taking turns exploring and caressing each other's bodies with lathered exfoliating gloves. By the time the shower ended, Ricardo had become fully aroused again. While she stood still dripping in the center of the bathroom floor, he rifled through the cabinet below the sink and found a bottle of almond body oil. Taking his time, he massaged the oil on her warm wet skin, then patted her dry. Then he lifted her from the floor, coaxing her to wrap her legs around his waist, and sat her on the vanity countertop. Seconds later, he plunged between her walls, slowly maneuvering his hips. At her whispered command, he gradually increased his momentum, causing her arms to tighten around him while her legs unfolded and spread far and wide, allowing him full access. Minutes later he eased into a stop and pulled away, leaving Genesis breathlessly clinging to him.

Once she regained her composure, she slipped back in and out of the shower, then padded to her bedroom where she found Ricardo pulling the tags off a pink polo shirt and a pair of golf shorts.

"What's that?" she asked, tightening her towel around her body and rifling through her underwear drawer.

"Your clothes for the day," he said, tossing the shorts on the bed.

"Since when did you start picking my clothes?"

"Since you started playing golf."

"Golf? I told you I have to get this work done."

"Not today, you aren't. It's your day off and you are going to spend it with me, not with your laptop." Ricardo pulled on a pair of slacks and a collared shirt.

"Ric, I really don't have time for this, not to mention that I don't even like golf." She slid into a pair of lavender lace French-cut panties and a matching bra.

"Sweetheart, you have to make time to enjoy life. . . . Okay, at least make time to enjoy me. Is that too much to ask?"

Genesis was trying her best to ignore his pleading eyes, but she found him irresistible.

"We're just going to go to the driving range. We won't actually play."

"I have to wear that?" She looked at the outfit in disapproval.

"Unless you want to go naked, yes. I picked it for you. You don't like it?"

Genesis held the polo up against her chest. "It's okay, I guess. How long are we going to be out?"

"A few hours." Ricardo shrugged nonchalantly. "Hurry up and get dressed. We need to get there before it gets crowded."

Genesis huffed but complied. "Do you have shoes for me too?" she said sarcastically, yelling down the hallway.

"Yep."

"What!" she whispered to herself. "That was supposed to be a joke!"

Ricardo appeared in the doorway holding a Nike shoe box and a pair of footie socks. "Here." He took a seat on the floor, slid the socks onto her feet, then opened the shoe box and helped her wriggle into the shoes. "Let's go." He grabbed her hand and led her down the hallway.

Once they reached the living room, Genesis's eyes shot over to her laptop and her unfinished work. "Hold on a minute, let me just check my e-mail before we go."

"No." Ricardo tightened his grasp around her hand and pulled her onward to the door. Genesis sighed in defeat, but didn't try to hide her attitude signified by a pout. "And put your lips in." She couldn't help but giggle.

The two only stayed at the range for an hour and a half, with Ricardo mostly coaching Genesis on how to swing a club. With his arms wrapped around her and his hands gently placed over hers, he whispered tips into her ear on form, foot positioning, and swing. Genesis found more pleasure in being in his embrace than she did sending ball after ball sailing into an open field. She wouldn't admit it to him, but she found herself disappointed when the bucket that had been once full of balls lay empty at their feet.

As they walked to the car hand in hand, Genesis's mind was far from her job responsibilities. *Ric was right, I do need to take some time to enjoy life.* "What are we going to do next?" she asked, not quite ready to return to her laptop. He opened her car door for her, then walked around to take the driver's seat.

"I need to go by my mom's house and pick up Dhani." He paused for a few brief seconds, staring straight ahead in pensive thought. "I'd like for you to meet my mom." Silence hung in the air for a few seconds.

Oh my goodness, he wants me to meet his mother, Genesis thought. "Really?" she finally said, unsure of what else she could say.

He nodded silently, puzzled about how to interpret her short response. "Is that okay with you?"

"Ric, I'd be honored to meet your mom," she said with a smile. "I don't really have on my 'meet the family' clothes, though," Genesis added, assessing the golf shorts and top. She pulled down the car's sun visor to check her appearance in the mirror, then used her hands to smooth her hair.

"You look just fine, babe." He winked with a widening smile. He pushed back into his seat and dug his hand into his pants pocket to get his cell phone. Using the speed-dial feature, he called his mom.

"Hey, Ma."

"Hey, Ric, you finally remembered you got a mama, huh?" Juanita teased, clicking channels on her remote, looking for the Christian broadcasting station.

"I could never forget you, Ma."

"Judging by the way you haven't called me in two days, I sure can't tell."

"I'ma do better, I promise. Listen, I'ma come by there in a little bit, do you need anything?"

"I was going to cook some hamburgers later on, but I don't have any onion. Can you bring me a couple, and a five-pound bag of sugar?"

"Okay, anything else?"

"Something to drink," she added.

"I'm bringing someone over to meet you." He looked over at Genesis and winked again.

"Someone like who? You must be serious about this one." Juanita turned the television down, wanting to hear all that her son had to say.

"Someone who is special to me, Ma. You know I wouldn't bring just anybody home to meet you."

"Can she use your comb?"

"Ma, you know I don't have any hair," he chuckled.

"If you had a patch of nappy hair on that dome of yours, could she use your comb?" Juanita playfully demanded.

"Yes, Ma, she can use my comb." Genesis stifled a laugh. "We'll be there in a little bit."

"Okay, I'll set the table for one more. See you then."

"Where's Dhani?"

"He's running around outside with Tiara's boys. They out there having themselves a good old time." Juanita lifted her size 4 frame from the couch to peer out the window at her grandkids.

"All right, well, let him know I'm on my way."

"Okay, baby. Don't forget to go by the store." Juanita said a few more things before ending the call. After hanging up, she went to her bedroom to shower and put on something other than the leggings and oversized T-shirt she'd been lounging in all day. She didn't feel like she needed to be impressive, but at the same time, she didn't want to embarrass her son.

She chose a turquoise sundress that showed off her well-taken-care-of bronzed shoulders, and a pair of matching thong sandals. A scarf was still wrapped around her head, which she removed, then used her hands to rub in a light hair oil through her locks. "I guess I look all right," she said out loud, glancing at herself in the mirror. On her way to the kitchen she stopped at her granddaughter's room. "Tiffany, get your lazy behind up and go straighten up that front room a little bit. Ricardo's on his way here with somebody."

"Okay," she answered without budging a single muscle. Tiffany was engaged in an episode of *Trading Spaces* and didn't want to miss the redecorated unveilings to the homeowners.

"Did you hear me, girl?" Juanita said through clenched teeth. Although she was a petite woman, she demanded and got respect. She expected her children and grandchildren to move when she said so, not when they got good and ready, no matter how old they got.

Tiffany, hearing the seriousness in her voice, switched the TV off right away. "Yes, ma'am."

Juanita continued to the kitchen and started on dinner, forming the ground beef into patties. She thought about how much Ricardo had been through and how much he'd grown in the past few years. It broke her heart when he had to spend time behind bars, but she was proud of how he seemed to be making strides to overcome his past. He'd been on his job for a good while, moved out into his own place, and made sure to take good care of Dhani. "I hope this girl adds to him. He needs a good honest woman in his life."

It was a little after four when Ricardo pulled into his mother's driveway. As soon as he recognized the car, Dhani bounded over to the driver's side.

"Hi, Dad!" he screamed, throwing his arms around him no sooner than Ricardo had stepped out onto the pavement.

"What's up, man? We gotta do something with this head of yours," he said, rubbing his hand over his son's hair.

"Tiffany said she was gonna cut it for me, but she kept watching TV all day."

"For real?"

"Yeah. I told her to hurry up and do it 'cause you was about to come and get me, but she just said she'd do it later."

"It's okay. Where's Gi-Gi?" he asked, referring to the child's grandmother.

"In the house cooking. Hey, Miss Genesis." Dhani threw up a hand, acknowledging Genesis's presence.

"Hey, sweetie," she replied. "I brought you something." Genesis dug in her purse for a novelty watch she'd picked up earlier that day while she and Ricardo were at the store and handed it to Dhani.

"Ooh!" he exclaimed, immediately tearing into the packaging.

"What do you say?" Ricardo suggested in reprimand.

"Thank you!" He beamed before running off to show his cousins.

Ricardo walked up to the front door, tapped twice,

then turned the knob to let himself in. "Ma!" he called. "Ma, we're here."

"I'm in the kitchen," she called back.

"Come on," he said to a slightly nervous Genesis, leading her through the living and dining rooms to the kitchen located in the rear of the house. "Hey, Ma!" Ricardo threw his arms around his mother, hugging her tightly, then kissing her cheek.

"Boy, get off me. You just showing off in front of this young lady!" she chuckled, swatting at him with a dish towel once he let her go.

"Here are the things you asked for." He placed a grocery bag on the kitchen counter, then turned to do introductions. "Ma, I want you to meet my special friend. . . ." He reached to grab Genesis's hand, beckoning her closer to where he and Juanita stood. "This is—"

Before Ricardo could finish his sentence, Juanita finished for him. "I know exactly who that is . . . that's Mo Nelson's baby girl, Genesis! Looking just like your daddy! How you doing, baby?" Juanita wholeheartedly wrapped her arms around Genesis as if she'd known her forever.

Genesis stood with her eyes and mouth stretched wide open.

Chapter 28

Taunya rolled over to her side, coming breath to breath with Milton. He slept peacefully on his back, his slightly parted lips letting out measured puffs of air, while his left hand rested against his chest. Just as Taunya thought to lean forward to kiss and arouse him, the glow of the moon peeked through the narrow slits of the blinds, illuminating and bringing attention to the wedding band that encircled his finger. In guilt, she turned away.

Feeling her stir, Milton rotated in her direction and dropped his arm around her, coaxing Taunya to nestle up against him. Not feeling like fighting against it, she obliged. His lips kissing at her shoulders, he moaned softly before he rested his head on the pillow and began to doze off again.

Her hand rubbed across her belly as she thought about the tiny life inside. She still hadn't told Milton that she . . . they were expecting, and couldn't quite put her finger on the reason why. After a few minutes of thought, she narrowed down her reasons: He would want her to abort the baby, he would ask her to leave his property, he would walk out of her life completely. *How did I get here?* Taunya asked herself, disgusted with her desire to have a man, even one who was married. She closed her eyes and tried to pray, but her feelings of unworthiness overcame her and she could not find the words. Instead an unhurried trickle of tears seeped from her eyes and rolled gently onto her pillow.

Milton's heavy and rhythmic breathing gave indication that he once again was in a solid slumber. Slowly she eased from beneath his arm and slid out of bed, then sauntered to the bathroom to shower, hoping it would make her feel better, although she knew it wouldn't. She didn't bother to put on her robe since the boys were away; she stopped at the linen closet on her way, grabbed a fresh towel, and tiptoed naked upstairs to the main bathroom.

Taunya stood idly under the hot stream of water for ten minutes trying to make peace with herself. Beneath the flow of water, her tears began to run more freely, although she fought against audibly gasping and sobbing. She hated whom she had become, realizing that she wasn't any better than a woman who sold herself on the streets. While she didn't charge men cash up front, she knew that she had many times sold her body for a steak and lobster dinner, a new pair of shoes, or for the price of a visit to the nail salon. Ridden with guilt and condemnation, she fell to her knees trying to think of something she could say to God that would redeem her. From out of nowhere a verse from Psalm 51 came to her mind and she spoke it from her lips:

"'Wash me throughly from mine iniquity, and cleanse me from my sin.' I don't want to keep living like this, God," she whispered. "And I need your help." The remainder of her prayer was in the form of tears, as she could find no more words to utter.

Prompted by the cooling water, she grabbed a guest washcloth from the towel bar outside the tub, scrubbed her body, then stepped out. Surprisingly, she did indeed feel a sense of relief, although it was short-lived, as heading back down the stairs to get something to put on, she remembered that Milton, another woman's husband, yet lay in her bed instead of his own.

Quietly she pulled open the drawer that housed her pajamas, grabbed the first pair she saw, then snuck out of the room, knowing that waking Milton would lead to her lying on her back with her feet spread apart in the air. She twisted her lips at the thought as she slid into her own bathroom to dress, then returned to the main floor.

Although it was barely four in the morning, she found herself in the kitchen pulling out a bowl, varied utensils, and the ingredients needed to bake a cake from scratch. Working as silently as she could, she began to visit in her mind the list of men whom she had shared her body with over the years, and challenged herself to produce the reasons why she had chosen to do so. She counted at least ten men she'd slept with in two years, under the explanation of executing her own sexual freedom and liberation, but it just wasn't working for her anymore; her conscience screamed against it.

Deciding not to use her electric mixer, she worked furiously against the batter while she tried to make sense of her actions. In her heart, Taunya wasn't satisfied by just any old man; neither did she desire another woman's man, but she wanted what she felt every other woman wanted, to be truly loved, cherished, cared for, and honored by a man who was totally and completely into her and her alone. She found that those desires could not be fulfilled in a relationship built only on sex.

She poured the batter into the greased pans, placed them on the center rack of the oven, then sat at her kitchen table, pulled out a sheet of paper, and just began to write. At first the words were just idle, but soon they began to form into a letter.

My Baby,

I've not felt you move inside me yet, but I know you're there. Right now, I owe you an apology. You deserve the best life, but you're already at a disadvantage, and you haven't even gotten here yet . . . and it's entirely my fault.

I've looked for love in all the wrong places and found lust instead. While love has been hard to find, lust seemed to have its rewards, money, things, even this place to live . . . and now you. Yes, you.

You come at a time in my life that I should be finished with this part of my life, and because you are my baby, I already love you, totally and completely. I think about you all the time and can't keep you from my thoughts. Only for a split second I thought about moving on without you, but I can't . . . I won't do that to you. I don't know exactly how we'll move on, but somehow, someway, we'll do it . . . together.

I'll see you in a few months.

The delectable smell of cake filled the room and reminded Taunya of its baking. She peeked into the oven, then smiled down at her belly, thinking of her cake baking in the oven. "It's time for me to make some right decisions," she stated out loud. "And I know just where to start."

Since she'd been seeing Milton, which had been well over a year now, she had long since stopped paying rent. Milton was carrying all of her expenses and providing her with spending money, as well as seeing to it that Nikki had everything she needed for school. He had even surprised Taunya for her birthday by opening a checking account in her name complete with five thousand dollars. Taunya had never seen that much money in one place before, unless it was a tax refund check where she was able to claim earned income credit for all of her kids.

Living out of Milton's wallet allowed her to save her paychecks and add them to her account. She walked over to her computer nestled in a corner of the den and logged on to her bank's Web site. With a few quick keystrokes, she accessed her account and took inventory. She had to be ready to stand on her own two feet if Milton cut her out of his life financially, even with the baby.

On her way back to the oven, she began to predict what Milton's response would be once she told him she'd not be able to see him any longer. She still had her Section 8 vouchers, which he'd received money from every single month. The fact that he'd give the money to her was beside the point. Taunya couldn't imagine that he'd put her out, but she could see him making her pay the portion of rent she should have been paying all along. That wouldn't be a difficult pill to swallow.

She turned the cake pans onto two plates, carefully lifted them, then placed the pans in the sink, humming the melody of "Hush, Little Baby." While the perfectly browned layers were still warm, Taunya topped them with slices of pineapple, and a sprinkle of cinnamon, then made a glaze from powdered sugar and drizzled it on top.

Returning to her computer, she began drafting a list of actions she would need to take to make sure that she made a successful transition from leaning on Milton to being on her own. She struggled in her emotions, being in love with Milton at this point, but at the same time knowing that she needed to let him go. Even if she wanted to keep him for the financial benefits, there was no getting around the fact that he had a wife, a wife whom he should have been in bed with right now. A wife who had probably spent many nights in tears.

She logged out of her computer and moved to the living room to recline on her microsuede sofa. Before she knew it, she fell asleep, drowning in a sea of thoughts.

"What the hell is this?" Milton held up the letter Taunya had written to her unborn child. Taunya's eyes peeled open slowly from the couch where she had fallen asleep, then stretched wide as she recognized her handwriting.

"Give me that!" she demanded, attempting to jump up and snatch the paper away, but as she stumbled back onto the couch, she realized it was for naught; he'd obviously already read it.

"You're pregnant?" he questioned, already knowing the answer from the look on Taunya's face. He came and knelt beside her and took her hands in his. "You're having my baby?" His voice was low and soothing, and a look of compassion covered his face. It was unlike any of the responses she'd gotten from the other fathers of her children. She felt both comforted and ashamed as she nodded. He lifted a hand and stroked the side of her face, then smudged away a tear with his thumb, all the while studying her eyes one at a time. "When, Taunya?"

"I'm nine weeks," she mumbled.

Gingerly, he rested his hand against her stomach, never taking his eyes from her face. "You're having my baby," he stated more for himself than for her. "When were you going to tell me?"

Taunya shrugged, knowing that she hadn't really decided to tell him, and was leaning more toward not letting him know. "I wanted to wait until the right time, I guess."

"And when was that going to be? You were just in my arms last night."

"I know, but I shouldn't be there, Lewis. Your arms should be reserved for your wife, not me." Her tears increased as she forced words from her lips. "And here I am living on borrowed love . . . really stolen love. And now . . ." She choked and sniffed. "And now I'm pregnant and you'll be going home to her, while I'll be here raising another baby," she squeaked through tears.

"Shh, shh." Milton wrapped his arms around Taunya and kissed her cheek. "Shh, stop crying." His eyes darted to several photos that Taunya had arranged on an end table, while his mind ran in circles. His emotions were mixed. He couldn't go home and tell Karilyn he'd gotten another woman pregnant, but at the same time, a part of him was excited that he'd be a father again. "We'll figure this out, okay?" He loosened his embrace and turned her chin so that their eyes met. "We'll figure it out. You let me worry about my wife. All I want you to do is take care of yourself, and take care of my baby." He paused and looked pensively at her. "Can you do that for me?" He nodded, encouraging her to give a positive response.

"Lewis, I gotta let you go," she blurted before she could rethink the words.

"Wha . . . ?" Her words stunned him. "What do you mean you gotta let me go?"

"I mean you're not mine, Lewis! Haven't we been playing this game long enough? Don't you get tired of lying to your wife?"

"Taunya I—"

"You what, Lewis? What do we have together other than a few memories from a trip or two, and wild sex? I need more than that!" Taunya's hands flailed wildly as she became more exasperated.

"Taunya, I love you." Milton's strong hands grabbed her shoulders to still her movements. "I love you," he repeated in a whisper with crinkled brows that expressed sincerity. "You are so much more to me than sex. How can you even say that?"

"You . . . are . . . married. Married, Lewis! That's not something that I can ignore. Are you going to leave her for me?" Taunya paused for two seconds. "Are you?" Milton dropped his head on her lap in defeat. A minute ticked by before she wriggled from beneath his weight and padded to the kitchen. "I didn't think so." Seconds later she heard his footsteps tread across the planks of hardwood, then the familiar creak of her front door opening and closing. She stood frozen at the sink fighting back tears, knowing she had made the right decision.

Chapter 29

The ride back to Genesis's home the night before had been incredibly silent. Even Dhani could sense tension hovering in the car's small interior and managed to sit still and quiet simply looking out of the window. Ricardo kept one hand on Genesis's knee while he drove with the other, occasionally patting as if to say "It's going to be okay."

It had been difficult for Genesis to enjoy her meal that evening, although Juanita had prepared a delicious spread of hamburger with onions and gravy, baked macaroni and cheese, steamed cabbage, and biscuits made from scratch. She found herself just picking at the food, emotionally overwhelmed about all that Juanita had shared about her father. At least three times Genesis had to excuse herself from the table in an attempt to hide her tears. When Ricardo took her home she was utterly exhausted, using her last bit of strength to change into a pair of comfortable pajamas and collapse in bed. Ricardo lay beside her, enveloping her in his arms, which was both the least and the most he felt he could do.

"Moses was a fine man who loved your mother dearly. His nose was wide open behind Angeline, and she used to treat that man like dirt." Juanita piled the cooked food into separate serving dishes as she talked. "The more he loved on her, the more running the streets she did, poor thing."

"Did he know about me?" Genesis asked with trembling lips.

Ricardo squeezed her hand beneath the table to show his support. "Yes, he did, and was proud of you too. Did all he could to be a part of your life until he was forced to back away."

"What do you mean?" Genesis just couldn't imagine any situation that would actually prevent a father from seeing his child if that was what he really wanted to do.

"Well, baby, Angeline had resorted to prostitution." Juanita shook her head sadly. "She'd lost her own place, and stayed in so much trouble that your grandmama was afraid to have her in her house. She got hooked up with a pimp who used her for all she had. When your daddy tried to rescue her, knowing she was pregnant with you, that no-good man of hers threatened to beat her to death if he showed his face again."

With the food now set on the table, Juanita called for the rest of her family, pausing the conversation at hand long enough for everyone to eat together at the table. She didn't believe in discussing grown folks' business in front of kids. The meal couldn't go by quick enough for Genesis, who was naturally anxious to hear more. Once the family filled their bellies, she helped clear the table.

"Baby, I'm going to go play with Dhani for a little while if that's okay with you." Ricardo wanted to allow

Genesis some privacy to let go of her emotions without feeling ashamed or inhibited by his presence, knowing that his mother had more to say. He leaned over and kissed her on the cheek, then squeezed her hand reassuringly once more. "I'll be right in the living room if you need me, okay?" It was all Genesis could do to nod with a weak smile on her face. As soon as the kitchen cleared, Juanita began again.

"I remember seeing Moses at church one Wednesday night kneeling at the altar just crying his eyes out, pouring his heart and soul out to the Lord. The poor man didn't know what to do. He knew that man meant what he said, seeing's how he'd slapped Angeline around a few times before, so he did the only thing he knew to do, he backed off. I have never seen a man so pitiful looking in all my life." Juanita put the leftovers into plastic bowls with lids and placed them in the refrigerator. "Angeline ended up going to jail for a while, which kept her off drugs long enough to carry and deliver you healthy, but once you were born, she was right back out there with you on her hip. Then the money he was sending to your mama went straight into her veins, up her nose, or to that pimp, chile. By the time your grandmama took custody of you, Moses was serving in the military, moved to Italy and a couple of other places, and lost contact. The one thing that she did do was honor him by letting him pick your name. He said he picked it because in the Bible that was where God created life, and you were his Genesis . . . the place where he created a life."

Genesis dabbed at her eyes with a paper towel, trying to stop the flow of tears brought on by mixed emotions. So she did have a daddy who knew about and possibly loved her; that in itself brought a mixture of joy and pain. Joy from knowing he existed, and pain because she'd missed him terribly growing up. "Do you know where he is now?" she asked, unsure if she was ready for Juanita's answer.

"Last I heard, he was living down in Atlanta, Georgia. Had gotten married and had a couple of babies, I think."

Equipped with that bit of information, Genesis contemplated launching a search to find and reunite with her father.

"Baby, I'm here to support you however I can," Ricardo whispered in her ear just before she drifted off to sleep. In a short while, her labored breathing signified to him that she was sleeping peacefully. He went to the guest bedroom and held his son in his arms, thankful that Sarita had been selfish enough to drop him off on his mother's doorstep. Ricardo wouldn't trade the joy of fatherhood for all the world.

Chapter 30

"I've got to get out of this house," she said to herself, retracting her hands from the dishwater she had just run and drying them on a towel. Determined not to remain in a funk all day, Taunya rushed to her bedroom and pulled on a pair of sweats over her panties and a T-shirt over her bare breasts, then put on a matching jacket and zipped it up to hide the fact that she wasn't wearing a bra. Taunya wasn't trying to be impressive, she was only driving over to Starbucks to get a cup of coffee, thinking that the single small luxury purchase would give her spirits a boost. She pulled a ball cap over her head, still covered by the satin scarf she wore each night to protect her hair. With her feet still covered by her bedroom shoes, she grabbed her keys and purse from the sofa table, but stopped dead in her tracks, as she took note of her reflection in the elongated mirror that hung in her foyer at the front door. Checking herself over in the mirror, she noticed how sad her eyes looked and how suddenly she looked weary and worn. Her red eyes drooped from the lack of sleep, and were magnified by black rings underneath. Dulled skin covered her usually radiant complexion, and she noticed a few wrinkles forming around her lips.

Without a second thought, she returned to her bedroom to spruce herself up just a little bit. She whipped the scarf from off her head, stuffed it in a drawer filled with all kinds of hair products, then plugged in her largest curling iron. In just a few seconds, the smell of burned hair mixed with hair pomade filled the room, a smell that Milton always crinkled his nose at, but seemed to be fascinated by. Sometimes he would sit on the lid of the toilet just watching her style her hair. With the removal of a few bobby pins, her hair, thickened by pregnancy, cascaded around her face and shoulders.

While the curling iron heated, she twisted a seamless push-up bra around her torso and slid her arms through the straps, giving her breasts an instant lift. Instead of the loose-fitting T-shirt and sweats she'd put on before, Taunya decided on a fitted tee by Bebe, and a pair of jeans, then traded her slippers for a classic pair of white K-Swiss. After running the hot barrel through her locks, she pulled the loose curls up into a ponytail, leaving a few tendrils to fall at the nape of her neck and at her ears. Taunya applied a bit of mascara and a lightly tinted gloss to her lips, added a pair of large hoop earrings that she found on Nikki's dresser, then smiled at herself having, in just a few minutes, rejuvenated herself and looked her usual ten years younger.

Feeling better about herself, she decided to continue on from the coffee shop to Williamsburg Outlets mall to do a little shopping. A few hours later, the cargo space of her SUV was occupied by bags of all sizes, filled with shoes, purses, and clothes. She had even picked up a few irresistible unisex baby outfits. Taunya rubbed her belly, thinking about both the baby and how famished she was. She started her car and headed for Cracker Barrel, almost licking her lips at the thought of a platter of pancakes, scrambled cheese eggs, and a side dish of hash brown casserole.

"How many in your party, ma'am?" the hostess greeted.

"Just one, thank you." Taunya had no qualms about enjoying a meal alone.

"Smoking or non?"

"Non."

"Right this way, please." Taunya was led through the restaurant to a table for two just in front of the window. As she settled in her seat and glanced over the menu, a familiar voice called out to her.

"Well, hello there."

Taunya looked up and was greeted by Karilyn's smiling face.

"You're dining all alone this morning?" she asked. *Or is my husband in the bathroom somewhere?*

"Oh, hi. Karilyn, right? Yeah, it's just me this morning. I was out doing some shopping." Taunya shrugged.

"Well, could you stand a little company? I'm traveling solo myself today, just running some errands, and got a little hungry."

"Uh, sure," Taunya agreed, taken a little aback, but not really minding.

"Thanks!" *Oh, this is gonna be too easy,* Karilyn thought. She still had the package she'd picked up from downtown in the zippered compartment of her purse. All she needed was for Taunya to have to use the bathroom. Remembering from the housewarming how much salt and pepper Taunya sprinkled on her food, she planned to add the gray substance to the shaker. Karilyn hid her chuckle as she turned to the hostess who had been standing by patiently waiting for her to finish her conversation to show her to her table. "I'll just sit here." The hostess nodded, then walked off.

"So, how've you been?" Taunya started.

"Pretty good!" Karilyn beamed. "Although things have been really hectic at work," she said, lowering her tone to a whisper. "I don't know what has been going on, but things have been really screwed up lately." Her eyes stretched wide with concern. "I'm not sure what is going on with Genesis, but she has been seriously under the gun. I'm doing all I can to support her, poor thing," she ended, dropping her eyes to the menu.

"Yeah, she was telling me that she'd been dealing with a lot of issues lately. What do you think is going on?"

"I have no idea. There're just a lot of mistakes being made, things missing . . ." Karilyn shook her head slowly, with a look of confusion on her face. "And it's so not like Genesis to be like this. I know she's been seeing someone new lately, but I don't think even that would make her careless." Feeling that she'd said enough, Karilyn flagged their server over as a segue to change the subject, not wanting to expose herself. "I'm sorry, did you decide on what you wanted?"

"Oh yeah. I'm ready."

The ladies placed their orders and chatted a few more minutes; then as Karilyn hoped, Taunya excused herself.

"Be right back, nature's calling."

Glancing around nervously, Karilyn wasted no time

adding the fine gray substance she had bought off the streets to the pepper shaker, then placed it back in the center of the table. Just as she retracted her hand, the server walked up with a large serving tray full of plates of steaming food.

"Wow! That didn't take long at all," she said, relieved that she had accomplished her mission prior to the food being set on the table. Moments later Taunya returned.

"Okay. I can concentrate on my food now," she giggled. She bowed her head for a few seconds of grace, tasted her food, and immediately reached for the salt and pepper, sprinkling both over her eggs and casserole. She dug into her pancakes first, drenching them with syrup. What she said next nearly caused Karilyn to fall over backward in her chair. "I've been eating like a horse since I found out I was pregnant." She picked up a glass of orange juice and took a large swallow.

Completely stunned, Karilyn was grateful that she had a mouthful of food that would not allow her to speak right away although she fought to keep it all in her mouth instead of choking and spitting it out on her plate. She held up a single finger, asking that Taunya give her a minute. *My husband has fathered a child by this woman! He got this whore pregnant? Hold it together, Karilyn,* she coached herself. *Keep your cool.* She cut her eyes down to Taunya's eggs, thinking about the poison that had been sprinkled on them, and feeling a twinge of remorse that she'd be killing an innocent child. She felt that Taunya deserved to die, but found it hard to justify poisoning a baby. After swallowing hard, she finally responded. "I didn't realize you were pregnant."

"Yeah, I just found out not too long ago myself. I'll be starting all over again. My baby is seventeen." Taunya pushed the pancakes away and pulled the eggs and casserole toward her. Karilyn's heart began to skip beats. She had mixed feelings, wanting Taunya to both scarf down and not eat the food at the same time. Taunya consumed a forkful of each dish. Between chews, she continued, "Although it wasn't planned, I'm excited about the baby."

"How does the father feel about it? Does he have children already?" Karilyn asked, pretending not to know. Had he told her about their son who was stationed in Japan.

"He actually has an adult son in the military. This is a surprise for both of us. I wish that I could get a marriage proposal out of the deal since he claims that he loves me," Taunya giggled. She didn't notice the flames that had ignited in Karilyn's eyes once she'd said that. In an instant, the guilt she felt for Tauyna's unborn child had been erased.

I hope you and your bastard baby die! she yelled internally. Karilyn cleared her throat, trying to get rid of any sounds of nervousness or anger. "Have you started picking out names yet? Eat up, honey, you're eating for two," she added, chuckling.

"Not yet," Taunya answered. As she chewed, her eyebrows began to crinkle. "It is funny how pregnancy makes you hate your favorite foods." She put her fork down. "Normally, I don't leave a single bite on my plate, the food is so good here, but today it just doesn't taste right. I guess the baby doesn't want any."

"Well, you know, sometimes you have to make yourself eat to make sure the baby gets its proper nutrition.

You should at least try to have a few more bites," Karilyn encouraged, desperate for her to eat more of her meal.

"Nah, I think I'm about done."

Eat the damn food! Karilyn cursed to herself. She made more small talk, hoping that Taunya would change her mind and nibble on the rest of her meal. She was disappointed when Taunya finally began to rise having not touched the food again since she'd put her fork down.

"Well, I better head back home. My boys are coming back from the state championship game today and I want to fix them a special meal." She stretched as she stood to her feet.

"You don't want a box or anything? You know a pregnant woman could get hungry at the drop of a hat."

"I'm stuffed to the gills," Taunya said, pressing into her stomach with her right hand.

Karilyn pushed away from the table. "I guess I'm done too." She grabbed her purse and walked with Taunya to the cashier's counter. "Oh, I forgot to leave a tip, be right back." Karilyn rushed away, headed for their table again. She looked around at the other patrons, as she dug in her purse for a couple of dollars. Keeping one hand in her purse, she reached down to leave the tip, then scooped up the pepper shaker and dropped it in her bag. She snuck another one from a vacant table to replace the one she'd taken, then walked back to the counter where Taunya was still waiting to pay for her meal. "Thanks for letting me eat with you. I enjoyed your company."

"Likewise," Taunya replied as they strolled to their vehicles.

Once Taunya got on the highway headed back to Hampton, she began to notice that she wasn't feeling so well.

Chapter 31

"I think this is the one right here." Ricardo studied the three-carat diamond closely, finally coming to a decision after being in the store for more than two hours. The single marquis-shaped stone could not be more perfect. "Yeah, I'll take that one," he repeated to Mandy, the sales associate.

"Sure," she acknowledged with a smile, happy that he wasn't leaving the store without having made a purchase. "So, have you decided how you will give it to her?" she asked, reaching beneath the display counter to get a ring box.

"I'm actually still trying to work through that. You have any suggestions?"

"Umm . . . well, what kind of person is she? I mean, does she like a lot of fanfare and noise, or is she more reserved?"

"I think she's kind of in the middle. I'm going to propose to her tonight over dinner, but I wanted it to be done in a special way. Something a little bit out of the ordinary."

"You could have a server bring it on a plate with, like, some lettuce and fruit and stuff," she suggested.

"Hmm. That's a thought." He chewed on the inside of his lip, partially thinking about how he would ask Genesis to marry him and partially thinking about the amount of money he was spending. It was a pretty penny, but Genesis was worth every dime.

The clerk gave him a total and he reached for his wallet, pulling out the amount in cash. Her eyes widened, unaccustomed to seeing anyone carry around so much money, and more used to swiping a card through a reader than having the customer sign a slip of paper. As in days gone by, Ricardo had saved the cash using the shoe box method after being denied by several banking institutions when he attempted to open an account. With a criminal record in his past, he had to work three times as hard to accomplish anything.

He carefully counted the dollar bills, then handed them to the young lady, feeling good about his purchase. She recounted the money after him, checking several of the bills for authenticity, then had her manager check behind her. Although Ricardo was offended at the gesture, he kept his cool and said nothing.

He turned his head away and began wondering if he would ever outlive his past. It was only by the grace of God that he had found and was approved for the home he was currently living in. He had prepared himself to get the typical decline response.

I'm sorry, Mr. Stewart, but with your criminal record, there is nothing we can do. I wish I could tell you something differently. He had heard it one too many times. When the property management company called him to let him know he could move into the home on Ivy Avenue, he fell to his knees in tears of gratitude and thanked God out loud as soon as he hung up the phone. He knew it wasn't because Genesis was trying to do him a favor; she hadn't even recognized him that day he viewed the property. He gave God all the glory and credit for providing him with a roof over his and his son's head.

He would never forget the day he had obtained the keys and moved in with nothing more than a box of clothes, two newly purchased air mattresses, and a small TV. While Dhani was at school, he went to Wal-Mart and bought a few household necessities, some food to put in the kitchen, a microwave, and a small arcade video game that plugged directly into the TV. A smile crept across his face as he drove home, inflated both the beds, covering Dhani's as best he could with the twin-sized comforter set, and cooked dinner. He made a pot of spaghetti, toasted some bread, made a pitcher of Kool-Aid, and warmed two individual-sized apple pies for dessert. If he'd had a table, he would have set it for him and his son, but tonight they would eat dinner sitting on pillows in the middle of the living room floor while playing Pac-Man.

"I got a surprise for you, little man," Ricardo said to Dhani as he took his hand and began walking in the direction of the house.

"What is it?" Dhani asked, half skipping, half walking.

"It's a surprise, I can't tell you," he answered, swinging his son up on his back. "You'll have to wait and see."

Dhani filled Ricardo in on his school day, then questioned him once they got to the door. "Who lives here?"

"Me and you," he said, fitting the key into the lock.

"We do?"

"Yep." Ricardo swung the door open, then placed Dhani on the floor, where he immediately took off running around the house.

"Oooh!" he screamed, looking at his Spider-Man–themed room, as he dove onto the bed.

After checking out the entire house, then coming back to the living room, he threw his arms around Ricardo's waist. "I love you, Daddy!"

His heart melted. It was just what he needed to hear. Dhani loved his father unconditionally and expressed his love and appreciation in his school art projects, often drawing pictures of the two of them and letting him know that the things he'd created were made especially for him. Many times Ricardo found his inspiration and strength to go on in the eyes of his son.

Now as he made this ring purchase, he had to admit that Dhani had further influenced his decision by giving his approval of Genesis.

"I like Miss Genesis, Daddy," he said one afternoon while he worked on a math worksheet. "I think you should marry her." Dhani hadn't even looked up from what he was doing. Ricardo stared at his son in disbelief, his attention broken from the bills he'd been focused on.

"What makes you say that?" he quizzed.

"Because she is pretty and intelligent," he said, still without looking up.

"Intelligent? Boy, you don't even know what that means." Ricardo pushed Dhani's head playfully.

"Yes, I do!" Dhani beamed, finally making eye contact.

"No, you don't. What does it mean, then, since you know so much?"

"Intelligent means you are a good thinker and very smart."

Ricardo burst into laughter at his son's vocabulary usage.

"What's so funny?"

He smiled back. "You, because you're so intelligent," he answered, rubbing the top of his head.

"So are you gonna marry her?"

Ricardo's laughter slowed into a chuckle. "We'll see, man, we'll see."

"Here you go, Mr. Stewart. Thank you so much for your purchase." Mandy handed him a small bag with tissue bursting from its opening, which held his purchase. "Good luck tonight!"

"Thanks."

On his way out of the store, it came to him how he would propose. He turned back around and started a search again for a smaller, far less expensive ring. It didn't take him long to find the perfect piece, which he quickly paid for with the money he had left over from the bigger ring purchase, and left the store with a smile on his face.

Chapter 32

Taunya's boys returned home that evening to find Taunya lying in the middle of the living room floor barely able to move or speak. They both rushed to her side; then Jonathan, the elder of the two, ran for the phone, calling the paramedics. Only one of the boys was able to ride along in the ambulance, so Jonathan hopped inside and gave instructions for his younger brother to call Genesis. After three rings, Genesis picked up the phone.

"Miss Genesis, my mom's in the hospital," David blurted.

"What? David, are you okay?"

"Yes, ma'am, but I don't know what happened to my mom."

"Where are you?"

"At the house. We had to call an ambulance to take my mom to the hospital and Jonathan rode with her. Can you give me a ride over there?" he asked, sounding as if he were on the verge of tears.

"Of course. I'll be right there in a few minutes." Genesis hung up the phone and brought Ricardo up

220 Kimberly T. Matthews

to date. "I'm sorry, baby, but we're going to have to do dinner another time," she said apologetically. They had been on their way out the door when David's call came in. Genesis looked exquisite in a powder-blue Vera Wang satin gown that she'd purchased from the clearance section on Bluefly.com. Both Ricardo and Dhani were handsomely dressed in suits, looking as if it were Easter Sunday.

"Do you want me to ride with you?" he offered.

"That would be great. Thanks."

In minutes they both were in the car headed for Taunya's house and then to Sentara Hampton Care-Plex. By the time they'd arrived, Taunya had been admitted. Genesis and Ricardo waited in the hallway, allowing David to go into the room and see his mom along with his brother. After ten minutes, she tapped on the door and opened it slowly.

"Hey, you," she started, catching eyes with her friend.

"Hey," Taunya said in a whisper. "You three look mighty sharp. Where are you headed to?"

"Don't worry about us, are you okay?" she asked, not really knowing what else to say.

"I think I'll be just fine. Hey, Ric," she said, acknowledging him standing by the door holding Dhani's hand.

"Hi, Taunya. What is the doctor saying?" he asked, cutting to the chase. "What happened?"

"He said I had traces of arsenic in my system."

"Arsenic!" Genesis shrieked. "Like arsenic poisoning?"

"Yeah." She nodded slightly.

"How did that happen?" Genesis asked, her facial expression revealing her perplexity.

"I don't know. I hadn't really eaten or drunk anything except some coffee from Starbucks and breakfast at Cracker Barrel. I saw your assistant in there, and we both sat down and ate together. I'm thinking if I got sick from either of those places, a whole lot of other customers would be in here with me complaining of the same symptoms or maybe even dead."

"Well, what about the . . ." Genesis stopped herself, unsure if Taunya had told the boys about her pregnancy.

"They have to run some tests to make sure the baby is okay," she said openly, having already shared the news with her kids. "The doctor said since I had only consumed very little, we both should be okay, but they want to keep me at least overnight for observation."

Genesis took a seat and stayed for an hour or so making small talk with the boys until Taunya began to doze off. "Well, I'm going to let you get some rest now. I hope everything checks out okay." Genesis stroked her friend's arm as she stood by the bedside. "And I'm sorry about the other night," she added after pausing for a couple of minutes. "I didn't mean what I said."

"I know you didn't. Apology accepted, girl, as long as you take my boys home and make sure they get in okay."

"Ma, we know how to go in the house," Jonathan chuckled.

"All right, then, Genesis make sure they get in the house by themselves and without them ragamuffins they call girlfriends." She reached for her throat, still feeling some pain from it being constricted by the poisoning. "Now y'all let me get some rest please."

The boys embraced their mom and said their goodbyes, then exited the room with Genesis and Ricardo. The drive back was still and silent, although Genesis had commented a few times that she couldn't believe Taunya had consumed arsenic. Ricardo signaled for her to be quiet until they dropped the boys off and Dhani had been put to bed.

Once Taunya's sons entered their house, Ricardo pulled out of the driveway and said, "I smell a rat."

"What do you mean?" Genesis asked, her mind still reeling. Ricardo turned and looked at Dhani, whose head was tilted to the side and mouth hung wide open in sleep.

"What's the common denominator?" he asked, looking at Genesis.

"The what?" She furrowed her brows trying to interpret his question.

"When there are a bunch of strange occurrences, the first thing you look for is a common denominator, a common thread that links the incidents together," he stated. "Now think about everything that has been going on at work . . . then think about what Taunya said she did today."

Genesis rolled her eyes around a few times in thought, then shrugged. "The only thing I can think of is Karilyn. I work with her, and Taunya coincidently had breakfast with her this morning."

"Bingo. The question is why? What have the two of you done to that woman?"

"I haven't done anything to her," Genesis exclaimed with her brows raised. "I am a good boss to her, plus you don't know if one has anything to do with the other anyway."

"I do know, there's just no proof . . . yet."

Chapter 33

Still frazzled from the happenings of the past week-end, Genesis could hardly get her thoughts together. She arrived in her office just in time to make her weekly conference call. As quick as lightning, she dialed the toll-free number, punched in the pass code, and announced herself.

"Good morning, Genesis, glad you could join us," Ray Anderson said with a bit of sarcasm, having already done a roll call. "Let's go ahead and get started with our first agenda item. Does everyone have the document I sent out last night?" Quickly, Genesis typed in her password to log on to her computer, but was immediately locked out of the system. While other call participants chimed in with yes responses, Genesis ran out to Karilyn's desk in need of help.

"Karilyn, I seemed to be locked out of my system this morning. Do you mind doing me a favor?"

"No, no problem," she answered.

"Can you call in a trouble ticket for my computer, let them know I've been locked out after one log-in attempt? Then I need you to see if you can get your hands on a copy of the new customer care document. We're reviewing it on this call this morning and I can't access it. You may need to call the Richmond location and have someone there forward it to you." Without waiting for a response, Genesis turned on her heels to go back to the call at her desk.

". . . so we still need to get responses from Williamsburg, Chicago, and Boston. Please get those to me ASAP so we can move forward." Ray was finishing, only allowing Genesis to catch the tail end of his sentence. She didn't have any idea of what he'd just referred to, or what she hadn't turned in.

What is he talking about? she thought as she checked the project calendar that lay on her desk where she recorded everything that had due dates and deadlines. Not finding anything outstanding, she made a mental note to review the minutes from the call to find out what she'd missed.

"Our next agenda item is Customer Comment Cards rankings. I want to give kudos to Aungie over in Stockton, who is at the top of the stack ranking with a 9.87 satisfaction rating, but right on his heels is Debra over in Killeen with a 9.85, followed by Timothy in Memphis at 9.84. Congratulations to these three locations. Now on the other end of the scale, I'm noticing some disappointing trends and areas needing improvements for our sites on the bottom of the stack ranking. Can you guys help us understand what's going on at your locations? Genesis, why don't we start with you, since the Williamsburg site is showing the most room for improvement?"

Genesis cleared her throat while her face became flustered. She had no clue as to why the Williamsburg location would be on the bottom of the Customer

Care stack ranking. Not wanting to make up something off the top of her head, she tried to give a vague but intelligent response. "Our site has recently undergone some changes in our housekeeping staff, and I'm not sure if the last group received proper training, but it's something I definitely have my thumb on, Ray." She immediately muted her phone, then tried to log in to her computer once more to no avail. A heavy sigh burst forward from her lips as she rubbed her temples.

"Here of late, we've just gotten all kinds of negative comments from the guests there that are not all related to housekeeping issues, so . . ." Ray let his comment hang in the air unfinished.

"Ray, maybe we should talk after the call so we can both be on the same path to understanding where our failures lie," Genesis replied, embarrassed that she was being called out.

"I think I'll have some free time this afternoon when we can get together and chat." Ray transitioned to another site, letting Genesis out of the hot seat. She muted her phone once more, then immediately called Karilyn in.

"I just got raked over the coals about our Customer Comment Cards. Have I been receiving them all?"

Karilyn looked surprised and confused. "Why, yes! I leave them on your desk every single week before they go off to corporate."

"Ray just mentioned that we've gotten an influx of negative cards, but I've not seen them." She tapped a pencil on her desktop, looking away from Karilyn and out the window, thinking about what Ricardo had suggested. The fact of the matter was that Karilyn was the sole individual who emptied the Comment Card box. "Okay, we can talk about it later," she said, dismissing Karilyn and refocusing her attention on her call.

"Genesis, do you mind reading for the group the paragraph in the shaded box on page twelve please?" Ray asked, facilitating the Train the Trainer portion of the call.

Genesis began to swear out loud, as she didn't have the document in front of her and had just been following along listening and taking notes. "Can this call get any worse!" she said prior to taking her phone off mute. "I'm sorry, Ray, we're experiencing some kind of virus this morning and I haven't been able to access the document. I've just been taking really good notes at this point."

"Okay, no problem. Rebecca, can you take that portion please?" he responded, moving on without hesitation. Ray didn't call on Genesis anymore until he was ready to wrap up the call. "Genesis, would you mind hanging on after the call? I just want to talk to you about a couple of things," he said right before he dismissed the other call participants.

"No problem." Genesis knew what was coming; it was obviously clear that she wasn't as prepared as she needed to be. Multiple duo-tones signaled other call participants hanging up. Once things grew silent, Ray started his conversation. "You there?" he checked.

"Yes, I'm still on," she answered, already dreading anything that he would say.

"Genesis, I have to tell you that I am very disappointed in what is going on at the Williamsburg location. Your customer complaints have tripled in the last month."

"Ray, I wish I could tell you what exactly was going

on. I think one of the things we have to look at is that although complaint cards have increased, there have been no increase on refunds or complimentary stay requests. We both know that one is a direct reflection of the other."

"You make an interesting point, and I was actually looking at that number, and you're right, your refund and complimentaries have been consistent month over month. Nonetheless, that is not my only concern. Your payroll has been off week over week, and I am seeing the same errors being made for the same individuals. Now, as your manager, I believe in your talent and capabilities, but I have to ask you, is your head in the game at this point?"

Ouch. Genesis resented even being asked such a question, but she couldn't fault Ray for questioning her the way he did. Had she been in his shoes, she would have done the same. "Of course my head's in the game, Ray. I do value my job," she stated, trying hard not to be cynical.

"Well, I've got to be honest with you, Williamsburg is getting a lot of negative exposure right now, and everything you do is being highly scrutinized."

"I fully understand."

"I'm going to be visiting in the next few weeks to see if I can't help you straighten some of this out."

"Sure. Right now I'll take all the help I can get," Genesis said diplomatically, even though she hated the fact that Ray found it necessary to schedule a visit.

"All right, well, I'll be keeping an eye on things from here in the meantime."

"I appreciate that."

"Take care, Genesis."

"You too."

Both Ray and Genesis disconnected from the call. Seconds later, Karilyn hung up from her desk.

"Did you hear back from the systems admin yet?" Genesis asked, coming out of her office.

"No. I've called, like, three times," she lied. She had yet to place the call, knowing that Genesis wouldn't be able to get any work done as long as she couldn't get in her computer. Before Genesis got in that morning, Karilyn had successfully logged in to her workstation, scrolled through her e-mail, and deleted messages, something she had been doing for close to six weeks now. Several items that required Genesis's attention and response had gone unaddressed simply because Genesis had not known about them. Karilyn had also reset many of her calendar reminders to have Genesis miss deadlines and conference calls.

Unbeknownst to Genesis, there were talks circulating in the corporate office about seeking her replacement.

"I just don't believe that Genesis is intentionally dropping balls like this," Ray argued with his boss. "I've worked with her for nearly a year now and have never seen such poor performance from her or such poor indicators from the location. There has got to be some reasonable explanation for it."

"All I know at this point is that she is single-handedly weighing down our numbers. Now, I like Ms. Taylor just as much as the next guy, but I have a business to run, and I would hope that she does too. If she can't effectively do the job and bring these indicators up, I have no choice but to replace her with someone who can," Marvin Waldron stated sternly after reviewing another report that reflected Williamsburg's substandard performance under Genesis's leadership.

"Just let me go out there for a few weeks and dig into what's going on, make a few observations, offer some development, and come back to you with some solid recommendations."

Chapter 34

Genesis opened her door to Ricardo dressed in a trench coat and hat and holding a briefcase in his hand. Right away, she burst into laughter.

"Dan-na-na-na-nant, Inspector Gagdet, dan-na-na-na-nant woo-hoo!" he sang, shuffling his feet. "Go, Gadget, go!"

"What in the world?" she giggled. "Boy, get in this house before somebody calls the men in the white coats on you."

"Go, go, gadget lips," he chuckled, leaning forward and kissing Genesis on the mouth. He stepped inside her condo.

"I think you missed Halloween."

"I have something for you." His tone suddenly switched from playful to more serious. He sat on the couch, put the briefcase on the table, and popped open the locks. Inside was a mantel clock and a motion detector.

"Okay?" she sang, confused about the briefcase's contents.

"We're gonna see what is really going on on your

job." He lifted the clock from the briefcase. "These are actually surveillance devices," he said. "See?" He pointed out to Genesis the tiny camera located on the face of the clock, then the one hidden inside the look-alike motion detector. "All you have to do is set these in your office and come back and view the tapes."

At a loss for words, Genesis studied the equipment for several minutes. "Can I really do that? I mean, is it breaking any kind of law or privacy act or something?" She turned the clock to the backside, then to the front again, staring into the camera's eye.

"I don't think so. Haven't you ever seen that show *Busted* where they catch people doing all kinds of stuff on the job? You aren't taking the camera to anyone's home, you'll be putting it in your office at work, a private place where everything should be on the up-and-up."

"I don't know, Ric. I'm scared."

"Scared of what? Which one are you more scared of, putting these up or losing your job behind that woman sabotaging you? She's already tried to kill your friend."

"Ricardo Stewart!" she nearly yelled. "How can you sit up here and accuse that woman of attempted murder?"

"Because I believe she tried to kill Taunya, that's how," he said with a shrug, fiddling with the cameras.

"Okay. Why would she do that? First of all, Taunya said she didn't know that she was going to run into Karilyn that morning. It wasn't like they planned to have breakfast together. Karilyn barely even knows Taunya."

"Okay," Ricardo replied nonchalantly.

"And Karilyn has never done anything to hurt me

at work. As a matter of fact, I couldn't ask for a better assistant," she added, clearly offended.

"Just do me a favor. When you go to work tomorrow, set this clock on your bookcase and let it stay there for about a week, maybe longer. We'll watch the tapes together and if I'm wrong, I will send Karilyn a dozen white roses and buy her lunch."

"I don't know how to set this stuff up," Genesis shot, angry at Ricardo's implications.

"I'll do it for you. Let's go," he said, standing and stripping out of the coat and hat that he'd worn purely for laughs.

Ricardo all but dragged Genesis to his car. She rode the entire way with her arms folded over her chest never uttering a word. Not fazed by her behavior, Ricardo switched on the stereo and started singing along with Anthony Hamilton, Mariah Carey, and Stevie Wonder. He pulled into the lot just as Stevie finished crooning about chocolate chip kisses. As he turned off the ignition, he took Genesis by the hand.

"Look at me." After a few seconds, she rolled her eyes and looked at Ricardo.

"What?" she said dryly.

What he said next upped his point value, even in the midst of her irritation with him. "I love you. I love you and I believe in a man protecting and taking care of his woman. Now, you might not like this, but trust me. Right now I'm protecting my woman." He leaned over and pecked her on the cheek, then opened his car door to get out.

Genesis sat there frozen in place by his words and her desire to want to stay angry that had been melted away by those same words.

"Stop poking your lips out and being so childish

and come on," he commanded, slamming his car door. He didn't come around to the other side to open her door, but started his stride toward the building. His value instantly shot up a few more points in his showing that he wasn't going to stand for her acting just any kind of way, but he had some "stand up and set things straight" in him.

After watching him from the car for several seconds and seeing that he wasn't going to stop to wait for her, she lifted herself from the seat, then jogged a few steps to catch up to him. Together they entered the building, spoke to the front desk attendants, and headed for the elevators. Genesis dug her passkey out of her purse while they waited for the elevator to reach the first floor. When it did, the doors eased open, putting them face-to-face with Karilyn standing there ready to step off.

"Oh!" she said, startled, then chuckled. "Hi, Genesis. I, uh. . . didn't expect to see you today."

Ricardo said nothing but just looked at Genesis knowingly.

"Yeah, it's my day off, and I generally don't come in on my day off. What are you doing here, isn't it your day off too?" she asked as nonaccusingly as she could although her suspicions were raised.

"I, uh . . . I left my wallet here on Friday and didn't realize it until today when Milton and I were going out to, uh . . . pick up a few things from the grocery store," she lied. "I wanted to do a little shopping on the way back. You know our anniversary is right around the corner, and I can't have him paying for his own gift." Karilyn laughed nervously, stepping past the couple.

"Right," Genesis said slowly, entering the elevator.

"So, did you find your wallet okay? I mean, it was right where you left it? Because you know a lot has been going on here lately. I would hate to hear of your things being stolen."

"Oh, no, no, no . . . I found it and it hadn't been touched at all," she said, digging in her purse and pulling it out. "I'm ready to shop now!" She smiled and started toward the exit, anxious to get out of the hot spot she found herself in. "Well, enjoy the rest of your weekend, and I'll see you tomorrow."

"You too," Genesis replied as the elevator doors slid closed. She looked over at Ricardo. He said absolutely nothing, keeping his thoughts to himself. Once they got to the administrative floor, he went to work placing the equipment and making sure they both were functioning properly.

"Ric, I—"

"Don't say anything. There are two things that don't lie . . . numbers and videotape." He turned the mantel clock on the bookcase to face the door. "We'll watch the videotapes."

Chapter 35

Moses Nelson stared out the window of the plane trying to figure out what he could possibly say to a daughter he'd never seen. As he'd done before, he thought back to the day that he had confronted Quinton Chappelle.

"I'ma tell you this, my brotha," Quinton said sarcastically. "You got one more time to bring your ass over here looking for my woman." Searching for Angeline, Moses cut his eyes around Quinton, who stood in the doorway in a clean wife beater and a pair of tailored trousers. While a belt circled his waist, the buckle was undone and hung at the closure of his pants. His chemically processed hair had been slicked down to his head by a superholding gel, and a single gold tooth gleamed in his mouth as he talked. "And the day you do is the day her mama gone have to plan a closed casket funeral for her. I don't give a damn how pregnant she is. I oughta beat her ass just for that . . . messing up my money lettin' a punk nigga like you knock her up."

Moses caught a glimpse of Angeline peering down

the hall toward him from the door of the small room
Quinton had put her up in. There was pleading and
sadness in her eyes as she stood there in a tattered pair
of shorts, a dingy T-shirt that revealed a belly that was
just beginning to round out, and no bra. Her natural
hair was covered by a frizzy lopsided wig. Quinton, noticing that Moses's attention had been diverted, took
a quick glance behind him.

"Bring your nosy ass up here!" he ordered. Right
away, a seventeen-year-old Angeline took quick steps
toward the door. When she got in reach, Quinton
quickly cuffed the back of her neck and squeezed
tight enough for Angeline to jump, gasp, and draw
her shoulders as high up to her ears as she could get
them. He forcefully pressed his lips onto the side of
her face. "Now I'ma let you decide what happens to
her," he said, staring as Moses. "Her fate lies in your
hands, big man," he taunted, letting go of Angeline's
neck and draping an arm over her shoulder, pulling
her into him, then rubbing on her belly, feigning
compassion. A cynical smile crossed his lips while he
narrowed his eyes.

Feeling completely helpless although his blood
boiled within him, Moses backed away never taking
his eyes off Quinton's evil face. His heart melted when
the door slammed shut and he could hear through an
open window Angeline suffering the repercussions of
his visit.

"What the hell he doing showing up at my house!"
he yelled. The sounds of Quinton's open-handed
slaps and Angeline's shrieks reverberated in Moses's
hearing. "Didn't I tell you to leave the nigga alone?
Huh?" Angeline begged for mercy, crying out in pain
and terror. Terrified that he would indeed kill her,

Moses ran to the nearest pay phone, dialed 911, then waited nearby for more than an hour for the authorities that never showed.

Although it had been nearly thirty years ago, it was a sound that Moses had never forgotten. Her screams were relived when he got the surprise phone call from Juanita, a high school alumna, some weeks ago.

"Ladies and gentlemen, we have begun our initial descent into the Newport News area. Please take your seats and make sure that your seat belts are securely fastened . . ." The flight attendant's message sent a nervous flutter to the pit of his stomach. Moses knew he would have to give an account for his absence, and as he pondered his excuses in his mind, it was crystal clear now more than ever that every one of them was weaker than a wet paper bag.

He hadn't called in advance, which he now had second thoughts about. He felt that showing up in person would position him for a stronger argument over a phone call, which, after thinking about it, seemed like the coward's way out. While the plane taxied to the gate, he pulled a small worn document from his shirt pocket, on which he had written Genesis's address. After examining it for a few minutes, although he'd already committed it to his memory, he flipped to the opposite side. Tears came to his eyes as he scrutinized the faded image of Angeline lying in a hospital bed holding a tiny baby girl. He could only see a mass of black shiny hair protruding from a bundled pink blanket. Angeline had mailed it before she left the hospital with a brief letter that he also had folded in his pocket and had read at least five times during his flight.

Dear Mo,

Here is a picture of our daughter that Mama took yesterday. She is beautiful and looks just like you. I named her Genesis like you asked me to. I wanted to give her your last name too but Quinton wouldn't let me. I know that you go to church and pray all the time. Please pray for me that I can get away from him. He doesn't know that I am writing you or sending you this picture. He would probably kill me if he did, which is why I am writing you from the hospital and sending it before I leave to go back home. I am still at the rooming house by the way but please don't come by. I will try to call you to meet you somewhere so that you can see the baby. Quinton doesn't work, so it might take me a little while. Also please don't write. Quinton reads all the mail. Sometimes I feel like my name is Ceilie from The Color Purple. *I wish we were still together. I know now that you really do love me and want the best for me.*
I still love you too.

Angeline

Moses had ignored Angeline's plea for him not to write; but instead of writing her, he wrote letters to the baby every week and included a money order for Angeline to buy diapers, milk, cute little pink clothes, and whatever else she needed for the baby. He didn't know it at the time, but Quinton forced her to sign the documents over to him and spent nearly every dime of the money while he accused and punished Angeline week after week for seeing Moses behind his back. Moses finally stopped when he received an envelope from Angeline's mother, Anna Marie. Its contents shocked him to his core.

Moses,

I know you love your daughter and are trying to do the right thing, but please, please stop writing Angeline. You mean no harm but you're going to be the death of that girl. I hope that one day soon Angeline will do the right thing, but for now, I'm trying to preserve my baby's life. You love your daughter, and I love mine too. I'm begging you to leave that child alone.

Ms. Anna Marie Taylor

Also included with Anna Marie's letter was a photo of a terribly brutalized and nearly naked Angeline lying in an alley. It had been the final factor in his decision to stay away. However, he knew that even that would not be enough to explain twenty-nine years of absence.

Chapter 36

Genesis and Karilyn sat at the round table working through a stack of reports, looking for errors. They had been going at it for hours, Genesis diligently and Karilyn simply going through the motions. Karilyn knew full well why there had been issues with payroll and other reports. She made sure that she held on to the pages that reflected that the numbers and codes had been manipulated, pretending to have found nothing.

"I would hate to think that ADP has made these gross mistakes," Genesis said. "And seemingly out of the clear blue sky. I've never had an issue with them before."

Karilyn shrugged. "But you are so careful about your work, I can hardly believe that something would get past you like this." She stretched her eyes wide, reviewing several columns, running her fingers across the printed ink. Hearing the phone ringing on her desk, she pressed her palms against the arms of her chair to rise. "I'll be right back."

While Karilyn was out, Genesis grabbed the stack of

documents that Karilyn had claimed to have reviewed and switched it with the stack she had personally gone through. She flipped through the sheets quickly, then set them aside for later review.

"That was Mr. Anderson. He just pulled up in the parking lot and will be up shortly," Karilyn said, returning and taking her seat.

Genesis let out a heavy sigh. While he said he was coming to help, she knew that she was really under some level of investigation and evaluation. "Okay, well, I'm sure I'll be tied up with him for the rest of the afternoon. Thanks so much for going over these reports with me."

"No problem. I just wish we had found something that could help us understand what's happening. It seems like everything is going haywire all at once."

"I'm sure I'll be able to uncover it pretty soon. With the way I've been busting my behind in here, something has to change."

"Do you want me to finish going through these at my desk?" Karilyn offered, knowing if Genesis said yes, she would just set the reports on her desk without touching them.

"No, don't worry about it. I'll finish them up this evening at home."

"Are you sure? There's a lot there."

"I'm positive. I'll take care of it."

"Well, I'll be at my desk if you need me." She turned to leave, coming face-to-face with Ray Anderson, the district manager. "Oh, hi, Mr. Anderson. It's good to see you again."

"Hi, Karilyn. Likewise," he said quickly, not stopping his momentum to enter Genesis's office. He relieved his shoulder of the weight of the laptop bag he carried, then extended his hand to Genesis. "How's it going there, Genesis?"

"Great," she replied out of habit, accepting his hand.

"So, I understand there's been a little trouble in the camp?"

"I wouldn't exactly call it trouble," she answered, trying to minimize the situation. "But there are some things I'd like to get to the bottom of." She closed her office door and took a seat again at the table.

Ray studied her face for several seconds as he seated himself in the chair that Karilyn had just been in. He chewed on his bottom lip, letting his eyes scan over the stack of documents on the table, then looked back up at her. "Genesis, I'm very concerned about your work performance here of late," Ray began, sitting casually with one ankle propped against his knee. "There are a number of things that have taken place that, uh . . . I just can't figure out what's going on and I'm really hoping that you can help bring some clarity to these situations."

"Mr. Anderson, I'm trying to understand some things myself," Genesis replied nervously.

"Now, initially when there were payroll checks missing, I was thinking that it was an anomaly, but since then, there have been three other incidents of not only checks being missing, but also employees not being properly compensated for their work performed." Ray stared at Genesis so intently she thought she could feel a hole being burned into her flesh. She cleared her throat and tried to defend herself.

"Certainly my job performance is important to me and I strive to be meticulous in carrying out my responsibilities, especially in an area as sensitive as payroll. I value my employees here and understand that this is their livelihood. Again, I'm not quite sure what these recent errors are attributed to, but please know that I am fully committed to doing stellar work."

Ray didn't comment immediately, but his facial expression reflected serious concern and doubt. "Well, I'm going to be here over the next few weeks just to ensure that processes are being followed as outlined in the Standard Operating Procedures manual." He paused for a brief second. "And I have to be honest with you, I'm going to be in your business," he added matter-of-factly.

"I'd expect nothing less," Genesis replied. "I'm just as anxious, if not more so, to have things resolved and running smoothly, and I appreciate your assistance in that effort."

Ray stood and tugged at the waistline of his pants. "Well, I'm going to go ahead and get set up in the area there." He pointed to a desk right across from Karilyn's. "And I'll be debriefing with you daily. Let's see if we can't get to the bottom of this thing as soon as possible." He lifted his computer bag from the floor and walked toward the door. "I hope you don't have any evening plans for the next several weeks." His tone strongly suggested that if she did have any, she'd better cancel them quick. At that, he left her, still seated, frustrated and massaging her temples. Karilyn immediately came rushing in.

"How'd it go?" she asked, disappointed that Genesis wasn't more shaken.

"Ray's going to be here for a while," she replied, slumping back in her seat. "And he's going to be digging through every little thing, not that that is a bad thing. But I just don't understand what in the world is going on. I know I double-checked that payroll and there were no errors on it. Whatever is going on is making me look careless and incompetent."

"Well, let me know what I can do to help. This will all be over soon," Karilyn said, feigning loyalty. "I'm going to head out for lunch. Milton and I are meeting for a bite to eat."

"You two sure are doing a lot of dating here lately.'

"Just trying to keep some spice in my marriage." Karilyn winked. "Do you want me to bring you anything while I'm out?"

"No, I'll just grab something from downstairs. Have a good time."

Ready to take a break, Genesis emerged from her office carrying her purse. "Ray, I'm going to get some soup from downstairs. Care to join me?"

"Sure, just let me finish up this e-mail . . ." His voice trailed off. He clicked the keyboard of his laptop for a few more seconds, then stood to his feet stretching. "I am a little hungry, I guess. Some soup would really hit the spot."

Together they took the elevator to the first floor and proceeded to the hotel's restaurant. Ray didn't hide the fact that he was keeping his eyes peeled for anything that was out of the ordinary or under par. He scanned the restaurant doing a quick guest count, then glanced at his watch. The lunch hour was just getting started and the dining room was slowly beginning to fill. Seated at tables and booths were single guests who looked a bit lonely, couples who looked in love, and groups of three or more discussing business over the clinking noise of forks hitting plates.

They took a seat near a window that overlooked the hotel's courtyard and perused the lunch menu. Just as they came to a conclusion on what they each would have, their server approached.

"Hi, Ms. Taylor. Decided to get out of the office for a few minutes, huh?" Genesis was relieved that Stephanie would be serving them today. She was one of the best servers at the hotel, which was reflected by both her reported tips and customer comments that frequently made it to her desk.

"Yes, just for a little while," she said, smiling. "This is Ray Anderson from the corporate office," she introduced. "Ray, this is Stephanie, who's been working here for a while now. She's awesome too."

"Nice to meet you, Stephanie," Ray said cordially. "So, how do you like working here at the hotel?" he asked, fishing for information.

"Oh, I think it's great. I love the hours, which allow me to go to school, I make pretty decent money, and my boss is great to work for and so is Genesis." She beamed, pleased at the way Genesis had quickly taken care of a payroll dispute that had shortened her check by ten hours. "I'd really like to get into the management training program here."

"Well, good. If you are as great as Genesis says you are, I'm sure you'll have no problem." Ray paused enough to smile, then transitioned into ordering.

"I'll be right back with your drinks," Stephanie said after memorizing what they'd ordered. She walked a few tables off and stopped to check on one of her other guests. "Is there anything else I can get for you, sir?" she asked as she picked up the gentleman's check and credit card.

"Um . . . actually there is." Moses cleared his throat,

"Did I just hear you call that young lady Genesis?" He motioned his head toward the table where his daughter was seated.

"Yes, sir, she's the hotel's general manager," Stephanie volunteered.

"Is that so?"

"Mmm-hmm. She likes to come eat down here every now and then to make sure things are going well here. Keeping us on our toes, you know." Stephanie winked as she giggled. "I'll be right back with your card and receipt."

Moses thought hard as he waited, unable to keep his eyes off Genesis, who hadn't even noticed him. He didn't quite know what to do. A part of him wanted to seize the opportunity and another part of him was terrified, although it was the reason why he'd come. He jumped, startled, as Stephanie slid his card back on the table.

"I'm sorry—didn't mean to scare you."

"Oh, it's okay. Just deep in thought, I guess. Hey . . ." His voiced faded away for a few seconds. "Do you think I could meet the general manager?" He grabbed his card and began fumbling with his wallet trying to cover the trembling of his hands.

"I'm sure she wouldn't mind meeting you. Let me go over and let her know."

Moses couldn't control the rapid beating of his heart no matter how hard he willed it to slow down. He watched as Stephanie walked over to the table, spoke a few words while she filled two glasses with tea, then met Genesis's eyes when she turned slightly to see who Stephanie was referring to. He gave a slight smile and nod, for which he received a professionally pleasant smile in return. Seconds later, Genesis stood and walked over to where he was seated. Immediately he rose to his feet.

"How are you doing, sir? I'm Genesis Taylor," she said, extending her hand.

Moses refrained from wrapping his arms around her, but could no longer hold back his tears as he grabbed her hand. "Genesis . . . I'm . . . I'm," he stammered. "I'm Moses Nelson." He watched as Genesis's eyes got as wide as dinner plates. "It's me, your father."

Chapter 37

Karilyn returned from lunch pleased to see that Ray was not seated at the desk he'd set up to work from. She quickly punched a code into her phone to route calls back to her desk rather than to her cell. She couldn't afford to miss the call from the college, which was scheduled to come in that day.

While the school hadn't yet called, she did answer a call that she found quite interesting indeed. She had been picking at Genesis for months now trying to find out who her secret love was, but found that Genesis wasn't one to discuss her personal business, particularly her love life, with her staff. She rarely got personal calls into the office, but today had been different.

During her lunch hour, Karilyn answered her cell just as professionally as if she were sitting at her desk.

"Yes, Genesis Taylor please," the male caller asked.

"I'm sorry, she's tied up at the moment, may I take a message?"

"Sure, can you let her know that I'll be working late this evening so I've changed our dinner plans to eight instead of seven?"

"And your name, sir?"

"Ricardo Stewart," he volunteered, thinking nothing of it.

She had planned to use her lunch hour riffling through Milton's banking information so that she could begin to transfer money from his accounts to her own private one. Instead she sat at Milton's desk and did a Google search on Ricardo. After a few clicks and visits to multiple Web sites, a wicked smile crossed her lips when she read what had been documented as public record. She printed what she'd found, carefully cut off the URL address and the time and date stamp along the bottom, then started typing a letter, which she planned to anonymously deliver later that day.

Mr. Anderson,

I am so very glad you are here to straighten out this mess that our general manager has made. She has shamed the name of our company many times over with her careless mistakes . . . or should they be called mistakes?

I am sure that you are aware of several things going not so well here, from things being missing or stolen, to guests being mistreated, to substandard and poor quality work being approved or overlooked.

I would like to bring to your attention that Ms. Taylor has been seen entering and leaving the building on her days off with a known convicted criminal, Ricardo Stewart. Enclosed you will find proof of this fact. I am sure if you review the front desk surveillance tape, you will see them entering and exiting the building.

I believe that on this fact alone, Regal Towers has become a less safe place to work. I sometimes leave the building in fear, not knowing whether I will meet some

*sort of doom or demise as I walk through the parking lot
and to my car.*
*I trust that you will handle this matter quickly and ap-
propriately.*
Anonymous Employee.

She stapled the public records printout to the
letter, then pulled a nine-by-twelve envelope out of
one of Milton's drawers and slid both documents
inside before sealing it.

Just as she was about to drop it on Ray's workstation, he came around the corner.

"Karilyn, I'm glad you're back. Genesis had to leave
for an emergency, so I'm really going to need your
help with a few things since she'll be gone for the rest
of the day." Ray had a legal pad full of notes tucked
under his arm.

"Oh my! Is she okay?" Karilyn gasped.

"I'm not sure." Ray's expression was puzzled. "She
nearly passed out at lunch after having a brief conversation with one of the restaurant guests. I don't know
exactly what happened, but she left in tears."

"Was she okay to drive?" Karilyn stretched her eyes
and laid her hand over her heart.

"She didn't drive herself, she actually called her guy
friend to pick her up. He practically had to carry her
to the car," he shared. "I'll give her a call later on this
evening to make sure she's all right, but in the meantime, I wanted to talk to you about your perception of
how the hotel is being run."

"Oh, I'd be glad to . . ." Karilyn paused for a
moment. "As long as it will be kept confidential."

"Of course."

Karilyn jumped at the opportunity, saying everything she could to defame Genesis's character. For thirty minutes, Ray sat behind the closed doors of a conference room listening and taking notes, only commenting with an occasional "hmm." By the time Karilyn finished, Ray wasn't sure if Genesis should still be employed. And then added to that was the fact that she hadn't respected his presence enough to tough it out through her earlier unexplained dilemma.

"Thank you for sharing, Karilyn. I appreciate your time."

"Let me know how I can help, Mr. Anderson," she replied, acting as if she were truly concerned.

Karilyn returned to her desk and worked steadily until 5:30 p.m., keeping an eye on Ray in her peripheral vision. She strained to listen to his phone calls, most of which she couldn't make out, and watched as he spent the rest of the day working fervently at his computer. Once he left for the evening, she stopped working and logged on to the Internet to see what else she could find on Ricardo. Before she could begin her search, she read an opening headline and article on the MSN page:

WOMAN AND BABY SURVIVE POSSIBLE ARSENIC POISONING

A woman in Hampton, Virginia, was recently treated and released at a local hospital after ingesting arsenic. "I'm not sure where I could have picked it up. I am just glad my baby is okay," a shaken Taunya Johnson stated to police. Thirty-nine-year-old Johnson recalled only having a cup of coffee from Starbucks in Hampton, then having breakfast with a friend at a Cracker Barrel restaurant located in Williamsburg, VA. A thor-

*ough investigation was executed at both estab-
lishments, but no traces of arsenic were found.
Ms. Johnson plans to deliver her baby in March.*

Karilyn had forgotten that she was still toting the
tainted pepper shaker around in her purse. Right
away she pulled it out to throw it in her wastebasket
but thought she should at least wrap it up first. Before
she could move for the restroom, shaker still in hand,
the phone on her desk rang. Out of habit, she answered although it was after hours.

"May I speak to Patricia Hines please?" the caller
asked. Karilyn's heart skipped a beat; it was the call
from North Carolina Central University that she'd
been expecting.

"Speaking."

"Yes, Ms. Hines, you had called some weeks ago
wanting to verify the attendance and completion of a
degree program for a Genesis Taylor?"

"Yes, that's right."

"Ma'am, we have no record of a student by that
name ever attending or being registered at our institution."

"Are you positive? Did you double-check the
spelling?"

"Ma'am, we checked thoroughly and there has
never been a student by that name on record."

"Well, thank you, miss," Karilyn said, attempting to
sound disappointed. However, she couldn't have been
happier if she had hit the lottery. "Would you mind
sending that over to me in an e-mail so that I will have
it in writing?"

"Sure, where do you want it sent?"

Karilyn rattled off an e-mail address, then hung up

the phone and laughed out loud to herself. "Well, I didn't get you, Ms. Taunya, but it's a done deal for your little lying friend!" Setting the pepper shaker on her desktop, Karilyn pulled her anonymous letter from her bag, dropped it on Ray's workstation, then scurried down the hall to the ladies' room to get paper towels. She pulled a few from the wall dispenser and headed back for her desk, but was sidetracked noticing that Genesis's office door had been left ajar. Looking both ways first, she entered, closed the door, and began her routine of digging through files, stealing documents, and deleting e-mail messages.

An hour later, with a smug look on her face, Karilyn emerged from the office, but was immediately horrified when she realized the cleaning crew had come through, emptied the trash, and taken the shaker from her desk. Frantic, she visited every floor of the hotel, hopping on and off the elevator, looking for the crew in an attempt to retrieve the shaker. Not able to locate them, she finally gave up, prayed that they had simply thrown the shaker away, and headed home.

When she crossed the threshold, a furious Milton was waiting.

"Why didn't you tell me John had been calling?" he bellowed.

"Oh, I forgot."

Her nonchalant attitude angered him even more. "What the hell do you mean you forgot! How did you forget to tell me? He said he spoke to you three damn times, Karilyn! How did you forget?"

"I don't know. I guess I had stuff on my mind." She dropped her purse and keys on the kitchen counter and stepped over to the refrigerator. "Are you hungry? How about some stir-fry?"

Milton was mad enough to choke the life out of his wife at that moment. "You caused me to lose a multimillion-dollar deal," he said just above a whisper, clenching his fists as he walked toward her. She nearly jumped to the ceiling when he brought his fist down on the countertop. "No, I don't want any damn stir-fry!" He swung his arm and sent a vase of tulips crashing to the floor, then stormed out to the garage, pulled out, and sped off.

"Well, now you know how it feels to be screwed over," she said out loud, taking a bottle of water from the refrigerator, stepping over the broken glass, and retreating to her bedroom.

Chapter 38

"So he just showed up at your job?" Ricardo asked, providing a listening ear for Genesis. He had driven to a park downtown to where they stood against the railing overlooking the James River.

"Yes!" She threw her hands up, expressing her disbelief. "I'm sitting there having lunch with my boss, and the girl says someone at another table wants to meet me. I walk over there and he says, it's me—I'm your father! How do you just walk up on somebody's job and make an introduction like that, Ric?"

"What did you say to him, babe?"

"I was totally speechless." Genesis shook her head slowly. "I couldn't think of one single word to say."

"Well, what else did he say?"

"He started apologizing about not being there and stuff like that," she blurted, waving a dismissive hand. "I was so shocked, I can hardly remember all that he said, but we're supposed to get together some time this week to sit down and talk." She sighed as she looked out onto the water.

"It's good that he is willing to attempt some type of relationship with you, even though it's been a long time coming."

"Yeah, I'm very interested in what he could possibly say to me that will cover the span of thirty years, Ric. Okay, I can understand him staying away initially, but at some point he should have come back to look for me . . . at least once . . . if he was serious about wanting me and all that."

"Well, sweetie, just listen with an open mind and open heart." Ricardo lifted her hand to his lips. "Give the man a chance."

"I will." Genesis nodded as she nudged away a tear before it could roll down her face. "This is going to be a hard week for me," she said. "Ray's in town, my dad is here, I don't have a way to get to work tomorrow." She giggled through her tears, remembering she'd left her SUV at work.

"Yes, you do. I'll take you. Don't even worry about that."

"I thought you had to be to work by six."

"I'll take you," Ricardo repeated. "Anything you need, you let me know, you hear me?" Genesis nodded like the little girl she felt like inside. "Stop trying to carry the weight of the world on your shoulders. . . let me do that for you," he finished, wrapping his arms around her and kissing her on the forehead.

She rested her head on his shoulder and smiled to herself. Ricardo had so many wonderfully filled pages in her Him Book that she, in her mind, had deemed him The One.

"Come on, let's go home. I'll run you some bathwater."

As promised, Ricardo drew Genesis a bath once he got her home. He found her favorite pajamas in the dryer, pulled them out along with the rest of the laundry, left the pajamas on her bed for her, then folded and put away the remaining garments. He then threw a towel in the dryer so that it would be nice and warm when Genesis called for it. While she soaked in the tub, he made her his favorite comfort meal—vegetable soup with a grilled cheese sandwich—which he placed on a serving tray, ready to bring her dinner in bed. Just as he got the food arranged, her voice floated down the hallway.

"Ric, I forgot my towel."

He yanked the towel from the dryer, folded it quickly, then presented it to Genesis, who bashfully stood behind the bathroom door. He smiled at her gesture of modesty, taking that as a signal that she wanted to rest tonight. "Here you go, baby."

"Ooh! This towel feels so good," she moaned.

"Can I have a kiss since you're hiding from me tonight?" Genesis poked her lips forward to peck Ricardo, then retreated and closed the door, leaving him chuckling on the other side. He shook his head at her antics, then went back to the kitchen to get her dinner. After she ate, he washed the dishes and saw himself out. "I'll see you in the morning, sweetie," he called from the front door. "Try to get some rest tonight, okay?"

"I will," she answered.

"Love you."

"Love you too."

Later that evening as Genesis settled into bed filling her journal with more details and points about Ricardo, and Karilyn sat at Milton's desk transferring money between accounts, Eedy Williams was pronounced dead after ingesting arsenic. The tainted shaker had been found in her smock pocket.

Chapter 39

"I think you should take a look at this." Ray slid the unmarked envelope across Genesis's desk.

"What is it?" she questioned, looking up at him as she picked the envelope up. Ray watched her expression change from curiosity to horror to shame. Her eyes bucked as she read the public record detailing the committed crime and conviction of the man she was in love with. Having viewed all the documents, she replaced them in the envelope. "Where did this come from?" She struggled to keep her diplomacy intact. Instantly she felt the onset of a headache.

"How about we start with you telling me what is really going on, Genesis?" Ray spoke calmly as he seated himself in front of her.

"What specifically are you asking me, Ray?" Genesis began to take offense but maintained her professionalism. "If you are asking me if I am purposely sabotaging my position here with the company, the answer is no. If you are asking me have I cheated, stolen, and lied for my own selfish gain and private agenda, the answer is no. If you are asking me who it is that I choose to see in my personal time, I don't believe that is relevant to the recent challenges that I've faced here, nor do I feel it's any of the company's concern."

"It becomes our concern when you are seen on the company's property with a convicted criminal. Surely you understand that."

Genesis was completely seething inside, not so much at the allegations that Ray made, but more so that Ricardo had not shared this with her, causing her to be totally humiliated.

"Well, the fact of the matter is, Ray, I can neither confirm nor deny the validity of this information, as I've never seen or heard of it prior to right now," she said, whipping the public record printout from the envelope again.

Ray inhaled, then sighed deeply, stretching his arms high in the air, then bringing his laced fingers behind his head. "Let me share with you exactly what my concerns are. While I want to believe—" Ray's sentence was cut short from a sudden shrieking coming from outside Genesis's office. They both looked at each other in silence for a few seconds, then rose to investigate. Ray swung the door open to be faced by four policemen.

"Ma'am, please calm down and come with us. I'd hate to have to use force, but I will do it," the officer said. Karilyn was frantic and in tears.

"Officer, what is going on here?" Genesis looked at each of the four uniformed men.

"We have reason to believe that this woman was directly involved in the recent arsenic poisonings that have taken place in this local area."

"I'm calling my lawyer!" Karilyn screamed, reaching for the phone.

"Ma'am, ma'am!" A second officer grabbed her

arm to prevent her from using the phone and twisted it behind her back, then slapped on a pair of handcuffs. Karilyn screamed even more loudly.

"I'm going to have your jobs! All of you!" she spat as tears streamed down her face.

"Please help me understand what is going on," Genesis said, begging the officer to continue.

"Last night one of your employees died after ingesting arsenic that had been mixed into a pepper shaker."

"Oh my God! Who was it?"

"Ms. Eedy Williams."

Genesis's mouth dropped open in disbelief. "What!"

"It was reported that Ms. Williams and another employee visited this floor yesterday evening to do routine cleaning, which is where it's alleged that Ms. Williams picked the shaker up. Specifically, the report reads she got it off Mrs. Lewis's desk. She apparently used the pepper later on in the evening and placed the shaker in her pocket. Fortunately for us, whenever she used the shaker, she still had on her cleaning gloves. We sent the shaker to forensics and the report came back revealing that Mrs. Lewis's fingerprints were all over it. Surprisingly, this shaker matches the style of shaker that the Williamsburg Cracker Barrel restaurant has on its tables, which was where the other arsenic victim reported eating when traces of the poison were later found in her system."

"That's a lie!" Karilyn screamed as she was being led down the hall. "Genesis, please call my husband," she yelled over her shoulder as she was escorted to the elevators and out of the building.

Ray stood with his arms folded across his chest processing everything he had just witnessed and remembering the conversation he'd had with Karilyn the evening before. Genesis stood with both hands clasped over her mouth, finally realizing that the Lewis whom Taunya referred to was the Milton whom Karilyn was married to.

Oh my God, she really did try to kill Taunya. Frozen in one spot for several seconds, Genesis tried to make sense of everything that was happening. She had yet to view the footage captured by the surveillance cameras Ricardo had set up in her office. She stared pensively at Ray, narrowing her eyes and tapping a single finger against her lips. "I think I may have something we might want to both take a look at." She turned on her heel and strutted toward her office. Ray followed in silence, took a seat, and gave Genesis room to talk. "I'm not sure how unethical this may be, but with so many unexplained things happening here, I thought it necessary to install hidden cameras in my office about two weeks ago. I hadn't had a chance to view any of the tapes, but why don't we take a look at them together?" Genesis pulled a few tapes from a locked drawer, walked over to the small TV/VCR combo that sat on her bookcase, and slid in a tape. Using her remote, she switched to the appropriate channel, adjusting the tracking, and fast-forwarded through several minutes of tape until she found what she was looking for. She and Ray watched in silence as the video revealed Karilyn entering her office time after time, logging in to Genesis's computer, stealing files, and manipulating records. The date and time tracker at the bottom of the screen showed that a few visits had been made after hours.

After several minutes of watching and replaying footage, Ray stood to his feet. "Well, well, well," he commented. "What a difference a day makes. We both have quite a bit of work cut out for us, don't we?" He walked slowly to the door, let himself out, and closed it behind himself.

Genesis sat idly in her chair for a few moments, then grabbed her purse and left her office. "I need to get out for a little while," she said, rushing past Ray's desk.

"No problem." Ray focused his attention back to his laptop and opened an e-mail with Genesis's name in the subject line from a sender he didn't recognize. He double-clicked to open it.

> *To Whom It May Concern:*
> *Per you recent request, we have researched our records to confirm the attendance and completion of a degree program of Genesis Taylor at North Carolina Central University.*
> *Upon thorough investigation, we have found that no student has attended our institution under that name. Please feel free to contact our Alumni Records office with further questions.*
> *Sincerely,*
> *Jasmine Baker*
> *Alumni Records Clerk*
> *North Carolina Central University*
> *Home of the Eagles*

"What else can happen today?" he sighed, picking up the phone and dialing Marvin's number. Once he answered, Ray sighed again and said, "I hope you have a few minutes."

Chapter 40

Ricardo had been practicing with Dhani for weeks to pull off his proposal. Although the script was short, Ricardo wanted it to go perfectly. Especially since it had already been railroaded once when Taunya took ill.

"Let's practice it one more time. I'll be Genesis," Ricardo said, taking a seat on the lower bunk of Dhani's new bunk bed set.

"Okay," Dhani agreed.

"Hi, Dhani!" Ricardo said in a high-pitched falsetto voice, mocking Genesis. Dhani burst into giggles.

"Miss Genesis doesn't talk like that," he laughed.

"Oh yeah? Well, how does she talk, then, smarty-pants?"

"She talks like this—Ric, can Dhani watch a movie?" Dhani mocked, sounding even more ridiculous, but cuter.

This time Ricardo burst into laughter. "You know what? You're right, she does sound like that." He wrestled his son onto the bed, digging his fingertips beneath his arms and in his sides. Dhani, laughing hysterically, struggled to get free. "All right, come on.

Let's try it." Ricardo sat a still giggling Dhani on the floor and gave him a few seconds to get focused. "Now remember what I told you. Go 'head."

Dhani tugged at his shirt, making sure that his appearance was neat, then dropped to one knee. He lifted Ricardo's right hand, then began to giggle again. "Miss Genesis, will you be my mom?" He pushed a small white ring of a broken seal from a soda bottle around Ricardo's finger.

"Yes! Yes, I will be!" Ricardo answered in falsetto, grabbing Dhani in his arms again. "That was perfect, man! Now I'm going to have to pay you with tickles!" Dhani screamed in laughter while Ricardo attacked, but was interrupted by the ringing of his doorbell. Out of breath he jogged to the door. "I'll be right back to finish you off." He opened the front door where Genesis stood with angry eyes filled with tears and an envelope in her hand. "Oh my God, baby, what's wrong? Come in."

Genesis stormed through the door not saying a single word and slapped the envelope into Ricardo's chest as she passed him. Glaring at him, she took a defiant stance in the middle of the floor, crossing her arms over her chest. Ricardo hadn't taken his eyes off her while his fingers fumbled with the envelopes, opening and pulling out the contents. It was then that he lowered his eyes and immediately his heart sank. Not needing to read the entire thing, he folded his lips inside his mouth and stared up at the ceiling.

"Hi, Miss Genesis!" Dhani beamed, running out from his bedroom.

"Not now, Dhani, go back in your room and close the door," he said calmly "You can play with some toys or read a book." Dhani did as he was told without questioning Ricardo's authority. Silence hung in the air as he searched for the right words—any words to say. "Genesis . . ." He looked at her with imploring eyes.

"Do you have any idea how humiliated I was to have my boss hand me that today?" she spat with narrowed eyes. "For him to, in so many words, accuse me of ripping off the company with my convict boyfriend?" The only thing that kept her from raising her voice and seasoning her words with profanity was the fact that Dhani was only a few feet away in the small house. "Ric, you're an ex-con?" she asked incredulously.

Ricardo covered his face with both his hands and exhaled. *Say something, say something.* He knew an apology wouldn't suffice. As a matter of fact, nothing would right now. He punched his fist into the palm of the opposite hand, and blew out a puff of air. "Genesis, you know that is not who I am," he argued softly.

She shook her head slowly. "You know what? I don't have a clue who you are."

"That is so far back in my past—"

She didn't allow him to finish his sentence. "And you are so far back in mine," she said dryly, stomping toward the door.

"Genesis, wait!" Ricardo reached and grabbed her arm. "Baby, please. Please don't do this to me, just wait a minute and let's talk this out."

Without turning to face him, Genesis spoke just above a whisper through clenched teeth. "If you don't want to go back to jail, I suggest you take your hands off of me."

Ricardo held on few seconds longer. "Genesis, please."

"Now!" she bellowed. Reluctantly he let her go and

she wasted no time striding to her vehicle, letting the storm door slam behind her.

Ricardo dropped his head into his palms cursing at himself. He closed the door, sat on the couch, rested his elbows on his knees, and brought his clasped hands to his lips. As he squeezed his fingers together, he felt a slight pinch from the soda bottle ring Dhani had placed on his finger. Slowly he pulled it off and studied it as if it were real. He jumped to his feet and paced the room thinking, swinging at the air, and trying to figure out what to do. He weaved and bobbed, jabbing at an imaginary opponent, but internally boxing himself until he broke a sweat. "I can't let her just walk out of my life," he coached, swinging more blows. "If I want her . . ." he grunted while he jabbed and motioned uppercuts. ". . . I'ma have to fight."

Ricardo had spent the better part of the evening dialing Genesis's number over and over again to no avail. Dhani walked past his father's bedroom and saw that Ric was lying across the bed staring up at the ceiling. He knew that was so not like his father to lie around the house doing absolutely nothing. He tiptoed in, slowly approaching Ricardo, noticing that his father's eyes were red.

"Dad?" Ricardo did not respond. Dhani gently touched Ricardo's shoulder. "Dad, what's wrong?"

Ricardo looked at Dhani and took his time sitting up. He held Dhani without saying one word as his tears began to flow again. Dhani became scared and confused because he had never seen his father like this. His mind took him back to a time when he'd fallen off his bike and was scolded for shedding tears.

Ricardo pushed Dhani back, held him by his shoulders, and looked him in the eye. "Son, I know I told you that a man is not supposed to cry, but sometimes when your heart is filled with pain, you just can't help it."

"What do you mean your heart is filled with pain? Do you want me to pray for you?" Dhani asked sincerely.

Ricardo couldn't help but chuckle. "Well, that always works, but it's not that kind of pain."

"What kind of pain is it, then?"

Ricardo sighed as he tried to think of a way to explain to his son what he meant. "Dhani, do you ever get sad about your mom?"

"Yes, because everybody at my school has a mom except me."

"And that makes you sad inside, right?"

"Yes."

"Well, that's kinda how I feel right now."

"But you have a mom, Dad," Dhani said, puzzled.

"Yes, I have a mom, but I'm talking about someone else that I don't have."

"Who?"

"Genesis."

"She left?"

"Not really. But I did something bad a long time ago that made Genesis not want to talk to me anymore."

"So what about me? She doesn't want to talk to me anymore either?"

"Of course she still wants to talk to you. You haven't done anything, have you?" Ricardo attempted to lift the mood, which seemed to be getting dark.

"No. I've been perfect. I'm glad she still wants to talk to me, because I still want to ask her to be my mom."

Oh Lord. Ricardo sighed. "Well, first I have to figure out a way to make her not mad at me anymore."

"Because if she's mad at you she won't want to be my mom?"

Man, how do I answer that? "I don't think so, son."

Dhani's facial expression changed from confused to sad to angry. "I'm not going to have a mom now and it's all your fault!" he cried in his six-year-old voice.

"Dhani . . ." Ricardo rested a hand on top of Dhani's head, but Dhani snatched away.

"Get off of me!" he shrieked, then ran to his room and slammed the door.

"Dhani!" Ricardo yelled, jumping off the bed to chase after his son. He tried to enter his bedroom, but the door was locked. As easy as it would have been for him to unlock the door and force his entry, he respected his son's feelings and privacy for the moment. "Dhani, please open the door." He could hear the muffled sounds of Dhani's whimpers and sobs. With a heavy heart, he leaned his back against the door and slid down, dropping his head in his palms. He had managed to lose the woman he loved and now his son was angry with him.

He sat there for several minutes trying to sort his thoughts. Finally, he heard the turning of the lock, then the doorknob. Ricardo shot to his feet and lifted Dhani into his arms.

"It will be all right, son. I promise you, I'm going to fix this and it will be all right."

Once Dhani gained his composure and Ricardo felt safe about moving on, he addressed him on another issue.

"Listen to me, Dhani, because what I'm about to

say, I'm going to say one time only. As long as you are a child, don't you ever snatch away from me, run from me, or slam and lock another door in my house." Dhani's eyes stretched wide open. "Do we have an understanding?"

"Yes, sir," Dhani said meekly.

"Good. Now let's go get some ice cream."

Chapter 41

After all the commotion in the office that week, Genesis had gone into hibernation the night before, resulting in her oversleeping. She rushed through her shower, ran her hair brush through her locks, securing them into a sloppy bun with a few bobby pins, and jumped into a basic black dress and pumps. She began to break a sweat as she searched frantically for her keys, knowing if she didn't leave home in the next two minutes, she'd be late for work, which wouldn't be a good thing. Turning the pillows over on the couch, she reached for her cordless phone after it rang three times.

"Hello," she huffed, trotting toward her bedroom to examine her dresser again, although she'd already looked there.

"Genesis, it's Ray. You okay there? You sound a little out of breath."

"Oh, I'm fine, Ray. Just trying to remember where I put my keys so I can get out of here. How are things there, is everything okay?"

"Well, actually, that is why I'm calling. I wanted to catch you before you left home."

Immediately Genesis slowed her pace. "Okay . . ." she said more as a question.

"Genesis, I hate to do this, but I'm going to have to suspend you."

"What!" she shrieked. "Suspend me? On what grounds?"

"As you know, several things have taken place here not only in just the past six months or so, but even in the past week that have just brought many things to light. With that said, I'm not sure if it's in your best interest or the company's best interest to have you report to work right now." Ray paused to allow a response from Genesis, but she kept silent. "There are a lot of things that have to be looked at and considered."

"I understand that, Ray, but I believe with the information that you have, and what we both have witnessed and experienced in the past week, it's pretty clear what has been going on," she argued, becoming angry. "I feel like the company is penalizing me for something that can be pretty much proven as sabotage by the hands of another employee."

"And in some aspects, you're probably right, but let me share this with you. There are some questions being asked about the validity of the personal information you submitted during your application process."

Genesis's heart stopped. "Oh," she said lowly, knowing exactly what Ray was referring to. "Information like what?"

"Well, that is what I need to look into, and while I'm doing that, I'm going to have to ask you to take some time off work," Ray said with a finality that suggested there was no room for further comments.

"I see. So how long am I to stay home?"

"I'll follow up with you in a few days and let you know how things stand."

"All right, Ray. Thanks for calling."

"Sure. Have a good day."

Genesis hung up the phone and took a slow seat on her bed. "I can't afford to lose my job," she whispered into the air, although she felt it was inevitable. She logged on to her computer and checked her savings account balance, determining that she had enough to carry herself for at least six months just in case Ray called back with bad news.

She wanted to reach out to Ricardo, but couldn't. They hadn't spoken in nearly a week, and while Genesis missed him sorely, she was still angry and disappointed. She picked up and flipped through the pages of her journal, reading over her notes and thoughts. She couldn't deny that Ricardo had been more than wonderful, but now she felt such a sense of uncertainty of who he really was. Before she could resort to tears, her phone rang again.

"Genesis, this is your father." Right away, Genesis pushed air through her teeth in a clearly audible sigh. Moses ignored it and continued. "I know you probably have to work today, and maybe it's asking a lot, but I would really like to spend some time with you this evening."

"I, uh . . . I really don't think today . . ." Genesis rubbed her temples as she kicked her shoes off.

"Genesis, please don't say no. Please. After today, you don't ever have to talk to me again if that's what you choose to do, but please don't deny me this one opportunity to at least talk to you. It would really mean a lot to me."

* * *

Moses closed his cell phone, looked up at the ceiling of his hotel room, and spoke out loud. "I gotta hand it to you, Man, you are truly a miracle worker!"

Not even an hour passed before Genesis received a phone call from corporate HR informing her that she needed to schedule a time to go by the hotel to collect her personal belongings from her office. Her purchase had caught up with her. "What am I going to do?"

Moses arrived at the park at three that afternoon, more than an hour before Genesis would show, to give himself time to think and calm his nerves. He fingered the picture that he'd kept through the years, which had been his only connection to his firstborn child. While he'd rehearsed words over and over again, sometimes only in his mind, and other times audibly in front of a mirror, he knew that nothing could truly prepare him for the encounter that would take place. He prayed, as he had done many times prior, that things would go well . . . that his daughter would have a heart of forgiveness and then find room in her heart and in her life where he could squeeze in. "A small corner will do, Lord," he whispered, looking toward the clouds that floated above his head.

He stood nervously to his feet as he watched his daughter make her way down the extended sidewalk leading into the park. He felt both joy and relief in his heart that Genesis did come out to meet him like she'd agreed to. He turned a corner of his lips up in a half smile as she approached with a smile. He reached out to hug her, and to his pleasure, she obliged.

"I'm so glad you came." Holding her at arm's length with tears in his eyes, he spoke softly. "I don't even know where to begin. I am just so grateful to God for the opportunity to lay eyes on you, Genesis," he started. "I know you have lots of questions, some that I may not have the answers to, but I just want to tell you up front that you're beautiful and I love you."

Just hearing her father say those words to her caused Genesis's eyes to well up with tears. They both took a seat on a metal bench with joined hands. Moses's eyes danced around wildly, absorbing her features.

"Your mother was right, you do look just like me." He reached in his pocket and pulled out the letter Angeline had sent him so many years ago. "Here. Your mom wrote me this letter the day after you were born." Included with the folded paper was the photo.

"You kept this all this time?"

"It was the only piece of you I had." He paused pensively. "And staying away from you was the hardest thing that I've ever done in my entire life."

"But somehow you found the strength to do it," Genesis stated, staring down at the photo although her vision was blurred by more tears.

"And I realize now that maybe that wasn't the best decision that I could have made, but under the circumstances and at the time, it seemed right."

"What circumstances? Okay, Miss Juanita told me that some guy threatened to beat Mom to death while she carried me, but what about after that?"

"Honey, I loved your mother dearly. From what I know, she stayed with that guy for a couple of years after you were born. He would beat her up so bad that your grandmother wrote me and asked me to please leave her alone. That broke my heart." Moses wiped his hand down his face, drying it of tears. "Once she sent me a picture of your mother beat up so badly and left behind a building to die, I knew I couldn't contact her anymore. I'd been sending her money for you, and actually wrote you letters, although I knew you couldn't read them," he chuckled, looking out at the water. "I was in love with you although I'd never even seen you." He turned his gaze back to Genesis's face.

"So you just decided to never come and see me, or even try to? Even after Mom gave me up to her mother? When there was no more Quinton to threaten her or me or even you?"

"By no means is this justifiable, honey, but after I moved away, I lost contact and . . . and just pressed on with my life. It sounds so hard, but I swear to you, baby, I never forgot about you."

"And I hear you saying that, but your actions have never supported what you're saying. How can I believe that?"

"Baby, sometimes a man just makes a mistake, he makes a bad decision. There's no way to explain it, undo it, or fix it, and all he can do is accept the consequences of it and make the best of what's left." He paused, studying her face. "And that is what I'm trying to do right now. I'm already your father because I fathered you, and I can't undo what's already been done or relive days gone by, but if you would have me, I would like to start right here . . . right now . . . being your dad."

Moses's words struck Genesis at her core as she considered the consequences she would now have to face for the decision she'd made when she applied for her job. A lie she told, a document she falsified and signed her name on its bottom declaring it as truth. And while the two situations didn't truly compare, she realized that the feelings of regret and consequence were the same. She reflected on the clipping she'd read on Ricardo. She hadn't given him a chance to even explain to her what had happened that put him in such a predicament. Now she felt that she owed him at least that, for the Ricardo she knew was no criminal. Her father's words played back in her mind. *There's no way to explain it, undo it, or fix it, and all he can do is accept the consequences of it and make the best of what's left.* She turned to answer him but was interrupted before she spoke the first sentence.

"Miss Genesis! Miss Genesis" She whipped her head around in response to the familiar voice. Tearing down the sidewalk was Dhani, dressed in a three-piece suit. Several feet behind him in a reluctant stroll was Ricardo. "Hi, Miss Genesis!" He ran up to her and threw his arms around her neck.

"Hi, sweetie! You look nice today. Where have you been?"

"I went to school, but then my dad came and got me out early and told me to put this on. Then we went to your job, but you weren't there. Then my dad drove to your house and you weren't there either. Then he drove down here and then we saw your car and then he was happy and started doing like this." Dhani punched in the air while he shouted, "Yeah! Yeah!"

Genesis began to laugh. "For real?"

"Yeah, and then he was, like, run down there and see if that's Genesis sitting on that bench. My dad is right there, see, look!" Dhani pointed although Genesis had kept her eyes on him while he talked.

Ricardo, also dressed in a suit, approached the three of them deliberately, nodding his head toward the gentleman who sat beside Genesis.

"How are you doing?" Ricardo asked cordially, but was less interested in getting a response.

"Fine, young man, fine," Moses replied.

"I know I'm interrupting, but please pardon me for just a moment. Dhani, come on, let's do this just like we practiced."

Without further hesitation, Dhani dropped to one knee in front of Genesis. "Miss Genesis Taylor, I have a mother, but I don't have a mom. She went away a long time ago when I was a baby, and a mother is a person that a child can only have one of. All my life, all I have had is my dad . . . until my dad met you. Miss Genesis, I would be so honored if you would do me the pleasure of being my mom." Dhani fumbled in his pocket for a very small diamond ring set in white gold, took Genesis's right hand, and did his best to slide it on her third finger.

Through both laughter and tears, Genesis looked at Moses and Ricardo. "Did you two plan this?" Moses shook his head as he shrugged, while Ricardo kept silent and dropped to his knee, fixating his eyes on Genesis.

"Genesis, words cannot rightfully express my love for you. You are an incredible woman who has impacted my life in so many ways. You complete me," he whispered. "I know that I have some explaining to do and I swear I will answer every single question you have. I love you, and I am in love with you, I need you in my life." It was then that Ricardo seemed to pull a ring out of thin air and slide it onto her left hand. "Miss Genesis Taylor, I would be so honored if you would do me the pleasure of being my wife."

Genesis could barely see for the streams that flowed from her eyes, and nearly choked on her words as she took hold of Moses's hand.

"Ric, Dhani." Her eyes bounced back and forth between the two of them. "I would love to tell you both yes, but first . . . you have to ask my dad."

Chapter 42

Taunya laid her baby in her bassinette, clicked on the television, and watched the midday news as she quickly got dressed for her day. Her paced slowed as she heard the anchorwoman's voice dictating the news.

"And now today's top headlines. A Williamsburg woman, Karilyn Lewis, was convicted this morning of both attempted murder and murder charges after two local residents ingested arsenic that had been planted inside a pepper shaker. The first victim, Taunya Johnson, was with child when she had breakfast with Lewis several months ago. Lewis apparently planted the tainted shaker on the table after becoming aware that her husband was having an affair with Johnson. While Johnson and her unborn child survived the incident, unfortunately, sixty-four-year old Edith Williams did not.

"Williams was an employee at Regal Towers Hotel in Williamsburg. During the routine cleaning of the administrative offices, Williams picked up the shaker and later used it to season her evening meal, and unfortunately did not survive the lethal ingestion. Investigators were able to trace the shaker back to Lewis, then tie the two incidents together. Lewis is being held in state custody until sentencing later this month." Sketched pictures were used to depict Karilyn sitting in the witness stand with a sullen expression on her face; then they showed a quick clip of Milton.

"I never would have thought my wife capable of murder." He shook his head slowly. "I just can't believe it."

The clip then switched to Edith Williams's daughter. "My mom is gone and that's something I'll never get back. I hope they throw her under the jail."

The anchorwoman closed the story by saying, "Ms. Johnson was not available for comments but delivered a healthy baby girl back in March of this year."

By the time Karilyn's story had gone off and the weatherman began to give the week's forecast, Taunya had pulled on her panty hose and dress. The sound of the doorbell drew her away from the TV. "Who is it?" she yelled as she neared the door expecting the babysitter to arrive at any minute. She heard a muffled response but couldn't make out who it was. Without looking out of the peephole, she swung the door open, where Milton stood waiting. She turned, leaving the door open for him to enter, then rushed back to her bedroom to finish her look, not bothering to speak a single word despite Milton's frazzled appearance. Fifteen minutes later, she came into the living room looking absolutely stunning, dressed in a strapless teal cocktail-length dress with a fuchia ribbon at the waist. There was no visible indication that she had just recently given birth.

"You look incredible," Milton complimented.

"So, why are you here?" she asked, ignoring his comment as she fumbled with her earrings.

"May I see my daughter please?" he asked, standing to his feet.

"She's in the bedroom. I'll get her in a minute, I'm trying to get dressed." Taunya's tone was short and snippy. It wasn't that she despised Milton. She was more so disappointed in her behavior that had landed her in the place that she was. She had long stopped seeing Milton, and was determined not to go back. "As you can see I'm on my way somewhere, so it's really not a good time anyway."

"Taunya, please talk to me."

"I just told you I'm on my way out and even if I weren't I still wouldn't be in the mood to talk."

"I had a long, hard day. I guess I just thought I could talk to you."

"About what?" She shrugged, taking a seat to strap on a three-inch teal stiletto sandal. "About your wife's conviction? I don't want to talk about that. She tried to kill me. She tried to kill us as a matter of fact. She knew I was pregnant and she sat right there and watched me sprinkle that poison on my food, smiling in my face while I ate," she said without raising her voice or looking his way. "You want to talk about the baby? The baby's fine and needs diapers and milk. You want to talk about the house? As you can see, it's just about empty and I'll be out next weekend per my letter to you communicating my intent to vacate." Taunya had already begun moving into Genesis's old house, since Ricardo and Dhani had transitioned out of it. "What else is there to talk about?" Taunya got up to answer the door again. "Come on in, Michelle, the baby's in the bedroom.

"All right, Lewis, thanks for stopping by—I gotta run."

"Taunya, wait a minute." Milton jumped to his feet and moved quickly toward the door. Taunya stopped and planted both hands on her hips, letting out a heavy sigh. "Taunya, I was serious when I told you that I love you," he said, studying her eyes. "I was just thinking that, uh . . . that maybe we could move forward with . . . with us."

"With us? What us? There has never really been an us. There was you and your wife, and there was me on the side. Now there's you and your convicted wife, and there is Andia and me. There is no us," she said, pointing back and forth between the both of them.

"But, Taunya—"

"There are no buts. And maybe we both got in a little too deep, you emotionally, which you'll eventually get over, and me obviously physically, but my baby's not going anywhere. But the bottom line is, there will never be an us. Look at how we got together in the first place . . . I was stripping in a club, and you were there cheating on your wife. What kind of foundation is that? If you did it to her, you'll do it to me." Milton dropped his head, looking totally defeated. "Now, I'm not going to stop you from seeing your daughter, Milton, but there can be no more us," she said, emphasizing the word "us" with quotation fingers. "Listen, I need to get out of here, but you can come back this evening to see the baby," she said sincerely as she coached him through the door, then closed it behind the both of them. "I'll call you when I get back in." At that she stepped quickly to her SUV, got inside, backed out of the driveway, and zoomed away.

* * *

Taunya waltzed elegantly past Ricardo giving him a slight smile and wink. He smiled back as he stood handsomely dressed in a black tuxedo with a teal cummerbund and tie, holding Dhani's hand. Tears came to Ricardo's eyes as he watched his bride approach him, escorted by her father. There could not have been a more beautiful sight to his eyes. Juanita, who stood beside Taunya, also wiped away a few tears, overwhelmed and pleased that her son was marrying such a beautiful woman.

Following a teary exchange of vows, Ricardo saluted his bride and they were presented to their family, Moses and his wife, Dionne, Taunya, Juanita, and Dhani, as Mr. and Mrs. Ricardo Stewart. It was then that Moses cleared his throat for an announcement.

"Genesis, you've always been the love of my life, and I truly never forgot about you. Today, on your wedding day, I'd like to present you with this." He handed Genesis a flat elongated box.

"Thanks, Dad, what is it?"

"Open it, sweetheart."

Genesis gasped out loud when she lifted the cover from the box and took out a fourteen-karat gold checkbook cover. She lifted it from the box and flipped it open, then gasped again at a check made out to her for a figure that made her hold on to Ricardo to keep from fainting. "I was forced to stop sending money to your mother, but I faithfully put money in an account for you every single week, right up until last Friday. I always knew in my heart I would see you again, and have an opportunity to show you that you've always meant the world to me. I know it can't buy back time, but maybe you can buy you something nice that will bring a smile to your pretty face."

He wrapped his arms around his daughter and hugged her tightly. "I love you, baby," he whispered in her ear.

"I love you too, Daddy."

"Take care of my little girl," Moses said, grasping Ricardo's hand and pulling him into his chest.

"Yes, sir. I will." The men thumped each other on their backs before breaking apart.

The intimate and private ceremony at the park was over in a matter of minutes, but would be remembered forever by the few people in attendance. Genesis had selected the location to honor and remember the day she'd let her dad and now her husband into her heart, realizing that while neither of them would really gain a superficial one hundred points, they were both number one in her book.

Epilogue

Genesis settled herself behind her desk, logged on to her computer, then spun her chair to the window to meet the rising sun as she'd done so many mornings before. She whispered a prayer of thanks similar to the same words she'd used on her very first day at Regal Towers, although she'd been back for at least six months. But this time her conscience was clear and her hands were clean; she wasn't thanking God for helping her to cover a lie.

Close to three months after her termination, Marvin Waldron had personally called Genesis to offer her position back, contingent upon her immediate enrollment in a degree program. Without thought, Genesis accepted, able to state that she'd already started taking classes at Christopher Newport University. With a few adjustments to her schedule and the convenience of online classes, she found the challenge of balancing work, school, and her man not as insurmountable as she'd imagined.

Before Genesis could delve into her day, Sonji, her new assistant, tapped on her door. "Good morning,

Mrs. Stewart. These just came for you," she said, setting the flowers on the table. "That man of yours is
something else," Sonji mentioned, whipping her
straight black hair away from her face, disappearing
as quickly as she came.

"Yes, he is," Genesis responded casually, refraining
from pulling herself from the window, not wanting to
miss a second of the sun making its appearance for
the day. Minutes later, a slow smile spread across her
face as she turned toward the arrangement and
thought about her husband, a wonderful father and
provider. Ric had been more than supportive of her
work and school scheduling and had even reenrolled
himself in school to complete his course of study.
They would spend several evenings together with
their heads buried in books and eyes focused on
laptop screens, Dhani included. Genesis had long
gotten rid of her Him Book, and replaced it with a
new red velvet journal to capture every moment of
her experiences with her husband and son . . . sans
scoring.

The fragrant scent of the roses filled her nostrils as
she searched the bouquet for the small card. She
pulled it from its plastic stem and slid her finger
through the seal. Much to her surprise, Ric hadn't
sent the flowers.

*Just thinking of my baby girl. Love you, sweetie. Dionne
and I will be back soon to visit.*

Your Dad

After reading the card, she pressed it to her heart
and thought fondly of her dad and Dionne. Although
Moses had returned to his home in Atlanta, he vowed

to never again lose contact with his baby girl. Both he and Dionne had been a wonderful addition to her life.

"Love you too, Dad," Genesis whispered into the air.

She lightly kissed the card and slid it in the crevice of the frame that held Anna Marie's photo. As she placed it back in its familiar spot, she took note of the beautifully familiar sparkle in her grandmother's eyes, smiled, then gazed back toward the window and admired the morning sky.

She truly had something to thank God for.